"You were in that plane," she said, some awe in her voice.

"I was flying that plane," he said. "It's mine."

She shook her head. "Dr. Weathers, since that very first turkey dinner, you continue to surprise me."

Yeah, well, she surprised him, too. He hadn't expected her to become this important to him in just a few days. Her voice was weak, strained. He offered her the bottle of water on the bedside table. "Small sip," he said.

She took it. "I'm glad you came back. I didn't want to die alone."

"Nobody is dying on my watch," he said. "That's why we're going back to Bigelow Memorial."

She shook her head. "No."

"Why?" he asked. He had a pretty good idea but he wanted to test whether she would finally be honest with him. If she chose not to be, well, that was going to be somewhat crushing. How could he ever hope that they could move forward together if one of them was lying about almost everything?

Dear Reader,

Her Dangerous Truth is the third and final book in the Heroes of the Pacific Northwest miniseries. Dr. Jamie Weathers is a local hero. Everybody knows he's smart, brave and committed to his patients and the world of emergency medicine. Layla Morant knows one more thing: that her truth puts him and all that he holds dear at great risk. Even though she desperately needs help, she won't let him make that mistake.

But fortunately, Jamie has never been one to give up easily on anything.

As always, when I end a series and say goodbye to the characters and the community that I've created, I'm a little sad. I find myself wanting to visit fictional Knoware, Washington, to have coffee at Gertie's Café, shop at Tiddle's Tidbits and Treasures, and eat tacos and drink fresh lemonade at Food Truck Saturday.

I hope you feel the same.

All my best,

Beverly Long

HER DANGEROUS TRUTH

Beverly Long

HARLEQUIN
ROMANTIC SUSPENSE

(H) HARLEQUIN®
ROMANTIC SUSPENSE™

Recycling programs
for this product may
not exist in your area.

ISBN-13: 978-1-335-73801-1

Her Dangerous Truth

Copyright © 2022 by Beverly R. Long

Harlequin Enterprises ULC
22 Adelaide St. West, 41st Floor
Toronto, Ontario M5H 4E3, Canada
www.Harlequin.com

Printed in U.S.A.

Beverly Long enjoys the opportunity to write her own stories. She has both a bachelor's and master's degree in business, and more than twenty years of experience as a human resources director. She considers her books to be a great success if they compel the reader to stay up way past their bedtime. Beverly loves to hear from readers. Visit beverlylong.com, or like her author fan page at https://www.facebook.com/BeverlyLongAuthor/.

Books by Beverly Long

Harlequin Romantic Suspense

Heroes of the Pacific Northwest

A Firefighter's Ultimate Duty
Trouble in Blue
Her Dangerous Truth

The Coltons of Roaring Springs

A Colton Target

Wingman Security

Power Play
Bodyguard Reunion
Snowbound Security
Protecting the Boss

Visit the Author Profile page at
Harlequin.com for more titles.

In memory of Jim Kavanaugh, my good friend and brother-in-law. I miss you every single day.

Chapter 1

"It was a dark and stormy night."

"Catchy. Except that it's two in the afternoon," Dr. Jamie Weathers said without looking up from his laptop. He had six more charts in his queue to review.

"Dark and stormy *day* doesn't evoke the same chilling response," Caitlin Rose said.

His administrative assistant was standing at the office window, peering through the tilted blinds at the outside world, where it was dark enough to be night. Thirty minutes ago the outside lights of Bigelow Memorial had automatically come on, illuminating the rain that was coming down in torrents and the wind that was absolutely whipping the trees, bending their almost bare branches to the point that Jamie was confident the hospital might have to invest in new landscaping come spring. "If we lose power, I'm blaming you," Jamie teased.

"The lights have dimmed twice," Caitlin said. "It's not looking good."

No, it wasn't. The emergency department as well as other critical parts of the hospital were on generator power in the event of an outage. But that was never ideal.

"I hate driving in the rain," Caitlin said.

"It'll let up." At some point, it had to, right? But the storm had been pounding them pretty hard for the last hour.

"I was going to make one last stop at the grocery store," Caitlin said.

"You and every other resident of Knoware. How many are coming for Thanksgiving this year?" he asked.

"Twenty-eight. But there's room for one more," she said.

It was the third or fourth time she'd issued the invitation. It was what nice people did for those who didn't have their own families around to share the holiday. His parents had moved from Knoware, Washington, years ago, in favor of the warm weather in Sarasota, Florida. His two younger brothers who'd still been at home at the time had gone with them and liked it enough to stay in the area once they'd married and started their professional careers. An invite had come his way from his mom, too. *Fly down, spend a couple days.* He'd considered it but hated commercial flying over the holidays. He could take his own small plane, but it would be eleven or twelve hours of flying time each way. He'd declined, promising that he'd get there sometime over the Christmas holidays.

"I am confident that there is always room for one

more at your table. But I think you've got your hands full with your six kids, their spouses and those sweet grandchildren."

"You're working?" she accused.

Yes, he would cover the emergency department and the flight program. The holiday wasn't a big deal to him, and if it meant that one fewer staff member had to give up time with their family, he was happy to do it. Without family, the holiday was just another day. "I'm off the whole next week."

"Well, then, you're going to miss out on the turkey and rice soup that I bring in on Monday," she said, her tone snippy. She thought he worked too much. And she was probably right. But she wasn't acting like she was happy about his vacation.

"I just said I'm taking time off." His boss, the chief medical officer of Bigelow Memorial, had insisted.

"You're not going anywhere," she said. "You'll spend the time alone. Probably reading medical journals."

"I will be at home, with my feet up, reading a bunch of crime fiction novels. So there," he added.

"Will you turn off your cell?" she asked.

Probably not. "Of course," he said.

"Right." She left her post by the window. As she passed by his desk, his cell phone buzzed. "Speak of the devil," she said.

He picked it up, scanned the details and pushed his chair back. As the director of emergency medicine for Bigelow Memorial, he got notified of every 911 call requiring a medical response. And as the physician on call today, it meant that he was going out in the rain.

"Car accident with injuries on Highway 6," he read aloud.

"The helicopter is grounded," Caitlin said.

Jamie grabbed the keys to Mobile One. "I guess that means I'm driving."

"I hope whoever it is appreciates that you're risking your life to help them," Caitlin said. "Don't be a hero."

She'd started saying that lately whenever he left on a call. It had something to do with a hemorrhaging patient being lifted via a litter into a hovering helicopter while he'd been perched on said patient's chest, applying pressure. "I wish you'd never seen that photo," he mumbled, already halfway out the door. Almost impossible, however, since it had made the Knoware newspaper.

In less than three minutes, he was pulling out of the underground garage where they housed Mobile One, the all-wheel-drive Chevy Tahoe that was outfitted better than some small hospital emergency rooms. In a rural community, where people lived in sparsely inhabited areas and traveled winding, hilly roads with some regularity, it was essential to be able to deliver care outside the hospital.

It was his baby, and he loved it.

Although today was not a great day to be venturing forth. The wind rocked his vehicle, making it hard to steer, and the rain-slicked roads would offer every opportunity to hydroplane. Yet he hurried. Because 4.6 miles away, according to his GPS, somebody needed him.

It hurt to breathe. And moving seemed rather out of the question. It did not appear, however, that she was dead.

She gave herself a moment to let that sink in, then took stock. She was upside down, the car on its roof. Her lower left leg was trapped between the crushed-in

driver's side door and what must be a collapsed portion of the bottom of the vehicle. It was hard to know for sure. Too dark to see much.

Layla Morant, cursing the blood that drained to her head and made it pound, wriggled the fingers on her right hand. Then her left. And she could feel her toes, at least in her right foot, in the too-big rain boots that she'd hurriedly stepped into three hours ago when she'd learned that Douglas Glass had been released, four months and three days early.

"How could that have happened?" she'd railed at her attorney, who'd called late the previous night with the news.

"It just does," he'd said.

It had been a pretty unsatisfactory answer, but he'd simply been the messenger. He did not understand that she had plans in the works. Plans that weren't quite ready. But fortunately, because she wasn't the type to wait till the last minute for anything, much had been done.

She would no longer be able to execute the final details over the coming months. It was now or never. She'd thanked the man for calling, hung up, grabbed her go-bag, added the last-minute essentials and, in just under twenty-two minutes, had driven away from her sweet little condo in San Francisco in the dark of night. It was almost as if she'd practiced it, which, of course, she had, a million times over in her head over the course of many months.

She couldn't let *this* derail everything. She needed to get out of the car and, if necessary, drag herself up the hill, regardless of how daunting the prospect of that sounded. She wasn't paralyzed. She was still able to

think, to reason. She'd get herself out of this. She'd made a vow the day Douglas Glass had been sentenced that she would depend only upon herself from that day forward to stay safe. This was not the first difficulty she'd faced. She'd found solutions along the way. She would find a solution today.

She'd driven for hours in the dark, stopping to sleep at a highway rest stop for a few hours once it was daylight. Then she continued north. She'd had good weather until she'd hit the border between Oregon and Washington. At first it had been a light rain. Then, about a half hour ago, it had turned heavy and had slowed her down considerably. It had also worn on her nerves. She'd decided that a break might be good and had gotten off at the exit that promised both food and fuel.

Now that didn't seem like such a good thing. She'd been on that highway, with its heavily treed sides, for just five minutes when she'd encountered the deer. She had swerved, managed to miss it and had just been bringing her car back on the road when her rear tire got caught in a rut or something at the side of the narrow highway, flipping her car. More than once. After the first roll, for a fleeting second, she'd been upright before things had gone topsy-turvy again.

If she didn't get herself out, how long would it take for someone to find her? How many hours could she survive?

Not long, she thought, less panicked than she might have imagined. Perhaps because this would be a better death than whatever Douglas Glass had in mind.

It was oddly soothing, she thought, listening to the rain hit the underside of her vehicle. Maybe she'd sit here, suspended upside down, and simply fall asleep.

And when they found her in a couple weeks, when she looked and smelled like a rotten apple, they'd remark that she seemed very peaceful.

Speaking of smells, the car already had a bit of a burned smell, but it didn't scare her. She'd been in one other car accident, much less serious, when she'd been seventeen. The airbag had inflated then, too. It was that same smell that she remembered.

She tried to move her left leg, the one that was trapped, and cried out with pain. Oh, that was bad. Very bad. She wasn't going to be able to simply pull her leg free. She needed to be able to pry apart the metal that was holding her. She could maybe slide her left arm down, but she would need both hands, and the seat belt was holding her so tightly that there was no way she could reach her right arm to help.

She was afraid to unlatch her seat belt, afraid that gravity would drop her on her head and she would break her neck in the process. But really, she couldn't just sit here. She didn't want to be an apple. She didn't want to be dead. That's what had sent her running in the first place.

That's what had made her willing to give up everything.

She'd have to do this in stages. First, she raised her left arm, bracing the palm of her hand against the roof of the vehicle, which was now on the ground. Her arm shook with the effort, but she trusted it would hold her weight. Then, very carefully, she reached down with her right arm and attempted to unlatch her seat belt.

She pushed and pushed, literally punishing her thumb with the effort, to no avail. It was jammed. It was the final straw. She started to cry.

"Damn it. Damn you, Douglas Glass, and your whole crooked family." Damn the law for letting her down. Damn the money that had made it possible for justice to be thwarted.

Damn the life that she wasn't going to get to have. She'd wanted—

What the heck was that? The flash of light. A siren. Oh God. Help was coming. She'd never been more grateful in her entire life.

Never more grateful in her *new* life, she thought. Because when her attorney had called, her new life had been jump-started. If she was going to get out of this alive, she'd better remember that. If she didn't, the rescue efforts would have been in vain, because she was going to be dead anyway.

The vehicle appeared to be in bad shape, Jamie thought, as he looked down from the road. He stood next to his best friends, firefighter/paramedic Blade Savick and police chief Marcus Price. It certainly wasn't the first time the three first responders had converged on a scene, but Jamie hadn't expected both of them, because he'd thought Blade was home with his wife, Daisy, and newly arrived twin sons.

"Why are you here?" he asked, pulling essentials from the back of Mobile One. He was going to have to carry them down the hill.

"We had a hole in the schedule. I said I could cover for a few hours. Wasn't expecting a monsoon to hit."

Jamie looked in Marcus's direction. "I thought the chief didn't have to do fieldwork." He handed him a bag to carry.

"Riding with a new officer," Marcus explained. "And I'm never giving up fieldwork," he added.

Whatever the reason, Jamie was grateful to see both of them. This was going to be tricky. The four-door sedan was on its roof, and the driver's side door was smashed in, as was part of the undercarriage of the vehicle. "Who called this in?" Jamie asked, hoping it was the driver. It meant that he or she was still alive.

"A hunter. He was in the woods and saw the vehicle go off the road."

So it had just happened. Sadly, it might already be too late. This kind of wreck could certainly have killed the driver or any passengers.

Fully loaded up, they started down the hill. Jamie watched his footing. One wrong step and he'd need to be carried out, too.

"Too bad the helicopter is grounded," Marcus said. "Could have been another photo op," he added, sliding about three feet in the slick grass.

"You fall on your butt and I'll make sure that makes the next edition," Jamie said. It was not the first time his friends had teased him about the photo. But he knew they didn't think he had been grandstanding. He also knew they'd both have done the same.

The trio was close now. Another ten feet. Finally, Jamie was able to drop to his knees and use his flashlight to see into the driver's side window. There was a woman staring back at him, her eyes big with fright. There were tears on her face.

"I'm Dr. Weathers," he yelled, hoping to be heard over the rain and wind. "There's a whole crew here and we're going to help you. Can you tell me your name?"

It seemed she hesitated, and he wondered about a head injury.

"Regan Jones," she said finally.

It was hard to hear her with the glass separating them. For some unknown reason, the windows had held. He moved his flashlight, trying to see inside the rest of the vehicle. "Are you the only one in the vehicle?"

"Yes."

"Okay, Regan, thank you. Are you injured?"

"Hurts a little to breathe," she said. "And my leg is trapped. I can't feel my foot."

Maybe a collapsed lung, but he didn't think so. She'd be sucking in air, and it didn't look as if she was doing that. He thought it was likely that ribs were broken. Too early to tell about internal injuries. And the leg—well, all he could see was a rain boot. He glanced around.

"She said her leg is trapped," Jamie said, standing and pointing. Blade and the other firefighters were already looking, assessing how best to crack open the car and extricate the victim. The officer who'd come with Marcus was taking photos. Marcus was talking to a man dressed in hunter orange.

"Yeah," Blade said after a quick minute. "We could roll the vehicle, but not knowing exactly how the leg is trapped, we're going to cut through this." He pointed at the undercarriage of the vehicle. "We'll start on the far side and open it up."

Jamie got on his knees again. "You're going to hear some noises. Don't be scared. We're going to get you out of there as soon as we can."

"Don't leave me," she said. She had the prettiest gray-blue eyes. Heavily lashed, they had an intensity

that made it hard to look away. Her hair was blond, cut short, with streaks of lighter blond.

"I won't. I'll be here the whole way." He heard the saws power on. "Hang on, Regan. You've come this far."

Chapter 2

The firefighters worked tirelessly in the pouring rain, cutting and tossing car pieces aside. As they got close to the victim, they had to be more careful, more precise.

As always, Jamie appreciated their efforts, their expertise. But he was, quite frankly, pretty worried about the woman. He kept talking to her, telling her she was going to be fine, telling her that the firefighters were making good progress, even joking about not being concerned about the rain because he was pretty sure he wasn't going to melt.

At first, she'd nodded and even given him a strained smile once or twice. And her eyes had never wavered from his face. He lay on the ground, not caring that he was getting soaked by the thick, wet grass, keeping his face close to the window.

But in the last couple minutes, he could tell that she was fading.

He felt a tap on his shoulder. It was Blade. "You need to move now. We're going to pull that final section off. You'll be able to get to her then."

"I'll be right back," Jamie said, scrambling out of the way. He watched as the caved-in door was pulled away and the firefighters cut her out of her seat belt. They put a C collar on her before they moved her, and then she was gently put on a board, moving her just far enough from the vehicle for Jamie to get to work. Then the firefighters, along with Marcus and the young officer, grabbed a tarp and held it over him and the woman, protecting them somewhat from the rain.

Blade stayed with him and leaned close to Jamie. "Take a look inside that boot."

Jamie quickly pulled the tall rubber rain boot to the side. With his flashlight, he saw immediately what had concerned Blade. There was blood—a lot of it.

"This has to be cut off," he said. He glanced at the woman's face to see if she'd heard. He wasn't asking permission, but she'd been through significant trauma already, with more ahead of her, and any effort to build a little trust was never bad.

She blinked. "They were always too big, anyway." Her voice was a mere whisper.

"That's the spirit," Jamie said, holding out a hand for the knife that Blade had pulled from the tool belt around his waist. And with sure, confident slices, he destroyed the black-and-white polka-dot rain boot.

Her tibia was broken. Didn't need an X-ray to tell him that. Bone was poking through skin and had caused significant bleeding. Hard to tell how much she'd lost. Blood was still oozing out but had likely slowed substantially from what it had been. "Your leg is broken,

Regan. You've lost quite a bit of blood. No worries, but I am going to put an IV in your arm to address that." He worked fast while he talked, and within seconds of providing her with an explanation, the line was in and blood was flowing. Then he quickly wrapped a tourniquet around her leg to stabilize it and prevent additional bleeding.

She would need surgery, likely some pins and screws to hold the bone together. But she was young—it would heal. He was more worried about the things he could not see. He listened to her lungs. Sounded okay. Checked her respiration. Her pulse. Somewhat thready. Put a pulse oximeter on her to monitor her oxygen levels. Pupils were the same.

"Whatever will I do with just one rain boot?" she wondered aloud.

"Oh, I don't know. Maybe punch some holes in the sole, fill it with dirt and make a planter?"

That made her chuckle. And she grabbed at her midsection. "Oh, my ribs," she said, breath hissing through her teeth. "Don't make me laugh."

If she could still laugh after this, she had to be pretty strong. The pain in her midsection wasn't good. It might be her ribs, or she also might have damage to her liver or her spleen, and she could be bleeding internally. He reached for his mobile ultrasound. The images would be transmitted back to Bigelow Memorial so that the trauma team would have a heads-up on what was coming in.

"We'll check them," he assured her. He didn't say anything about his other concerns. She needed to save her strength to deal with the things that were known.

Her eyes closed.

"Stay with me, now," he ordered.

She blinked fast. "Just catching a little nap. Love the sound of rain on the roof."

She got points for gutting this out with some humor. "I'm going to give you something for the pain," he said. "Any allergies to medications?"

She shook her head.

He ripped the wrapping off a preloaded syringe and stuck her in the arm. Then he started the mobile ultrasound. It took just minutes for him to see something that concerned him. There was blood in her abdomen coming from her liver. They needed to get her to Bigelow Memorial now. He glanced upward at the road. An ambulance had arrived to transport.

"Time to travel," he said, covering her with a light blanket.

"I need my bag," she said. "I can't go without my gym bag."

"We'll get it later," he said. "Be a few days before you're at the gym."

"No," she said. "I need my bag."

She sounded panicked, maybe even desperate. *Just a gym bag*, he was tempted to say. But he knew that offering logic when somebody was responding with emotion was a waste of time. It never got through. "Okay, I'll get it."

In a second, he was back. He placed the black duffel next to her. It was heavier than his own gym bag. But then, all he generally packed was a pair of shorts and a T-shirt. She might have a hair dryer, a curling iron, makeup. His brother, who'd married last year, referred to it as "girl stuff," otherwise known as the things that make it impossible for women to get ready in less than

thirty minutes while men were in and out of the shower, dressed, and on the road in ten. "I grabbed your winter coat off the front seat, too," he said. He folded the jacket and laid it on top of her duffel. "You're going to Bigelow Memorial. I'll be right behind you, and I'll see you in the emergency room. Lots of folks are waiting there, ready to help."

She lifted her hand, reaching for his. She locked her fingers with his, and he felt the connection rip through him. The bones in her hand were fine and delicate, and her skin was very fair. "Thank you," she said.

On impulse, he ran the top of his thumb across her knuckles and then gently squeezed her hand. "You're doing great," he assured her.

If this was *great*, then good or fair really sucked.

"Jamie?" The new voice belonged to a good-looking man in a police uniform. "Can I have a minute?"

Layla got the impression he wasn't asking to talk to Dr. Weathers. The police officer wanted to talk to her.

She pressed her hand to her stomach. "I don't feel well," she said. "I think I might throw up," she added, her cadence fast and rising at the end.

"At the hospital, Marcus," Dr. Weathers said. He looked at the paramedics who had come to carry her up the hill. "Let's go." He walked alongside her all the way to the ambulance.

She was grateful that he'd helped her put off the police officer's questions. But it dawned on her that she was operating with a lack of information. "Where am I?" she asked.

He looked surprised. "Five miles outside Knoware. Hang on, here we go."

Five miles outside nowhere. Nowhere. That thought bounced around in Layla's head as she was loaded into an ambulance. If she was nowhere, then it was going to be hard for Douglas Glass to find her.

That was funny. In an odd, where-did-that-come-from way.

The doctor had been funny, too. Had been joking with her while she was hanging upside down. Maybe it had been the blood running to her head, but she'd felt almost lighthearted, which was not a feeling that she'd experienced since the whole sick situation with Douglas Glass had begun.

But Dr. Weathers's sudden appearance in the storm had literally been a lifeline. She'd wanted to give in to the pain, the terror, maybe even give up, but his presence, his calm voice, his steady gaze had made the difference.

The pain was still there but significantly better now that he'd given her that shot. But she was so tired. It was hard, so hard, to stay awake.

She had to try. Had to stay alert. Would need to be alert for the rest of her life. Or at least until she was sure that Douglas Glass was no longer a threat. When would that be? Once she was safely hidden, had fully assumed her new life.

People did it. It was hard, sure. But people did it. She could, too.

But she needed to stay sharp. No more pain medication. Too easy to let something slip. Dr. Weathers's first question had almost tripped her up. *What's your name?* Old name? New name? The options had danced before her. But he'd just said that there was a whole crew of people there to help. That had to mean po-

lice. The car she was driving was registered to Regan Jones. The driver's license she was carrying was that of Regan Jones.

Regan Jones, she'd said. It had felt weird, and she'd realized that even though she'd been carefully planning and executing for months, actually saying it for the first time was harder than she'd anticipated.

"We're here," said the paramedic.

"Where?" she asked.

"Bigelow Memorial. It's a good hospital. Not big like you'd find in some cities, but the people who work here care, and they're every bit as qualified as any healthcare worker you'll find."

She sounded proud. That was nice. It was good to be proud of your work.

She'd always been proud of her work. But now— Well, she was going to have to a find a new job. But she'd thought ahead, had planned for that eventuality. Had the necessary documents in her go-bag, along with scissors and hair dye and all the other things that she'd purchased in readiness of going. There were also two prepaid phones that couldn't be traced to her.

She did feel very bad about the chaos that Douglas Glass's early release would cause her coworkers. Before she'd left, she'd sent the carefully composed email that she'd drafted months earlier, explaining that her mother back east, whom she'd deliberately mentioned frequently at work, had taken ill and she was needed immediately as a caregiver. She'd wished them a happy Thanksgiving and a blessed holiday season, saying that she'd likely be too busy for much communication in the coming months.

They would believe her, not realizing that her par-

ents had, in fact, been dead for several years. They might not even be too angry that they would have to rely upon the notes she'd been making in the computer system to wrap up her pending projects. Her sudden absence would slow them down, but it shouldn't derail next steps in the clinical trials. She hoped not. The work they were doing was too important.

The back doors of the ambulance opened, she was unloaded and Dr. Weathers was there. He'd kept his promise that he wasn't leaving her. It was the nicest thing that had happened to her today.

"How you doing?" he asked. They were moving fast through a set of double doors. She was flat on her back, so the angle was bad for seeing much of what was going on around her. But it didn't much matter, she realized pretty quickly. They were in charge and she was simply going along for the ride.

"Just swell," she said as her ride abruptly slowed.

A middle-aged woman with a laptop approached. "Dr. Weathers?" she asked, her tone deferential.

"The bare essentials," he said.

Huh?

He looked down at her. "This is Janet from Patient Registration. This won't take long."

It didn't. Within minutes, she'd used the stylus pen to scrawl *Regan Jones* on consent for treatment and do not resuscitate forms.

"Do you have a photo ID?" Janet asked.

She did. But she was going to avoid handing it over if possible. "Can I get it for you later?" she asked, making sure her voice trembled. Her eyes sought those of Dr. Weathers.

"Let's do that," Dr. Weathers said. "We need to keep moving."

They were at least twenty feet down the hall before he leaned down. "Listen, is there anybody you need us to contact?"

It was a reasonable question, and he had no way of realizing it set off a rampage of doubts that she'd thought she'd put to rest months ago. She'd made her decision. "No, no one," she said.

"No one?" he repeated.

She nodded.

"Okay," he said. He reached for the duffel bag that was still lying next to her. She put her hand on it just in time.

"I'll keep this," she said.

"Trust me on this. It's not going into surgery with you. Personal items can be stored in our security department."

It was likely the best alternative. It had been packed so carefully. Any loss would be important. It had a combination lock on it, but a determined thief could cut the heavy canvas or break the lock. Most of her cash was safely hidden in the lining of the bag. For months, she'd cut her living expenses to the bare minimum to save as much money as possible. That, along with what had already been in her savings account, had been converted to cash, and she'd laboriously stuffed bills of varying denominations into the lining of the bag and then resewn the loosened seams. She'd been very grateful for her seventh-grade home economics teacher, who had insisted that everyone perfect a tight and even stitch. The only cash that was loose was what she'd grabbed from her house prior to hurriedly leaving. Then there

were the phones. Each had been activated, but not in her name. There were no calls on either, so they wouldn't tell anybody much. Most important were her driver's license, Social Security card and prepaid credit card.

Dr. Weathers motioned over a security guard who was on the other side of the room. She handed over her go-bag, hoping that his promise that all personal items were locked up until the patient retrieved them proved true.

Then things moved fast. She was stripped of her wet clothing, given a thin white gown and hustled through the process, which included a CT scan, an MRI and another ultrasound, along with assorted blood draws. Evidently, as the MRI technician had explained, they were anxious to get her into surgery to fix her leg but wanted to rule out other injuries first. If she was under anesthesia, it was best to fix everything that needed fixing.

Finally, when all the testing was over, they parked her in a room in the emergency department. Now she waited. She was freezing but couldn't exactly hop off the table and search for a blanket.

She heard a knock on the door and hoped it was handsome Dr. Weathers. But it was a young woman, Kindra from Patient Accounts, who needed her insurance information. "I don't have health insurance," she lied. The words felt odd and distasteful. As Layla Morant, she had really good health insurance. And she felt bad because her lack of insurance meant the hospital wouldn't get reimbursed for their expenses. But Regan Jones was uninsured. "I suppose that means I'll just have to hope for the best with this," she said, forcing lightheartedness.

"Of course not," Kindra said. "There are payment

plans and even opportunities for some charity care. Your medical care is never influenced by your ability to pay."

Maybe that was true at Bigelow Memorial, she thought. If so, good for them. She was confident that it wasn't that way everywhere. It was one of the reasons she'd always valued the benefits that came along with her work at the lab. "If the hospital is Bigelow Memorial, then is the town Bigelow?"

Kindra shook her head. "The hospital was named after a very wealthy family who donated the land and much of the start-up money. The town is Knoware." Then she spelled it, and Layla finally got it.

Knoware, not nowhere.

"There's a note in your record that we still need your photo ID."

"It's in my bag that was taken to security. Once I have that, I'll give it to the nurse," Layla promised.

"Okay, then I have everything I need," Kindra said. "I think Dr. Weathers is waiting to come back in."

She hoped so. She just felt better when he was near. "He seems nice," she said.

"Dr. Jamie Weathers is a super nice guy, super good doc. You really couldn't be in better hands."

Layla smiled to herself after Kindra had left. Now she was destined to think of the man as Dr. Good With His Hands, or Dr. GWHH, forever, and that had such a naughty connotation that she could practically feel her blood pressure rising. Likely not a good thing before surgery.

It was less than a minute before Dr. GWHH came in. His hair was dry. It was still brown but a little lighter than she'd imagined. And instead of straight and plas-

tered to his head, it was thick and had a slight wave. She just bet that when he'd been a baby and before his first haircut, he'd had curls. He wore a white lab coat now versus the dark rain jacket he'd had on when they'd first met. He had a lean physique, like maybe he was a runner. GWHH was really quite a nice package. Before Douglas Glass, she'd certainly have given him a second look.

Now, because of Douglas Glass, she was simply looking for a way out of here. "What's the verdict?" she asked.

"How's your pain?" he asked, not answering her question. "On a scale of one to ten, with ten being the worst."

"A two," she lied. It was a solid ten, but she didn't want any more medication.

"You must have a high pain tolerance. That will probably come in handy. Here's what's going to happen next. We've got a surgical team ready to fix your leg. You do also have two cracked ribs. No intervention required. It'll take a while but they should heal fine on their own."

"That doesn't sound so bad," she said.

"You also have some internal bleeding."

Oh, definitely bad. "From?"

"You've got a small slice in your liver. Sometimes, internal bleeding will stop on its own. And then the blood in the abdominal region will simply dissipate. If that doesn't happen, you'll need a second surgery to repair the liver. But right now our trauma surgeons are advocating a wait-and-see approach."

That implied that she'd be waiting around. No way. She'd avoided the insurance record and she was some-

what confident of the confidentiality of her patient record, but there was no way to stop the police report that her accident had surely generated. It was under the name of Regan Jones, and that gave her some protection but she knew, had always known, that the real Regan Jones was her Achilles' heel.

She'd have the leg surgery. No choice about that. But the first chance she got, she was going to disappear like a puff of smoke.

Chapter 3

Jamie scrolled through the online chart for the fifth or sixth time. Regan Jones's surgery had gone well. Given that she was young and seemed generally healthy, there was every reason to be optimistic.

But still, he worried. Not only was there the internal bleeding to be concerned about, it was the fact that sometimes things went south without much explanation or forewarning. And he felt strangely protective of this woman. *Is there anybody you need us to contact? No, no one.*

No one cared that this young woman was traveling alone, had been injured and was about to have surgery? How could that be?

When she'd demanded her duffel bag be retrieved from her damaged vehicle, he'd assumed it was because of her phone. After all, our phones connected us to the

rest of the world. Held all our contacts, relieving us of the necessity of ever remembering a phone number. Gave us immediate access to our texts and emails and the internet, so that every question could be answered. At many accident scenes, the first question the victim would usually ask was *Where's my phone?*

Then again, she wouldn't have given up her duffel bag later if he hadn't insisted. The idea that it would be locked up and protected in the security department had seemed to appease her.

It was no wonder he couldn't help wondering just what the heck was in the duffel bag.

He was the head of the emergency medicine department at Bigelow Memorial. Outside the hospital, he didn't use the title often, but inside these doors, it carried some clout. He probably could go to the Security Department and request to view the contents of the bag.

They would have to break the combination lock. That would get the request elevated to the head of security. Jamie really should have a better reason for asking than insatiable curiosity about an interesting woman.

He'd connected with Regan Jones. That didn't happen with every patient, regardless of his or the patient's effort. Sometimes, medicine was simply transactional. Didn't mean it wasn't quality care.

So, yes, there'd been a connection. But with Regan Jones, it had been something more. Connection had been surpassed. It felt, somehow, as if they had *merged* on that grassy, rocky slope in the pouring rain. She'd reached for his hand and he'd felt...changed.

He shook his head. It was lucky he wasn't blabbing this nonsense to Caitlin Rose. It would be the following

Thanksgiving before his assistant let him live it down. If Blade or Marcus got ahold of it, he'd have to leave town.

"Dr. Weathers?"

He looked up. Clarice, the recovery room nurse, stood at the doorway. "You wanted to know when she was awake," she said.

"Thank you," he said, getting up from his chair. He carried his laptop with him as he followed Clarice back to Regan's bed. She was the only patient in the recovery room. No one had surgery the day before Thanksgiving unless it was an emergency.

The nurse turned at the exit door and smiled at him. "I'll step out for a minute as long as you're here. We've got a holiday potluck going in the break room, and I need to pull my salad out of the refrigerator. I'll be right back."

"No hurry," he said. He pulled the chair next to Regan's bed a little closer and sat down. Her eyes were closed, but she seemed to be resting comfortably. He automatically glanced at the monitors continually assessing her vitals and didn't see anything that alarmed him. He settled back in his chair.

"If they have spinach dip and that Hawaiian bread, I'll take some," she said softly, not opening her eyes.

He laughed. "Okay. But I'm going for the little meatballs in BBQ sauce that they swear is made out of grape jelly."

She slowly opened her pretty gray-blue eyes. Blinked—her long and dark lashes catching and holding his gaze. "So, they tell me my leg is somewhat bionic," she said.

He shook his head. "A few screws, a plate. You won't even set off the metal detectors at the airport."

"Or play professional soccer," she said.

"Did you play professional soccer before this?" he asked.

"No."

"There you go. The more things change, the more they stay the same," he said.

"That should go on a coffee cup," she said, her eyes closing once more.

"I think that's where I got it."

She smiled but did not open her eyes. "Am I okay? Really?"

"Truly okay," he said. "All you need right now is some rest. You'll be in here for another hour or so and then moved to a regular room."

"I need my bag," she said.

The bag again. "I'll make sure it's in your room. I'll personally see to it."

She opened her eyes. "Thank you. For everything. Do you need to leave right away?"

He shook his head. "I can stay for a while." He didn't mind. It was turning out to be the nicest Thanksgiving eve that he'd had in a very long time.

When Layla woke up, she was in a hospital room. A nice one, for sure. She could tell that even though there was only one small light on to brighten the room. There were pictures on the walls. Ceramic tile flooring. Just one bed. That was nice. When her mother had been ill, she'd had to share a room with a complete stranger. There was a window with blinds, which were slanted just a bit. It was nighttime, and it was still raining. She usually wore a watch, but it had been removed before surgery. She'd been told that her things would be in

her room. She opened the bedside table drawer. Sure enough, her watch was there.

It was two in the morning. She'd been on her way to grab a late lunch when the accident had occurred. She'd been in surgery and recovery during the dinner hour. Now she was simply going to have to wait awhile for breakfast.

There was a closet in the corner. The door was open. On a hanger hung her winter jacket. On a luggage rack sat her go-bag. Dr. Weathers had been true to his word. She wanted to get up, to check her bag, make sure everything was still secure. But there was no way that was happening. She was afraid to put any weight on her injured leg and didn't feel up to hopping to the closet and back.

Everything she owned was in that bag. She realized now that might not be the smartest way to be traveling. She could easily have been separated from her bag if Dr. Weathers had not been so good about getting it for her.

It would be better if she was able to carry more on her person. She eyed her coat in the closet. Perhaps that was her best alternative. It wouldn't be too difficult to create a new hiding place with some needle and thread. As soon as she got out of here, she'd get to it.

She lifted the sheet and peeked at her leg. She couldn't see much, truthfully, even though there was no cast yet. They'd explained to her prior to going under anesthesia that they would splint and wrap her leg post-surgery and the cast would come later, once swelling had diminished and they were confident that the incision was infection-free. The splint itself was some sort of firm elastic that ran from midthigh to midcalf and was open in the front, allowing her to bend her knee

slightly as well as access the wound, which appeared to be wrapped in multiple layers of gauze. She imagined there was a whole line of lovely stitches hidden away.

She'd been disappointed by the news that she wouldn't have a cast right away. It would have been more durable, more forgiving of the strain she might put on her leg. But she would make do. She'd had a broken collarbone once. No way to cast that, and it had healed fine. Her leg would, too. In truth, her cracked ribs hurt nearly as much.

She remembered waking in the recovery room with Dr. Weathers sitting by her side. Asking him if he could stay. And he had.

The fear that she'd managed to keep at bay at the time of the accident and throughout the mad rush after that had finally caught up with her. She could have died in the wreck. It wasn't a stretch of the imagination.

Him being in the chair, in his quiet and watchful way, had calmed her. She'd fallen asleep again. She wasn't sure how long he'd stayed, but when she'd awakened, he was gone and the nurse was back. Disappointed, she'd closed her eyes and gone back to sleep.

It was frustrating that after hours of rest, she still felt terribly fatigued. It did not bode well for any escape attempts. Could she risk waiting another day? As was her habit, she started making a mental list of to-do items. Get a pair of crutches. Mobility was key. Find a cab or car service that could pick her up at the hospital and take her someplace nearby to hunker down for a few days. She was going to be too tired to travel—

"Happy Thanksgiving." Dr. Weathers was at the door, holding two trays. "I brought you turkey."

"Where did you get turkey?" she asked, not minding the interruption. She was really happy to see him again.

"The cafeteria serves turkey with all the trimmings to all three shifts on the holiday. I've got turkey, dressing, sweet potatoes and cranberry sauce. And pumpkin pie for dessert."

She motioned him to come in. "I thought I'd have to wait hours to have some cold scrambled eggs. This is wonderful."

"Nobody wants to eat alone on a holiday, right?" He put her tray on the table that swung across her bed. He took the chair in the corner and held his tray on his lap.

She'd been expecting to join her friend Becky for the holiday. When the call from her attorney had come in and she'd gone in flight mode, she'd been coherent enough to pull out the checklist that she created and refined for months. What she did not want to have happen was for caring friends to get worried about her disappearance and publicize it. Everyone had seen those stories. They went viral on social media. She certainly didn't want her picture out there, making it harder to stay hidden.

To Becky, she'd sent the following text: Terribly sorry for late notice. Due to last-minute vacancy, I have a great opportunity to join a group of scientists traveling abroad to study vaccine development. Not sure duration of trip but will be in touch when I'm able to. Might not be for a while. Thanks again for the invitation. Truly appreciated. Initially she added, just like your friendship. But she had erased that. She was saying goodbye, but Becky couldn't know that.

Once she'd gotten on the road, she'd anticipated that she'd reach Seattle by sometime early Wednesday eve-

ning. She'd assumed that she'd spend most of Thursday recovering from the drive and then on Friday get busy securing an apartment and starting the process of looking for a job.

She had certainly never anticipated being in the hospital, having a Thanksgiving dinner.

She took a bite. It was not bad, not bad at all. Maybe needed a little salt, but they were probably stingy with that in a hospital for good reason. "Do you work twenty-four hours a day?" she asked.

"I'm responsible for the emergency medicine program here at Bigelow Memorial. You'll find me around here quite a bit."

He'd sort of answered the question. "So you eat most of your meals here?"

"Here or I meet friends at Gertie's Café. It's this great little restaurant in Knoware owned by Gertie Biscuit. She'll close the place down today to give her employees time off with their families."

That was nice. "Is the hospital busy at this time of year?" she asked.

"There's always patients but a light surgery schedule on holiday weeks."

She held up a bite of stuffing. "They probably don't know about this."

He laughed. And took a bite from his own plate. "So you were traveling when the accident happened. Going somewhere for Thanksgiving?"

Literally, since the moment he'd first asked for her name, she'd been preparing herself for this question. She shook her head. "Just passing through the area. On my way to Canada. For work."

"What do you do?"

"I'm a graphic artist. Part of the gig economy."

"That has to be a fun job," he said.

It was a fun hobby, to be sure.

"Have you worked on anything I might recognize?" he asked, finishing his plate and moving on to pie.

"I don't think so. I do a lot of contract work for advertising companies." That would be almost impossible to check.

"So where is home?" he asked.

"Los Angeles." Her vehicle had California plates. He might have noticed.

"My friend Marcus Price was a cop in Los Angeles for about ten years. He was the officer at the accident scene. Actually, he was recently promoted to chief. I imagine you'll meet either him or one of his officers at some point soon. They'll want a statement about the accident."

She hoped it wasn't Marcus. If he wanted to exchange information about Los Angeles, it would be hard to hide that she knew next to nothing. "I appreciate them waiting to talk to me. I just wasn't up to it right after it had all happened."

"Understandable," he said. "What did happen?"

"I swerved to miss a deer. Then lost control of my vehicle and it rolled. More than once, likely less than five times," she added with a smile. "I thought I might be in the car for days before help came. I was afraid that I couldn't be seen from the road."

"A hunter called it in."

"Oh, thank goodness."

"Your gratitude may be misplaced. He likely was the person who scared the deer onto the road. Hunting season and all that."

"Nevertheless, I'm grateful," she said. "I had a vision of hanging upside down for days until I rotted, like an old apple." She'd been scared, and it felt freeing to actually give voice to that fear. For the last twenty months, she'd been afraid every day and unable to tell anyone. Unable to let anyone know what she was thinking, doing.

"I'm grateful, too," he said, standing and gathering the now-empty trays. "Old apples don't have a good prognosis."

"Speaking of which, when do you think I'll be good to resume my travels?"

"We'll do some more testing later today to monitor the slice in your liver, just to make sure that the bleeding is either stopped or significantly slowing."

It was an incomplete answer, but she couldn't press without the possibility of making him question her interest in leaving.

"I guess I'll have a chance to catch up on my sleep," she said, letting her eyes flutter shut.

"Best medical treatment there is," he said. "I'll stop by later to see how you're doing."

She wouldn't be here. She wanted to be gone before the police decided to follow up. "Thank you, Dr. Weathers. I really do appreciate everything."

"Of course," he said. "Get some sleep."

He left the room and she lay in the bed, staring at the ceiling. She'd done okay in her conversation with him. Had given reasonable answers to his questions, so he likely wasn't too curious about her. She did feel bad about lying to him. He would think poorly of her when he showed up to check on her and she was simply gone.

But better to be thought poorly of than to be dead.

She couldn't let emotions rule the day. She had to be precise, logical, tactical. She had to outsmart Douglas Glass.

"You're looking quite smart, Dougie." Francine Glass sat by the pool. She'd awakened and pronounced it too cold for swimsuits but definitely warm enough for a light sweater and a strong Bloody Mary.

Douglas had concurred that the pool would be perfect. He'd been less concerned about the weather and more about the nine-foot fence that would prohibit the most earnest of the paparazzi from snapping photos and selling them to any number of magazines that would pay for the privilege of seeing him back at his home.

He mixed the drinks, extra spicy, and drew in a deep breath. Damn, it felt good to breathe. He'd hated the air inside the prison, thick with the odor of too many men taking too few showers.

After his second week there, he'd understood being leery of that space where the water was never hot enough and the atrocities inflicted upon the lesser went unreported and unpunished.

He'd been a lesser. For the first time in his life, Douglas Glass had not been in control, had not been able to have his way, had not been able to simply demand an action and walk away with confidence that the request would be carried out.

He was never going to tell anyone about what had happened to him and the things he'd been made to do for others. It would kill his mother, and it would diminish him in everyone else's opinion.

He knew whose fault it was—Layla Morant's. He'd gone to prison because of her. His family's resources

had not been able to prevent that, although it had helped
bring a potential sentence of twenty years down to two.
And then he had just been lucky to be released more
than four months early. Sometimes overcrowding was
a very good thing.

She would pay. He'd promised her that. *I will come
for you and I will kill you. It will be my new mission
in life.* That's what he'd told her. Of course, he'd been
smart enough to say it in private. She'd repeated the
threat, but there'd been no proof.

But she knew. And he knew. That was all that mattered.

And Douglas Glass was a man of his word.

"Dougie, you're not thinking about that woman, are
you?" his mother asked. She'd always been able to read
his mind.

She'd asked him once, on one of her infrequent visits to the prison, if he'd truly said it. "You can tell me
the truth, Dougie. You know you can." They'd been
at a small table in the visiting room. She'd been ill at
ease, clearly hating being in the room with the type of
people she'd spent a lifetime avoiding. He remembered
how she'd kept her hands in her lap as if afraid to touch
the chairs or the table. Afraid that prison germs would
accompany her home.

When she'd asked the question, he'd looked around.
The guards had been far enough away, but still, he'd
been guarded. He was going to tell no one. "Of course
not," he'd said.

And because she was his mother and really did know
him best of all, he was confident that she'd not believed
him but was relieved that he was man enough to stick
to his story at all times, even in the worst of situations.

"I try never to think of her," he lied now, sipping his drink. Oh, what a luxury to be able to eat and drink whatever he wanted, whenever he wanted. He was never, ever giving it up again.

"I can't lose you to prison again, Dougie. You must forget about her. What's done is done."

What had been done to him could never be undone. He could not look in a mirror and not remember the mind-numbing fear of what each new day would bring. Somebody had to pay for that. *She* would pay.

He'd already called her work. Late last night, after his mother had gone to bed. He'd known it was way past business hours, but he'd wanted to make sure she was still employed at the same place. Sure enough, he'd worked his way through the company directory and into her voice mail. He'd heard the very standard greeting that Layla Morant was not available and to please leave a message.

He had a message, all right. One that he intended to deliver in person.

Chapter 4

Layla skipped the cold scrambled eggs on the breakfast tray but ate the fruit and the toast and drank the coffee. She'd slept off and on after Dr. Weathers had left her room in the middle of the night. Each time she'd awakened, she'd hoped to see him, but it hadn't happened. She knew he was either working or catching up on what was likely much-needed sleep as well.

And it was a foolish hope, because she was simply delaying the inevitable. She was going to slip away and never see him again.

The door opened and a nurse entered, carrying a pair of crutches. She put them in the corner of the room and proceeded to check Layla's vitals and the incision on her leg. Layla got her first peek at it. It was bruised and scraped and painted with a strip of color that she assumed was some type of topical antibiotic. But it was

the long stretch of stiches, at least three inches, that made her quickly look away. Black and ugly, pulling at the edges of the skin, they were a chilling reminder of the accident. "How's it look?" she managed to ask, thinking it looked pretty darn horrible.

"Just fine," the nurse said. "We'd like to get you up for a bit, let you visit the restroom. How does that sound?"

Sounded like a truly excellent idea. "I'll give it a shot," Layla said.

It was a slow process, and she felt light-headed at first as she swung her legs over the side of the bed. The nurse handed her the crutches, and she managed to stand. Got used to the feel of them under her arms.

Five minutes later, the bathroom trip, which included a glorious brushing of her teeth, was successfully completed and she was back in bed. Exhausted. How could it have been so taxing to walk twelve feet? She had to accept the sad reality that there was no way she was ready to leave yet. It was Thanksgiving Day. Her best hope was that the police department was lightly staffed and responding only to emergency calls, that something as routine as following up to get a statement about a car accident would be low priority. If they came, she was going to pretend that she was sleeping.

She vowed to use the day in the hospital to regain as much strength as she possibly could. She closed her eyes, slept for another few hours and was awakened for lunch. It was a duplicate of what Dr. Weathers had brought to her during the middle of the night. Oddly enough, it didn't seem to taste as good as it had then. But she ate most of it, wanting to stay fueled.

Sometime after lunch, she was wheeled somewhere in the hospital, where they did another scan of her ab-

domen. The physician who reported the results was not
Dr. Weathers. That was disappointing. It was also disappointing to hear that there was still some bleeding
from her liver. "Your vitals are good," said the woman
who'd identified herself as Dr. Ono. "We'll look again
tomorrow and make a decision."

The decision was already made. She was leaving tomorrow. "Thank you," Layla said. When she got back
to her room, it was being cleaned.

"Hello," Layla greeted the older woman.

"I'll be done in just a few minutes," she said, checking the garbage can.

"No hurry. Happy Thanksgiving, by the way," Layla
said.

"Same to you. Did you get turkey for lunch?"

"I did. It was good."

"The cafeteria does a wonderful job. Good thing I
love turkey, because I'll have it with my family later
tonight, once I'm home."

The woman was nice. Friendly. Maybe she was the
right one to ask. "I was wondering if you might be able
to help me with something," Layla said.

"I will certainly try."

"I'm not familiar with Knoware and was wondering where people might find temporary lodging, like a
hotel or maybe even a short-term rental."

"There's lots of that around," the woman said. "Being
that this is such a tourist trap in the summer. Some
places close in the off-season—it's just not worth it for
them to keep their doors open. But there's some hotels
and other rentals on Trigger Road near the beach that
stay open year-round. There's three, right in a row. Their
names all start with a C."

"Great. Thanks."

"Sure, no problem. What happened?" she asked, looking at Layla's leg.

"Car accident."

"You get patched up at the scene by Dr. Weathers?"

"I did."

"He's as nice as he is handsome. He's real tight with two other guys in Knoware, and people always said they were the three most eligible bachelors in town. The other two recently got married, so that only leaves Dr. Weathers. Not for a lack of trying on the part of lots of women, though."

"I imagine," Layla said.

"I shouldn't be gossiping, but in a small town, everybody does sort of know everybody else, and it's all in good fun."

"I'm sure it is."

"He's a local hero, you know?"

"Dr. Weathers?" Layla asked.

The woman nodded, her eyes dancing. "I'll show you. There's a copy on the desk in the nurses' station."

She was out of the room before Layla had a chance to say anything. But she was back in just a minute, holding a newspaper article that had been laminated. She handed it to Layla.

It was a photo of a helicopter. In the air. A patient, she presumed, was getting loaded, and there was Dr. Weathers, continuing to provide care. It was a perilous-looking situation, reinforced by the headline of Local Physician Hero Risks Life to Save Patient.

Wow. Just wow. "That's impressive," Layla said, handing it back to the woman.

"I'll say. It's fun because when the nurses tease him

about it, he blushes." She gave one final look around the room. "I think that's it. Hope you feel better soon."

The woman left, and Layla tried to relax. It was hard because her leg ached. She thought of the newspaper article. *Local physician hero. Who blushes.* That was very sweet.

When the nurse came in later, offering pain medication, she reluctantly accepted it. It was likely the only way she was going to be comfortable enough to sleep.

It was much later and dark outside when she woke up. The very heroic Dr. Weathers was sitting in the chair in the corner. "Hi," he said.

Was it wrong that it felt so very good to see him? "Hi. Have you been there long?" she asked, self-conscious that she'd been unaware of him. What if she'd been drooling in her sleep?

"Nope. I made a little noise to see if you'd wake up. If you hadn't, I'd have come back another time. How are you feeling?"

All things considered, not that bad. "On the mend," she said. "I had another scan."

"I know. I checked the result. No cause for alarm," he said. "We'll watch it."

She just smiled. "Have you been working all day?" she asked.

"I was covering the emergency room," he said.

"Busy?"

"You know, the typical odd assortment—everything from sore throats to sprained ankles to gallstones. Then there's always the extra holiday effect. A few burns from the folks who decide to deep-fry their turkey. A finger almost cut off by a carving knife. A couple trav-

elers like yourself with minor injuries from a vehicle accident."

Travelers like yourself. She didn't think so. Just how many people could be on the run from a homicidal narcissist?

"When do you sleep?" she asked.

"Soon. There will be somebody in to relieve me at eleven tonight. By the time I finish up charting, I should be home by two or three at the latest."

What a crazy life. "Some holiday," she said.

"Well, you probably weren't expecting to spend it like this, either," he said.

"No, not really," she said. She thought he might delicately be fishing around for an explanation of what she had been expecting. That would not be forthcoming. She'd already lied to him when she'd said that she was headed to Canada. She hadn't wanted to offer up Seattle.

"I spoke with Chief Marcus Price this afternoon. He'll be by in the morning to get your statement. Your vehicle was towed to Savick's Garage. You saw Blade Savick at the accident scene. He's a paramedic/ firefighter. His parents own the garage. This is their contact information." He hesitated. "I…uh…put my number on it as well."

He stood and passed over a sheet of paper where he'd written the information. She took it, because a reasonable person would be interested in following up on their damaged vehicle. But she didn't intend to make an insurance claim. No sense inviting that kind of scrutiny into her life. And with regards to his number, well, that was sweet, but she wasn't going to be calling him.

"I'll stop in and see you tomorrow," he said, his hand on the door.

"Great. See you then."

She closed her eyes once she was alone again. How many lies was she going to tell over the next months, the next years? It was overwhelming, really. She'd plotted and planned and conceived the whole idea of disappearing and starting over, but she'd absolutely underestimated the toll of lying, of being a deceitful person. How did people do this? It filled her with despair.

You'll do what you have to do.

How many times had she told herself that in the previous months? Now she was being tested.

She had better not fail.

Jamie Weathers was running on fumes. On Wednesday night he'd managed to grab a couple hours of sleep before he'd been back on duty in the wee hours of Thanksgiving Day. It was now almost twenty-four hours later.

He was about to drop. And still, he took a minute to think about whether he wanted to go upstairs again and see Regan Jones one more time. She had to be sleeping now. And it wasn't good for her recovery to continue to be awakened.

Maybe he could watch her sleep. He'd enjoyed that earlier before she'd awakened and caught him in the chair. He'd had the chance to really study her face— the absolutely perfect oval shape, the wide-set eyes, the finely arched eyebrows that were darker than her hair. It had been nice to chat with her when she'd awakened, but he would have been happy just watching her.

However, if he tried that now, it was a foregone con-

clusion that, ultimately, he'd fall asleep in the chair and sometime later a nurse would find him. She or he would be circumspect to Jamie's face, but then later the news would hit the hospital grapevine and spread like a virus. *What was Dr. Weathers doing in the patient's room?* Ultimately, somebody would get up the nerve to ask him.

And what would he say?

It's not weird. You see, we merged. He didn't think that was going to fly. He'd best head home.

He pulled his keys from his pocket and walked out the staff entrance toward the employee parking lot. It was a cold night, in the low twenties. There was a thin layer of ice on his windshield, and he had to scrape that. Once inside his car, he turned the heat to high and started home. His vehicle barely got warm before he pulled into his garage and killed the engine.

He liked his two-bedroom, two-bath condo. It was clean and sleek and totally different than the houses his two best friends were living in. They were both in big brick monstrosities. He felt comfortable in their homes but was never envious. He didn't need that much space.

But then, it was just him. Maybe when he had a family, he would change his mind.

And just like that, he was thinking about Regan Jones again. He was attracted to her. Which was stupid, because she was on her way to Canada. A long-distance relationship was one thing, but an intercountry one would take some real effort.

But, he told himself, as he went inside and immediately headed for the shower, he was pretty good at tough stuff.

Ten minutes later, warm under the heavy quilt, he re-

flected on the day. Another Thanksgiving in the books. He'd had the full turkey-and-dressing meal twice today. Once in the middle of the night with Regan and again at noon. For dinner, they'd ordered pizza in the Emergency Department, and he'd snagged a couple slices of that.

The middle-of-the-night feast with Regan had been sort of a spur-of-the-moment decision. He'd been going through the line in the cafeteria, loading up his tray, thinking about her. Wondering how she was doing. On a whim, he'd picked up a second tray and carried it upstairs. Had she been asleep, he'd not have awakened her.

But she'd been awake. And he'd been very grateful that he'd taken the chance. One, she'd been hungry. And two, it had been awfully nice to have a twenty-minute break in the middle of the night with someone he found attractive and genuinely nice.

When he'd seen her later in the day, he'd wanted to ask about her plans after she was released. They wouldn't want to cast the leg until they were confident it wasn't going to get infected. That meant that if she wanted it done in Knoware, she was going to have to stick around.

He supposed she could continue her drive to Canada and get it casted somewhere up there. But truly, people underestimated the toll a surgery and general anesthesia took on a body. She would get tired very quickly. He'd been hoping that she'd offer up a few details so that he could give her an opinion in the form of medical advice.

That hadn't happened, but when he went to the hospital today, he'd have that conversation with her. While he was officially on vacation, there was nothing to pre-

vent him from stopping in and making sure she was doing okay.

Nothing except that he was not the assigned physician. She had a hospitalist managing her care. He was... overreaching, possibly. Making things personal.

Making a mistake.

His gut told him that he wasn't.

He was not expected back to work until Monday of the following week. Ten full days off. It was an unheard-of amount of time off for him. But he was smart enough to know that he needed it. He'd been burning the candle at both ends and sometimes striking a match in the middle of it for the hell of it.

Now for days on end he could do whatever he wanted.

He closed his eyes. And his last thought before falling asleep was that of a pretty blonde with white streaks in her hair and gray-blue eyes.

Layla felt better when she woke up on Friday morning. Certainly not a hundred percent, probably not even a passing seventy percent, but definitely well enough to move her plan forward. She would have liked having more information about the internal bleeding, but she really couldn't afford a delay. The police were coming today. They needed to find an empty bed. With that in mind, she quickly ate most of the breakfast that they brought her and waited impatiently while the nurse checked the bandage on her leg.

Finally, alone again, she used her crutches to make her way over to her go-bag in the closet. The clothes she'd been wearing when she'd had the accident had not been returned. She assumed they were in the trash

somewhere. But she had two additional outfits with her. She took out underwear, jeans and a long-sleeved T-shirt, moving slowly and carefully, because her ribs evidently didn't want her moving any other way. If she tried, they protested.

She got her clothes on, finishing with two socks but just one tennis shoe. Her left foot was still so swollen that there was no way she was getting a shoe on. Even a sock was a challenge. By the time she was dressed, she was sweating as if she'd run a 5K.

But still, she was grateful for the winter coat that Dr. Weathers had grabbed off the front seat when he'd retrieved her go-bag. Without that, she'd be very cold later and also, she'd attract some attention. The opposite of what she wanted. She wanted to fly under the radar as much as possible from here on out.

She reached into the pocket of the coat and pulled out a gray stocking cap. She put it on, pulling it low on her forehead. She was going to have to exit the hospital without anybody stopping her. Best way to do that was to look like a visitor.

She wasn't sure how nursing units worked, but she suspected it was only her assigned nurse and perhaps a doctor who would realize that she'd not yet been officially released. She just needed to get past them.

She adjusted the straps of her go-bag so that she could wear it as a backpack. It felt heavy on her back and her ribs weren't happy about it, but it made it easier to use her crutches. She took one more glance around the room to make sure she had everything. She saw the slip of paper that Dr. Weathers had given her so that she could retrieve her car. With his number, too.

She hesitated. He'd been so very nice, and in differ-

ent circumstances, well… The possibilities might have been endless.

But this was her circumstance now. She left the paper on her bedside table. Maybe housecleaning would throw it away before he saw it. Or maybe he'd see firsthand that she never intended to contact him again. Maybe that would sting a little.

She couldn't let that matter.

She eased open the door and checked the hallway. The nurses' station was between her and the elevator. There were two young men standing there, both in scrubs. One was holding a laptop; the other had a tray of something. She did not see the female nurse who had been in her room that morning. She watched for another three or four minutes, her agitation growing.

It was now or never.

The man with the laptop looked up as she passed and smiled. She smiled back, feeling as if the muscles in her jaws were strung so tightly, they might snap. She got to the elevator, pressed the down button, and waited impatiently.

She felt hot. It was too warm inside to have her jacket on, but carrying it and fiddling around with crutches was a disaster in the making. Her hat was trapping her body heat, but she left it on. Blondes were remembered. A gray stocking cap was forgettable.

Finally, the elevator arrived. She had to wait while two people exited, and then she was inside and on her way to the first floor. The elevator door opened and she looked for an exit sign. She found it and made her way down a long hallway. There was a big lobby with a water feature. A male security guard sat behind a desk near the door.

There was a male police officer standing next to him. He was young and talking in an animated manner. He had a deep voice, and it seemed to echo in the big lobby. Something about football. Neither one of them was paying her any attention.

That was good, because she was pretty sure the cop was one of the two officers who'd been at her accident.

She crossed the lobby. It seemed to take forever.

She pressed the silver pad on the wall to operate the automatic door. It opened slowly. She was going to make it.

"Excuse me, miss," the police officer said from somewhere behind her. "Can I have a word?"

She'd always been a pretty quick thinker. At work, she'd been counted on as the one at the table who could offer up some reasonable options on the spot.

And absolutely nothing was coming to her.

She stopped, just shy of the now-open door. So close. She turned. "Yes?" she said, hoping that her voice did not betray the absolute fear that was running through her body. She'd assumed another woman's identity. Had paid for it. It was a crime.

She would be punished. More importantly, if found out, it would undo so much careful preparation. It would put her back in the crosshairs of Douglas Glass.

"How's your day going?" the young officer asked.

Not great. "Fine. Nice sunshine," she added, looking over her shoulder.

"I was wondering if you'd be interested in buying any candy bars. It's a police fund-raiser to help kids get bike helmets."

Fund-raiser. Her heart was galloping in her chest because of candy bars. "Of course," she said.

"Two bucks apiece," he said.

She handed him a five that she had in her jeans pocket. "I'll take two, and you can keep the extra dollar as a donation."

"Thank you," he said.

Oh no, thank you! "Officer, I am here from out of town, visiting my mom, and unfortunately, my phone went dead so I can't call for a ride. You wouldn't be able to help me with that?"

"Oh, sure. There aren't that many services in Knoware. But my younger sister and her friends use this guy." He was thumbing through his contacts as he talked. He punched a number. "Hey, Connor. It's Rick. I'm at Bigelow Memorial, and there's a woman who needs a ride." He listened. "Great. I'll let her know." He put his phone back in his shirt pocket. "He's pretty close. Will be here in less than ten minutes. Tan Toyota Corolla."

The stocking cap on her head felt as tight as shrink-wrap. She could feel the heat in her cheeks. The chocolate she was holding in her hand was going to melt. "Thank you," she said. "Good luck with your fundraising."

She turned. The automatic door had long since closed, so she once again pushed the silver button on the wall. It opened. She walked through.

She fought the urge to keep going, to push her body as far as it would go. First of all, she wouldn't get far. Second of all, she needed to wait for her ride. To do otherwise would raise an alarm with the officer. She'd taken a big chance asking him for help. But she'd known getting a ride from the hospital was going to be the toughest part of her getaway plan. She'd considered

using the phone in her room to contact a service but hadn't known whether they would be able to trace the call once she left. Had considered doing the same with one of the phones in her go-bag but wanted to wait to turn them on until there were no other options.

She'd hoped that there would be some nice old lady volunteering at a registration desk near the front door. When that hadn't materialized and the police officer hadn't seemed to realize who she was, it was an opportunity she could not pass up.

She sat on a bench that was thirty feet from the front door. Lifted her face to the warm sunshine. Prayed.

For time to advance swiftly. For her strength to hold out. For a place to stay. For the police officer to remain oblivious.

Lately, her praying had become so very practical. World peace and harmony were beyond her. Survival. That's what mattered.

Finally, she saw her ride arrive. He pulled to the curb and stopped. She got to her feet. Suddenly, the young driver got out and ran around the car to open the back door. "Hi, I'm Connor. Didn't see the crutches at first," he added. He offered up a slightly lopsided grin.

"No worries," she said. She'd kept her backpack in place when she'd sat on the bench, simply leaning forward to accommodate its width. Now she'd need to take it off to sit back and buckle the seat belt. She leaned against the car with her good leg, keeping all the weight off her broken one. Then she shrugged it off.

"I can toss that in the trunk," Connor said.

"In the back seat with me is fine," she said.

"These, too?" he asked, holding up her crutches.

"Sure."

He nodded, and once she was settled, he helped her shut the door, then walked around the car, opened the rear door on the other side and put her go-bag on the seat. There was enough headroom for him to put the tips of the crutches on the floor, then lean them back, over the duffel.

He shut the door and, unconsciously, she reached out, rested her hand on her go-bag. When you had almost nothing, what you had was important.

For months, she'd packed and unpacked the bag, over and over again, as she'd made decisions about what would make the final cut. Had looked for things that were multipurpose. A tool that could be a weapon that could also open a can or bottle. Had considered the weight of everything. Had envisioned the possibility of illness or injury, so first aid supplies had made the list. Survival gear. A waterproof blanket that folded up into a small pouch.

Connor opened the driver's door and got behind the wheel. "Destination?" he asked.

"Trigger Road," she said, remembering her conversation with the woman who'd cleaned her hospital room. "That stretch where all the hotels are," she added.

"I got it," he said confidently. "Knoware isn't that big."

That was a problem. Easier to disappear in a big place. But last night, an idea of how she could make this work had started to formulate.

She sat back, taking stock of the area around her. She'd seen none of this when she'd arrived. The hospital itself was three stories and, based on the different

shades of brick, looked as if it might have been added
on to once or twice. There were multiple flower beds
located around the property. Right now, they were bare
and brown, but she suspected that in the spring and
summer, it was quite pretty. There were big parking lots
that were about half-full. The streets around the hospital
were lined with modest, well-kept homes.

"New to Knoware?" Connor asked, keeping his eyes
on the road.

"Visiting my mother. She's ill," Layla answered.
That's what she'd told the cop.

"Bigelow Memorial is top-notch. Tough to travel on
crutches."

"Not ideal," she said. No, indeed. She glanced at her
watch, noting the time.

Twelve minutes later, he slowed the vehicle. "Which
hotel?" he asked.

She had made it to the right place. She saw the Coat-
tail Inn, the Crosswinds Hotel and the Creekside Hotel.
"That one," she said, pointing to the Creekside Hotel.
It was the biggest.

She hoped she was making a good decision with
this. She leaned forward as he pulled into the circular
drive that fronted the building. "What do I owe you?"
she asked.

"Sixteen dollars," he said. "That's my minimum,"
he added, almost apologetically.

She'd have gladly paid many times that. "Cash
okay?" She didn't want to use her prepaid credit card
in the name of Regan Jones unless it was absolutely
necessary.

"It's what I prefer," he said.

She handed him a twenty. "Keep the change," she said.

"Thank you. Let me get your things and help you with the door."

Two minutes later, she was standing outside his vehicle, ready to go.

"I hope your mom feels better," Connor said. He handed her a card. "Call me again if you need another ride."

"I'll do that," Layla said. "Thank you, Connor."

She walked into the hotel and scanned the layout before moving forward. There was a woman, fifties, behind the desk, staring at a computer screen. She looked up as Layla got near. "Good morning," Layla said and proceeded to walk past the desk toward the elevator at the far side of the lobby.

The woman smiled and returned her gaze to the computer.

Act like you belong and people will think that you do. That had been advice that her mother had given her when she'd attended her first science camp, three years younger than most of the other participants. It had served her well then. It seemed to be working now, too.

She got in the elevator, pushed the button to go to the second floor. Once there, she headed down the hallway, her crutches seeming to thump loudly with each step. Her leg ached, no doubt about it. And this was exhausting.

But she couldn't give up now. She was so close.

At the end of the hallway was a second elevator. She took it back down to the first floor, then exited the building via a side door. She glanced up, looking for a camera, but didn't see one. She walked down the narrow service drive that ran between the hotel and the property next to it. There was a linen truck idling

in the alley. An older man, dressed in gray work pants and a matching shirt, was unloading a dolly stacked high with freshly washed and folded towels that were wrapped in clear plastic.

It was such a risk. Could she take it?

If she didn't, what other alternatives did she have? None.

She approached. "Excuse me, sir."

Chapter 5

Jamie knocked on the door. It was ajar but closed enough that he couldn't see into the room. At Bigelow Memorial, all staff knocked before entering. Right now, he wasn't technically staff—he was simply a visitor—but the habit was locked in. He knocked again, a little more loudly.

Still no answer. Concerned, he pushed the door open. The bathroom door was open. She wasn't there. Two more steps into the room and he could see the empty bed. The closet door was closed. He yanked it open. Empty, with the exception of a discarded white cotton gown.

What the hell? He took one more look around the small room. On the nightstand was the slip of paper he'd given her the night before, with the information for Savick's Garage. With his cell number that he'd de-

bated for ten minutes before adding. He hadn't wanted to seem pushy or over the line.

He ran out of the room toward the nurses' station. "Room 224. Patient name of Regan Jones. She's not there."

The young nurse behind the counter tapped keys on his computer. Then he looked up. "I don't know. She hasn't been discharged. No tests were ordered, so she's not in lab or X-ray."

"Call security," Jamie said. "She can't have gotten far." Not on crutches, with a heavy duffel bag to carry. He went behind the counter and sat down in front of a computer. He signed on and pulled up her medical record. A nurse had charted her vitals at 8:12 that morning. Temperature, blood pressure and pulse had all been normal. Swelling in her left foot had gone down and incision was not draining. All good things. It did not mean that she was ready to leave.

"Dr. Weathers?"

It was Drake Porter. He'd worked security for more than two years. He also played in the hospital basketball league with Jamie. They always got along well. Now he looked young and scared, no doubt because the nurse had warned Drake that Dr. Weathers was upset. "They said a young woman left AMA."

He knew to take a patient leaving against medical advice as serious. "Yes. Were you working the lobby desk this morning?"

"Came on at seven."

"She's young, maybe thirty, blonde, slim. On crutches. Had a black duffel bag. Did you see her?" Jamie asked.

Drake shook his head.

"She might have needed a cab or information about car rentals," Jamie prompted.

Drake continued to shake his head. "There was a woman, but she wasn't a patient. She had on a gray stocking cap, but she could have been a blonde. Said she had been visiting her mother. No duffel bag. She had a backpack."

Jamie envisioned the bag he'd grabbed from the front seat of the vehicle, then later tossed into the closet in Regan's room. By changing the straps, she could have converted it to a backpack. "Yes," he said. "Did someone pick her up? Did you see the vehicle?"

"I...I don't know," Drake said. "I'm sorry. I can tell this is important to you. But you could ask Rick Daniels. The two of them talked."

What? Rick Daniels was the newest officer on the Knoware Police Department. He'd been at the accident scene with Marcus. Surely he'd have recognized Regan as the accident victim. Although, come to think of it, he hadn't come too close. Marcus had been the one to actually try to talk to her. "Where and when were they talking?"

"This morning, maybe around eight thirty. Right by my desk. She bought some chocolate from Rick."

Jamie knew immediately what he was talking about. Marcus had hit both him and Blade up for the police fund-raiser the last time they'd had breakfast together. He'd bought ten bars and left them in the staff break room.

"I think Rick might have helped her get some transportation. But you'd have to ask him. I got busy with a call at the desk while they were talking, and then he

left shortly after that. I think there was a police matter that he needed to respond to."

The only police matter that he was interested in was a missing woman. He needed to talk to Rick Daniels. Now. And he knew just the guy who could make that happen.

"Thanks, Drake," Jamie said.

"Listen, I'm sorry if we should have stopped her," Drake said.

Jamie held up a hand. "You didn't know," he said simply. He waited until Drake had left the area before dialing Marcus. Drake had no way of knowing, but the young cop should have been smarter.

"Marcus Price," his friend answered.

"Regan Jones left Bigelow Memorial this morning AMA after evidently being assisted by one of your officers." The words rushed out of his mouth. He had a horrible feeling that there was no time to waste.

"What? Slow down," Marcus said.

"Regan Jones," Jamie repeated. "She left the hospital this morning, and Rick Daniels evidently helped her find transport."

"That makes no sense," Marcus said. "Like I told you the other day, we needed to talk with Ms. Jones to finalize the accident report. Rick and I had arranged to meet at the hospital to do that this morning, but then we got a 911 call about another break-in on Main Street. That had a higher priority, so I called off the meeting, thinking we'd circle back later today."

"Well, you missed your chance, I think," Jamie said bitterly.

Marcus was silent, clearly absorbing Jamie's irritation. "Where are you?" he asked finally.

"At the hospital."

"I thought you were on vacation."

"I came to visit Regan Jones."

"Right."

He could practically hear the gears grinding in Marcus's head. "Look, I feel bad for this woman. It's tough to be traveling and get injured."

"Right," Marcus said again.

This time he sounded less convinced.

"Fine. I liked her. I wanted to see her again," Jamie admitted.

"Okay. I'll find Rick and figure out what happened. Give me five minutes and I'll call you back."

Jamie considered going to his office. He could pace there as well as anywhere. But he returned to her room, as if he could learn something from the empty bed. He picked up the slip of paper that he'd given her, put it in his pocket. What had compelled her to leave before she'd been medically released? What the hell was her hurry? Was she simply going to leave her wrecked car behind?

Had their *merge* been in his head? Had she felt nothing when it had about knocked his socks off?

She'd said that she was headed to Canada. As a licensed pilot who flew regularly, he had contacts that could help him with that. Flight manifests for both commercial and private flyers could be checked. Security footage of airports reviewed.

He pulled up his contact information on his phone. Then typed his message: Need assistance ASAP. Looking to find a Regan Jones (female, age 30, blonde, gray-blue eyes) who might have been flying from some-

where in Washington State to Canada today. Injured leg, likely using crutches. Can you check?

He got a reply in less than twenty seconds. Yes, will check and advise.

He let out a breath. He'd served in the army with his contact. The man would know that the request hadn't been made on a whim, that if Jamie had felt compelled to ask, there was a good reason.

His phone rang. Marcus. "Tell me you know where I should look."

"No," Marcus said. "But I know who picked her up and I've got a contact number. I was going to call him but I thought you might want to."

"You thought right. Let's have it." Jamie wrote it down as Marcus recited it. "Thank you."

"Yeah, for what it's worth, Rick feels bad about this. He said that she looked very different from the woman he remembered from the car accident."

No doubt. Then, she'd been wet and bloody and in pain.

"And he said that she was very convincing that she'd been visiting a patient."

That bothered him more than he wanted to admit right now. If she'd rehearsed that story, what else had been a performance? He pushed the thought away. He wanted her found. Wanted her to have the medical treatment she needed. They weren't even confident yet that she didn't require surgery for her internal bleeding. "I have reservations that he's going to make it as a cop," Jamie said, redirecting his thoughts.

"Yeah, me, too," Marcus admitted. "Call the guy," he said.

Connor Kissner. That was a mouthful. He dialed.

"Hello."

"Connor, my name is Jamie Weathers, and I'm a physician at Bigelow Memorial."

"I know who you are."

There was little anonymity in small towns, especially when your photo made the front page. "This morning you picked up a blond-haired woman from the front entrance. She was wearing a gray stocking cap. The ride was arranged by Rick Daniels. She was on crutches."

"Of course, I remember. Nice woman."

"I need to know where you dropped her off."

"Well, I…"

He was hesitant. Likely meant he was a decent guy.

"It's a medical emergency," Jamie said. "We have information that we need to pass along to her as soon as possible."

"In that case, she's at the Creekside Hotel."

"Thank you, Connor. I appreciate the help." Jamie hung up and was whistling as he made his way out of the hospital.

"Morning," the man replied. He shut the back door of his linen truck.

"I have a huge favor to ask," Layla said, aiming for charming versus desperate. "I'm having a bit of trouble negotiating these crutches, and I've got a distance to walk. Is there any way I could grab a ride with you?"

"What direction are you headed?"

She'd come from the south. The west was water. Her true destination was east. "North," she said.

"I'm only going as far as Widow's Peak before I head home to Olympia," he said.

She had no idea how far north that was. "That would still be very helpful," she said.

He shrugged. "I had a knee replacement last year. Those crutches are a bitch. Get a walker instead."

"Sounds like good advice," she said.

"Give me a minute to drop these off inside and I'll be back."

When he was gone, she stood outside the vehicle, figuring the best way to negotiate the high step to get inside. When he came back, she was ready. She opened the door, tossed her go-bag on the floor and stood on one leg as she shoved her crutches inside. Then she turned around, reached behind herself, braced her hands on the seat and awkwardly jumped onto it.

It would have been a 2.6 on a ten-point scale, but she was inside.

She had voluntarily gotten into a stranger's vehicle. What the heck was she thinking? If he attacked her, she'd have no way to defend herself, no strength upon which to draw.

She drew in deep breaths and reminded herself of basic truths. Most people were good people. Most people would help someone else when asked. Most people would never ever harm another person.

It didn't totally calm her nerves, but by the time the driver walked around his vehicle and got into his own seat, she was no longer in danger of hyperventilating. "Thank you again," she said.

"Yeah, probably against company policy to offer a ride, so don't put it on social media," he said, checking his mirrors before pulling out.

"No worries there," she said. She took off her hat and stuffed it into the pocket of her coat, which she consid-

ered removing, but if she needed to move quickly, she couldn't manage crutches, a backpack and a coat. Better to leave it on.

He glanced at the time on the dashboard. "Forty-five minutes, give or take a few," he said.

They would arrive by ten. Midmorning. How could she be so weary?

"Name is Mickey, by the way."

"Regan," she said.

"How did you hurt your leg?"

"Fell off a ladder while I was trimming a tree," she said.

"You know, there are people you can hire to do that."

She'd learned this past year that there were people you could hire to do most anything. "Good advice. Busy day?" she asked, wanting to shift the conversation away from herself.

"Busy enough. Not like in season, when I regularly work twelve-hour days. This evening I'll be home for dinner, with maybe enough time for a cocktail beforehand. I'd normally go another sixty miles north of Widow's Peak, but everything that direction is closed."

She couldn't tell if Widow's Peak was a physical place, like a hotel or a restaurant, or maybe it was a town. She couldn't ask, because earlier she'd acted as if she knew the spot. She turned her face toward the window, hoping to avoid more conversation. The less they talked, the less likely he was to remember her or to later reflect that their conversation had been odd.

He turned on the radio, to a talk radio station, where the topic of the day was coastal erosion. It was mind-numbing noise in the background of her thoughts that were running a mile a minute. Once she got to Widow's

Peak, she was going to have to find a place to stay, to rest. It was painful to admit it, but she was spent, truly spent, and she'd been away from the hospital for less than an hour.

They'd have figured out she was missing by now. What would they do? Notify the police? Shrug their shoulders and move on with their day? She couldn't be the only patient who ever walked out prior to discharge.

Would they contact Dr. Weathers?

Would he care that she'd suddenly disappeared?

If he did, what did it really matter? *Not one damn thing*, she thought, blinking fast as her eyes filled with tears.

It took Jamie less than ten minutes to drive to the Creekside Hotel. He parked on the street and went in the front door. The woman behind the desk looked up and smiled at him.

"I'm trying to connect with one of your guests. She checked in just this morning, probably within the last half hour."

The woman pursed her lips. "I'm sorry, but no one has checked in yet this morning. Perhaps her arrival was delayed."

"No. She was dropped off here this morning. Her name is Regan Jones."

The woman tapped the keys on her computer. "I'm sorry. We don't have a Regan Jones registered."

This was like quicksand, sucking him in. He pulled a business card. "I run the emergency medicine program at Bigelow Memorial. It's a matter of grave importance that we find her."

"You're friends with Marcus Price, aren't you?" the woman asked.

It wasn't the question he'd been expecting. "I am. You know Marcus?"

"He used to date my daughter. I always hoped things would work out between them. I was disappointed to hear that he'd gotten married," she said with a smile.

"Pretty confident you weren't the only one," he said.

"Let me take a quick look at our security feed from this morning." She tapped on computer keys and within minutes was turning her screen so that Jamie could see. "Is this her?"

"Yes," he said. It was an outside camera, pointing at the front door. She was outside, on the sidewalk. There was a clock in the corner of the screen, ticking off the seconds. He looked at his watch. He was less than thirty minutes behind her. So close.

He watched as she walked into the hotel. Then the woman clicked a few keys to switch the view. There she was in the lobby. She was getting around on the crutches fairly well, but he could tell that she was weary. She did not stop at the front desk. Instead, she made her way to the elevator at the far end of the lobby. When she got in, she disappeared from view.

"Where does she go?" he asked.

A few more key clicks. Another image popped up. "That's the second floor," the woman answered. They watched the screen. Saw Regan approach a second elevator and punch the down button. She got inside, and the door closed. The woman switched the feed back to the lobby area. At the far side of the screen, Regan could be seen stepping from the elevator and then quickly exiting the building via a side door.

The woman looked up. "That's all I'll have. That door exits on the side of the building onto a service drive that we share with the hotel next door. It automatically locks behind the person, with no way to re-enter. Delivery vehicles text us when they are here and then we let them in. Otherwise, it's not used. We've never bothered to set up video cameras. There's been no need."

The disappointing words registered but seemed inconsequential in the face of what Jamie had just witnessed with his own eyes. Regan had had Connor drop her off at the Creekside Hotel. She'd walked in as if she was a paying guest, taken the elevator up, then down, exiting from a side door. He wasn't a cop like Marcus, but he recognized a subterfuge when he saw one.

But why make the effort to get dropped off somewhere where you weren't staying?

The only plausible reason was that she didn't want anybody to track her movements post the hospital. Because?

She'd lied about the accident? She was wanted by the police? She was a secret agent? The possibilities floating in his head were getting crazier and crazier.

"Dr. Weathers?"

The woman behind the counter was looking at him expectantly.

He wasn't ready to give up. "You said the drive is used for delivery trucks. You didn't have any of those this morning, did you?"

She shook her head.

It was one dead end after another. "You have a parking lot behind the hotel, right?"

"Yes?"

"With cameras?"

"Of course. There's a guest entrance back there." She said it as if she was insulted that Jamie was implying that they might not be doing everything in their power to provide security for guests.

"Can we look at that feed?" he asked. "Please. I know this is taking your time, but it really is important."

She nodded and touched screens. "I went back to just a few minutes before we see her exit the side door."

He watched. A time in the corner of the computer screen ticked off the seconds. There was absolutely no activity in the parking lot. No one coming in the guest entrance. Three minutes went by. Four. Based on when she'd exited the side door, she'd had plenty of time to walk down the service drive and into the back parking lot. She should be on-screen by now. Five minutes. Six. Seven.

Nothing. He was pathetic. "Thank you," he said finally.

She shut down the camera feed. "I'm sorry that we can't find her."

"Uh…thank you. Can I just go out that side door and take a look around?" he asked.

"Of course. But again, you can't get back in that way."

"No problem." The answers he was looking for weren't here. "I appreciate your time."

"Tell Marcus that Dinna Lowe says hi."

"Will do." He had a feeling he was going to need to talk to Marcus pretty darn soon if he intended to find Regan.

She doesn't want to be found, the walls practically shouted back at him.

Tough. Anybody who knew him knew that he didn't give up easily. Just about everything in life that he'd attempted, he'd been successful at. Most probably thought he was pretty lucky. It wasn't that. It was hard work, maybe some innate talent and dogged determination.

He walked out the side door and stood in the service drive. It was typical of what could be seen between a lot of the lodging properties in Knoware that were grouped together. Trucks needed to be able to get close to efficiently make deliveries, so narrow driveways between buildings had been established.

He walked across the paved road and tried the door of the Crosswinds Hotel. It was locked. Likely a similar situation to that of the Creekside. He walked down the alley, toward the street. Then entered the Crosswinds Hotel by its front door.

"Good morning," said the young man behind the desk. "Checking in?"

Jamie shook his head. "I'm trying to find a woman who was dropped off this morning at the Creekside Hotel. She exited via their side door. It's possible that she came in here. She's approximately thirty, blond-haired, on crutches. Dark coat and gray stocking cap."

The young man shook his head. "I've been here all morning. Haven't seen anybody who matches that description."

It had been a long shot. "You don't have a camera in the alley that runs between here and the Creekside?"

"No."

An even longer shot. "Any deliveries this morning?"

The man just shook his head.

The fat lady had sung. "Thank you for your time."

He walked back to his car and got in. He pulled his cell phone from his pocket. Dialed Marcus.

"Did you find her?" his friend answered.

"No. I tracked her as far as the hotel where the car service dropped her off. She wasn't a guest there. She entered via the front door, took the elevator upstairs, took another elevator back down and walked out the side door."

Marcus said nothing.

"Tell me what you're thinking," Jamie demanded.

"I'm thinking it doesn't look good for Regan Jones. Those are not the actions of somebody doing the right thing."

"She could literally be in mortal danger," Jamie said. "She may be bleeding internally."

"I'll have somebody check street cameras. Maybe we'll get lucky."

"She said she was from Los Angeles," Jamie said.

"I know," Marcus said, surprising him. "I got her address from her vehicle registration."

That was good that the information all matched, right? But then again, maybe that, too, was rehearsed. He was so unsure of what to do. All he knew was that he didn't want to have lost her. "You still have people in LA who could be helpful to us?" he asked.

"I do. I don't think it would be a big deal to ask for a drive-by, a knock on the door. Maybe they get a little more information that might help us track her down."

"You think I'm crazy for pursuing this?"

"No," Marcus said immediately. "Maybe before I met Erin. But now I fall firmly in with the other lovesick puppies who are convinced that there really is the perfect mate. You sometimes just have to look really hard."

"What if they don't want to be found?" Jamie asked.

"Despite what I said earlier, I'm willing to assume good motivation here. For now. But if we get some information that causes us to think differently, my advice is going to change."

"Call your friends," Jamie said.

Chapter 6

Widow's Peak was a massive stone structure that perched on land that jutted out over the road below it. It had turrets and balconies and exquisite fall landscaping. Off to the side, she could see a patchwork of paved pathways that led through a golf course that seemed to practically reach the back door. There were golfers, all wearing some kind of jacket. "Kind of a cold day to golf," she said.

"This is one of the nicest golf courses within a hundred miles," Mickey said. "There's a small private airfield on that side of the property," he said, pointing to the north, "and lots of big-money types fly in for a round of golf. There are people playing here unless there is snow on the ground."

Given that it was the day after Thanksgiving, that might not be too far in the future. She had to get to Seattle before

then. This needed to be a quick stop, just long enough to get her strength back and for her leg to heal a bit.

"I can drop you off in front. I use a back entrance," Mickey said.

"That works," Layla said. She was making up the plan as she went. There was no row of hotels like there had been in Knoware. Widow's Peak was a standalone attraction. "This is really a lovely place."

Mickey nodded. "Impressive, for sure. Did you know that a hundred years ago, Widow's Peak was originally a private residence? The owner made his fortune in railroads. He had a big family, and he built a bunch of cottages, anticipating that his children would use them when they returned to visit him in his old age. If you're inside and looking out the big bay window in the lobby, you can see them."

She looked where he pointed and, from this vantage, could see rooftops. "Are they still part of the hotel property?" she asked, thinking the place was more massive than at first glance.

"Nope. The man died earlier than expected, there was a blowup within the family over the estate and ultimately the property was split up and sold. Widow's Peak sat empty for years until the right buyer came along. He's the one who put the airfield in. The cottages, however, sold fast. It's a nice place to spend the summer. I suspect they're all boarded up for the winter now. It gets pretty isolated here. Even Widow's Peak closes after New Year's Eve and doesn't reopen until April."

"I can't remember how far the next town is," Layla said.

"Oh, that's Kingsbury. Ten miles, probably. I have

a couple accounts there during the season." Mickey brought his truck to a stop. "The restaurant here is pretty good," he said. "In case you're hungry."

"Appreciate the tip. And I appreciate the ride." She pulled a twenty from her pocket and offered it to him.

"Nonsense," he said. "I was coming this direction anyway. It was nice to have the company. Although," he said, "I've got a daughter about your age. Worries me whenever I see a young woman traveling alone."

He was a nice man. She could have done much worse in picking a ride. "I'll be fine," she assured him.

"Where you going to go from here?" he asked, still obviously concerned.

From her go-bag, she pulled out one of the burner phones. "I've got a friend who lives farther north. I'm going to call her and she'll be able to pick me up." She hated lying to the man, but she was afraid he might not be willing to leave her here if he thought she was stranded.

"Well, I'm glad I could get you this far," he said.

"Me, too," she said. "And I know my friend appreciates the shorter drive." She opened the door. "This will take just a second."

"Take your time."

She got her crutches planted and slid to the edge of the seat. Then to a standing position. Tried for a deep breath, but her injured ribs prevented that. She was just going to have to be content with shallow breathing. She reached back for her backpack. She got it on and carefully stepped away from the truck. "Thanks again, Mickey," she said. Then she made her way inside.

It was equally grand there, with high ceilings and ornate walls. Big mirrors had been strategically placed

to make it look even larger. When Mickey had been explaining about the property, she had thought that it might be a good place to hunker down for a night or two, just to rest and regain more of her strength. But it would be expensive to stay here even for a few days. She had many thousands of dollars with her, but her cash was going to have to last her a very long time, so she didn't want to use it up unnecessarily. And she definitely didn't want to use her credit card and create a paper trail. It might be better to move on now.

But first she could afford an early lunch, or a late breakfast. Whatever they were serving. What she really wanted was a good cup of coffee. The beverage that had arrived with her breakfast at the hospital had supposedly been coffee, but she'd remained unconvinced after taking a few sips. She headed toward the restaurant sign.

"Table for one?" the hostess asked as she entered.

"Please," she said. She followed the young woman through the airy and well-lit room to a table next to a wall of windows. Within seconds of her sitting, a server approached, wearing dark slacks and a white shirt. She ordered coffee and scanned the menu that the server left.

The coffee was strong and delicious, and she practically sighed when she drank it. From the menu, she picked a cinnamon roll and a fruit plate.

It was really quite peaceful, she thought five minutes later as she ate her food and watched the golfers through the window. The restaurant had—purposefully, no doubt—been situated at a spot where the front nine of the golf course ended and the back nine started. It was a perfect break spot for golfers in need of sustenance.

She watched as a group of four men approached the green and putted around, finally getting all four balls in the hole. Then they got in their golf carts, drove them just a small distance before parking them again, and entering the restaurant by the back door. The way they were greeted by the hostess, Layla had a feeling that they were frequently at the course.

She'd golfed many times over the years. Still considered herself a novice, but she could hit the ball and it generally went in the right direction. She'd played in a golf league this summer with friends from her work. Once a week, it had been golf, then drinks and dinner. It had been fun.

Just one more thing that she'd miss.

Not forever, she told herself. *You'll find a place to settle in. Find new friends. Find another golf league.* But never again as Layla Morant. Only as Regan Jones.

Layla had been left behind, permanently.

In dreaming up this plan, she'd told herself that she'd bear that if it meant that she could stay alive. What was a name, after all?

But it wasn't just a name. It was Layla's life that had been left behind. Layla's work. Layla's sweet little apartment. The ache of loss was real.

She'd tried to avoid it. Had told the police, her lawyer, a few select others about Douglas Glass's threat. The police had dismissed that he'd said it. He was a white-collar criminal. Had no history of crimes against people. *Was she sure she'd heard him correctly?*

Her lawyer had been less dismissive. *He'll go to prison,* he'd said. *He'll have time to cool off and he*

won't want to do anything that will jeopardize his pa-
role once he's out.

She'd tried to find some comfort in that. But she'd
seen his face, heard the hate in his voice. Glass had
been serious, and she knew that he had the resources to
distance himself from the crime unless she did something drastic.

Becoming Regan Jones was about as drastic as it got.

She pushed away her half-eaten cinnamon roll. The
server had just refilled her coffee, and she drank that,
watching as another group of golfers approached. Two
men, two women. The women were better golfers,
which was fun to see. They made nice, long putts and
then waited patiently as the two men chased the little
white ball around the green, overshooting the hole at
least twice.

They also parked their golf cart and came into the
restaurant. But instead of taking a table by the windows,
they went into the bar, at the far end of the restaurant.
They took off their coats and accepted a menu from the
server who delivered water to their table.

They were going to stay awhile.

She signaled her server that she was ready for her
bill. Once it was delivered, she calculated a nice tip and
left the cash on the table. Then she wrapped what was
left of her cinnamon roll and put it in her backpack.
She did not have the luxury of wasting food. Then she
walked out the back door, directly to the golf carts.
She looked first at the two that had been parked by the
four people now in the bar. The key had been left in
one of them.

Act like you belong. Act like you belong. The words

reverberated in her head. She quickly shrugged off her backpack and put it and her crutches on the passenger side. Then she slid behind the wheel and started it up. She took the path leading away from the hotel, praying that no one else had been paying attention, that no one else had noticed that she'd taken a golf cart that some-one else had arrived in. Praying that she didn't hear, *Hey, lady. What the hell are you doing?*

Five minutes later, heart pounding, she'd reached the end of the path and presumably the end of Widow's Peak property. The coastal road loomed ahead, offering a choice of right or left. She knew what lay left. That was the direction she and Mickey had come from. She turned right. Golf carts did not belong on the road, but unless she was willing to steal a car, it was her best bet. It was a risk, though. A passing car would see her and maybe report her to the police. But it was a risk she needed to take. Mickey had said that the closest town was ten miles north. If she could get that far, surely there would be someplace she could stay. Heck, if not a hotel, maybe a vacation rental unit.

As she checked for oncoming traffic, she glanced across the paved highway. Sitting at least a hundred yards back from the road were the cottages that Mickey had described. She put her hand up to her eyes, protect-ing them from the midday sun. And counted. There were eight. All the same size and shape. One-story frame bungalows. Maybe twelve to fifteen hundred square feet with sharply pitched roofs that could be seen from Widow's Peak.

They varied only by paint colors, and Layla suspected that was a reflection of new owners wanting to differ-

entiate themselves somehow from their neighbors. Pale yellow. A bright green. Robin's egg blue. Beach colors.

There were no garages. Just narrow gravel driveways that in some spots were more grass than gravel, leading up from the road. She saw no vehicles parked outside, lending credence to Mickey's perspective that the places were closed up for the winter.

She quickly realized that one of them could be the perfect place to hide out for a few weeks until she got stronger. Widow's Peak was open until New Year's Day. That meant she had about five weeks before the area would be shut down for good and there'd be no easy way of getting a ride to somewhere where she could hop on a bus to Seattle. She'd need to be ready to go before then.

Her decision made, she focused on finding a nearby spot where she could hide the golf cart. The underbrush was rough and rutted, and it was a bumpy affair. She drove with one hand and slipped the other under her thigh to support her injured leg as she lifted it a couple inches off the floor of the cart, hoping to avoid jarring it unnecessarily.

Finally, behind two big trees, she came to a stop. She used the sleeve of her coat to wipe off any fingerprints on the steering wheel and the key. She'd had a low-level security clearance for her work at the lab, and her fingerprints were in the system because of that. She'd bemoaned that fact early on when she'd first decided to disappear, thinking it could be her Achilles' heel. But then had come to the realization that it might be for the best. She could be careful along the way, but in the event that Douglas Glass ever did find her and fulfill what he'd claimed to be his *new mission in life*, in death there would at least be some final proof of her real

identity. It was a morbid thought, but when one contemplated erasing herself, morbid thoughts were the norm.

She got out, strapped on her backpack and made her way back to the side of the road.

She crossed the road and headed for a light purple cottage in the middle. It had long been her favorite color and right now it seemed as good a rationale for a choice as any. She avoided the gravel, which was going to be tough on crutches, and walked through the rather scrabbly yard. Finally, she reached the front of the cottage, which faced the ocean. There was a porch that ran the length of the structure, and was at least four feet deep. Empty of furniture, but in her mind, she could see herself on a warm summer day, sitting in a soft chair, her feet on the railing, watching the surf roll in. The ocean was less than two hundred yards away. And while the cottages were likely advertised as beachfront property, there wasn't much beach. It was mostly rock and wild grasses. When the surf hit the rocks, it sprayed up.

She thought it was beautiful. Nature at its finest.

But she wasn't here for that. She turned and studied the cottage. Made her way up the two steps and tried the door. Locked. Of course. There was a window on each side. Just glass, no screens. She suspected those had been removed in advance of winter. She pushed up on each window. Both locked. She could not see inside. There were blinds on the windows.

She shrugged off her backpack. Opened it and found the tool that had been so carefully selected. Studied. Practiced with. Opened the blade she thought would work best. Then methodically etched a line. Another. Made a square. Then methodically traced the edging, over and over, to wear through the glass. When she was

able, she used the blunt end of the tool to punch out the square. It fell inside, presumably to the floor.

She shrugged off one arm of her coat, leaving just the one sleeve. She pulled it down to cover her hand. Then very carefully stuck her arm through the hole, used her fingers to feel around, located the latch and managed to flip it.

It was probably thirty degrees out, and she was sweating like it was ninety.

That went about as well as you could have hoped. She congratulated herself, feeling the need to bolster her confidence before she tackled the final hurdle. She was going to have to get herself and her crutches inside, all without banging her injured leg.

Now that she had the window open, she reached down for the bottom of the shade. Pressed up. It was a cordless shade, and it easily retracted upward. She pulled her flashlight from her bag and used it to see into the house.

She would be entering into a small living room. There was a couch and two chairs. And climbing in through a window was really not too big of a deal when one had two good legs that could bear equal weight.

But that wasn't the case now. And she really couldn't see how she was going to manage the next part. She blinked fast, feeling tears threaten. She'd come so damn far this morning. Had avoided any doctors or nurses intent upon stopping her. Had avoided the police. Had gotten a ride, then another. Taking the golf cart had been a spur-of-the-minute decision, but it had gotten her here, to this point, with minimal fuss.

She was damn well not going to give up now.

But the longer she remained on the porch, the more

likely it was that she'd be seen. While it was late November and the beachside cottages were empty, that did not mean that people didn't stroll on the beach to get their exercise.

She looked again at the window and the distance to the floor. She had a genius IQ. She should be able to figure it out.

After a long minute, she made her decision. The best way in was going to be headfirst. Well, actually, hands first. She had good upper-body strength. She could do this.

She also had cracked ribs. It was going to hurt.

She put her flashlight back into her backpack and tossed the bag through the window. Then, more carefully, her crutches. She was going to need them to be close. Then she bent over the windowsill at her waist and extended her arms inside the house. In order to touch the floor, she had to lift her legs off the ground.

Balanced on her pelvis, she teetered on the windowsill, half-in, half-out. She put her hands on the hardwood living room floor. Edged forward a bit more. She could see the piece of glass that she'd knocked out of the window. It was in one piece. She reached for it and tossed it aside.

Now she was more in than out, but here came the hard part. She needed to get inside without banging her lower leg on the sill. If she rebroke her leg or busted her stitches, it would be game over.

She took her left hand off the floor, balancing her weight on her right arm. Then she reached her left arm up and over her body, turning herself in the process.

Ribs screamed. She hissed and shut her eyes to stop the dizziness, praying that she didn't pass out. She

didn't. And after a moment, she opened her eyes, swallowed hard, and accessed.

She'd done a 180 and flipped from her stomach to her
back. Her yoga teacher would be impressed. Now that
she had both arms under her again, she slowly, holding
her entire body weight on her arms, lowered her butt to
the ground. Her legs were now inside, propped against
the windowsill, at a ninety-degree angle to her body.

She scooted her butt back until she was flat on the
floor. Her whole body shook with fatigue. She knew
she needed to get up, shut the window, pull down the
shade. But she simply couldn't move. Not yet.

She closed her eyes. She'd take a five minute
breather.

Then she'd get on with the rest of Regan Jones's life.

Jamie had too much time on his hands. A rare problem, to be sure. But once he'd left the hotels, he'd driven
the streets around the two properties. Over and over. He
had proof that she'd gotten as far as the Creekside Hotel.
She hadn't simply vanished. And he was confident that
she'd not have had the strength to go far.

All he got for his efforts were some odd looks and
a few horns from drivers with the bad luck to come
upon him. If they were locals, they gave him a bit of
an awkward wave when they went around him. If they
were visitors, he got a less friendly hand gesture. He
hadn't given up. Had simply widened his search until
he'd covered all of Knoware, multiple times. Late afternoon, he finally returned to his house for a shower and
something to eat.

When his phone rang and he saw it was Marcus, he
snatched it up. He'd wanted to call him multiple times

during the day but had resisted. Marcus would call him when he had news.

"What's going on?" he asked, trying to sound casual. Knowing he failed.

"I'm not sure," Marcus said. "Are you at home?"

"Yes."

"Good. I'm coming over. Blade, too. I think the three of us need to think this through."

When his friends got there, he offered them beers, which they accepted. He opened one for himself. "Is it bad news?" he asked. As an emergency medicine physician, he'd delivered his share of bad news. He could certainly take it.

"Earlier I said that we had her address from her vehicle tags," Marcus began. "I also found her driver's license in the system." He pulled a sheet of paper from his pocket and offered it to Jamie. It was a photocopy of a California license issued to Regan Jones.

He stared at the photo. "Her hair is blonder now," he said. In the photo, it was brown.

"Right," Blade said. "Hair changes."

"And it says on here that her eyes are blue," Jamie said. He looked at his friends. "They're really more gray than blue."

His friends exchanged a glance but said nothing.

"A name search produces eight Regan Joneses in Los Angeles," Marcus said.

He wasn't surprised. Regan might not be as common, but Jones certainly was.

"None of the eight were associated with the address that was on record with Motor Vehicles and also her

driver's license. Even so, that's where they started. This address is an eight-unit apartment building."

There was no apartment number in the address. Just a street. "They checked every apartment?" Jamie asked.

"Yes," Marcus said. "She's not there. And nobody in any of the apartments admitted knowing her. According to my friends, it's a building in a questionable area, pretty transient, and the people who live there aren't that friendly with the police."

"I had told her that the police were coming by to get her statement," Jamie said. "Maybe she was trying to avoid that."

"Maybe," Marcus acknowledged. "But I ran a background check, and there's no criminal history and no current warrants. I checked her education. A Regan Jones with the same Social Security number graduated from Los Angeles Public High School. I saw her senior photo. It's a decent match to her driver's license."

"College?" Jamie asked.

"No record," Marcus said. "And the limited work history that I was able to uncover doesn't suggest that she had additional education. Earnings were reported from a series of jobs in the service sector. Restaurants, retail, that sort of thing."

"Okay."

"I was able to reach a couple of the prior employers. They verified that she'd worked there, but…they weren't complimentary," Marcus said. He paused.

That didn't seem right. She'd seemed very polite, very nice. But he wasn't at all sure right now what was real. He said nothing.

"Anyway, I was able to get a cell phone number for

her from one of them," Marcus continued. "It's been disconnected."

Jamie gave the photocopy one last look. Then glanced up at Marcus. "So they checked out all eight of the other Regan Joneses?"

"Yeah. That's why it took a while. Nobody else matches. I'm sorry, Jamie."

"But she said that she was from Los Angeles," Jamie said.

There was silence in the room. He guessed he appreciated that his friends weren't pointing out to him that Regan didn't exactly have a track record of being a hundred percent truthful or trustworthy.

He put his beer down and stood up, started to pace around his living room. "Regan Jones went to high school in Los Angeles and had an address in Los Angeles. She worked there, had a driver's license and registered a car. But now, there's no trace of her still living in Los Angeles. Do I have this right?" he asked, looking at Marcus.

"Yeah."

"So she moved. Hasn't updated her address everywhere," Jamie said.

"You just told us that she said she lived in Los Angeles," Blade said, his voice soft.

Damn, it was inconvenient to be reminded of things. "Maybe it was so recently that she still considers it home."

"Then why didn't anybody in an eight-unit building remember her?" Marcus asked.

"I don't know," Jamie admitted. He picked up the photocopy of the driver's license. Studied it. Then looked at his friends. "So, there's another option. Now

that I've seen this photo, I'm confident that I'm not off track. Regan Jones is real. But the woman I met, that we all met, isn't really Regan Jones."

No one said anything for a long minute. Finally Blade leaned forward in his chair. "This woman was seriously injured, and immediately after being extricated from her vehicle, she was able to start what appears to be a path of lies. That's some pretty significant composure."

What Blade was trying to say in a nice way was that the woman Jamie knew as Regan Jones was likely a very experienced liar, perhaps even pathological. "She's not here to defend herself," Jamie said. "We can't know her motivations."

Marcus ran a hand through his short hair. "That's the problem, Jamie. She's not here. She fled. You need to let this go. We know that you're a devoted physician. Plenty of people in Knoware can tell you stories about how Dr. Weathers saved their lives, or their kids' lives, or their friends' lives. You go above and beyond. Always. But this one is a mistake."

Perhaps a logical part of him understood the arguments and advice being offered up by Blade and Marcus. But they hadn't spent time with the woman. They hadn't *merged*.

He wasn't going to be able to convince them. The reverse remained true. *They* couldn't convince *him*. "I appreciate everything you and the LAPD did today," he said. "And I appreciate the two of you coming over tonight. You're good friends."

"But—" Blade prompted.

"But nothing," Jamie said. He stood up. "I'm sure you

guys would like to be home for dinner. Let's call it a night."

Marcus and Blade exchanged a quick look, but neither lingered.

Jamie closed the door behind them, his mind already moving ahead. He was going to find her. Whatever her name was. She needed medical care.

And he needed, well... He wasn't ready to go there yet. Suffice it to say, he needed to find her. That was all there was to it.

Chapter 7

When Layla woke up, it was dark. She was on the floor, on her back, her legs stretched out in front of her. She had a hand on her go-bag.

God, her leg hurt. She had packed some pain medication. It wasn't as strong as what they'd given her in the hospital, but it would be better than nothing. She entered the combination, opened the lock and unzipped her bag. First thing she pulled out was her flashlight. She kept the light low, not wanting it to be seen by anyone who was crazy enough to walk a rocky beach at night.

Hopefully, there wasn't anybody that crazy.

She pulled out her first aid kit, found the extra-strength acetaminophen and shook out several pills into her hand. Then used her flashlight to inspect the house.

She'd already seen the living room through the window. Beyond it was a kitchen. One side was a long

counter, chopped up by a refrigerator, a sink and a stove/oven combination. A wood table with four chairs took center stage.

She was going to have to get up in order to see what was beyond that. She reached for her crutches and dragged them and herself toward the chair. Then she used the chair to awkwardly aid her progress to her feet.

She put the flashlight in her mouth in order to free up her hands. She thumped her way across the room, hating the crutches but knowing that they were just about her most important tool right now. Down a very short hallway, she found two small bedrooms and a bathroom. No bathtub, just a shower, toilet and small vanity.

There were no sheets or blankets on any of the beds, but there was a plastic tote in each room containing the items she'd need. She made her way back to the kitchen and immediately went to the sink. She'd debated for weeks over how much water to pack. It was heavy to carry and took up space. Ultimately, she'd settled on two bottles. Not enough to keep her going for very long.

She lifted the faucet and water, blessed water, poured out. She found a glass in the cupboard and drank greedily. Popped the pills she still had gripped in her hand into her mouth and drank some more. She prayed that they kicked in quickly. Then she opened the refrigerator, wincing when the bright light almost lit up the kitchen. She closed it quickly. It was empty but cold. Not that she had anything that needed refrigerating. She'd packed bread and peanut butter and jelly. That's what she'd live on for the foreseeable future.

There was a closed door at the end of the long counter. It opened into a small utility room, with a washer and dryer and a small area for tools and main-

tenance items. There was a hammer and a saw. Some
screwdrivers. Extra lightbulbs. Batteries. Nails and
screws. Odd pieces of lumber. Some plywood. That
got her attention. She examined that closer. They were
the right shape to cover the windows. She suspected
that there had been a few times over the years when big
storms had been predicted to blow in and the cottage
owners had covered the windows just in case.

When she'd woken up on the floor, her first thought
had been about the hole in the window. Probably because she'd been cold. It was likely about thirty-five
degrees outside, and the hole in the glass was letting
the cold in. That was a problem, and it was a problem
in another big way. If somebody checked on the property, it was going to be a dead giveaway that all was not
right. If she put the plywood over the windows, she'd
have more privacy, she'd be warmer and nobody would
immediately conclude that someone had broken in. The
risk, of course, was that somebody was going to notice
that there was plywood over windows now where there
hadn't been before and be curious enough to investigate.

It was a risk she thought she ought to take.

Believing that and actually getting it done were two
different things. It took her twenty minutes just to get
the plywood from the mudroom to the windows. She
couldn't carry it, of course. She had to drag it behind
her using a loop of heavy-duty twine that she wrapped
around her waist and nailed both ends into the plywood.
She was like a little kid dragging a sled behind her. It
was awkward and slow. But it worked.

In the dark, with only the light of the moon, she balanced on her crutches on the porch and more or less felt
her way around until she finally got the plywood tacked

up to both windows. She was grateful for all the minor repairs she'd made at her various apartments over the years. She'd honed a few basic carpentry skills.

She was absolutely exhausted by the time she finished. But strangely, almost euphoric.

It looked as if her luck was finally changing. She'd gotten away from the hospital before the police had come to take her statement. Therefore, she hadn't added to the complexity of her already screwed-up life by lying to them. And she'd found a place that appeared to be locked up for the winter where she could rest and recuperate for a few weeks. Her leg would heal. She knew that she was ignoring the possibility that she still had internal bleeding. But there had been little choice. She couldn't stay in the hospital and let everything she'd meticulously planned for disappear.

Now, she just had to hope for the best.

Jamie glanced at the time on his phone. Just before midnight. Twenty minutes later than the last time he'd checked. He lay in his bed, irritated beyond belief that he couldn't let the day go and simply fall asleep. He was a master at this—had been grabbing twenty-minute naps for years on demand. But now, like everything else in his life, there was little evidence of cooperation anywhere.

His friends thought he was crazy to be chasing after a woman who clearly didn't want to be found. But for most of the evening, after they'd gone home to their wives, he'd contemplated his next steps.

She hadn't simply disappeared. That meant he'd missed something. As a physician, when he missed things, there could be a very bad outcome.

It was no wonder that it was almost impossible to sleep. But he focused on deep breathing, every breath in for six counts, out for six counts. He needed to recharge his brain.

When he awoke the next morning at just after six, he felt pretty rested. He showered but didn't bother making coffee. He would get some at Gertie's, along with some breakfast. He'd been working way too much lately to have much of anything in his refrigerator that wasn't sour or moldy.

When he walked in, he took a spot at the counter and waved at Sheryl. She'd been in the same graduating class as him, and they'd been friends for nearly as long as he'd been friends with Blade and Marcus.

"Dining alone?" she asked, placing a set of rolled silverware in front of him. She automatically poured him a cup of coffee and slid a container of coffee creamers in his direction.

"Yeah." It wasn't normal for him to want to avoid Blade and Marcus, but right now, he didn't want his friends telling him that he was being a putz. Or, worse, maybe they wouldn't say it, but he'd be able to tell in their faces.

"Pancakes, two eggs over easy and bacon, please," he said without looking at the menu.

"Got it."

While he waited for his food, he glanced through the Knoware newspaper. This time of year, it was only published twice a week, so it wasn't much good for catching up on national or state news. Nobody read it for that reason. They read it to learn the local news—what was happening in the community, the schools, the various clubs that kept the community moving forward. They

read the obituaries, the wedding announcements and the police blotter.

Jamie generally didn't spend much time there, but he glanced at that section, aware that the paper had come out the afternoon of Regan Jones's car accident. Sure enough, there was a small mention. Traveler Flips Car was the headline. And the article was a whole three sentences: "A one-car accident on Highway 6 resulted in serious injury to the lone driver, Ms. Regan Jones. According to police, Ms. Jones rolled her vehicle multiple times. Updates on the condition of Ms. Jones were not currently available."

He should call the reporter. Let him know that updates on the *whereabouts* of Ms. Jones were not currently available. Sheryl set down his plate, refilled his coffee cup and lingered for just a minute. He glanced up. She was looking at him with concern.

"You seem a little down, Jamie," she said.

He shrugged and cut his pancakes. "I'm fine. These look good."

"I wondered if it had anything to do with what happened at the hospital yesterday. My nephew Drake said that you were pretty upset about a patient who walked out of the hospital."

He'd forgotten that Drake Porter was Sheryl's nephew. "Drake didn't do anything wrong," he said. "He's a good kid and a good security guard."

"For being just twenty-two, he does okay, I think," she said, trying not to sound too proud. "I know he would have hated to disappoint you. Did you find the woman?"

Jamie shook his head. "I haven't given up. I lost her somewhere on Trigger Road, in the C's," he said.

"I don't think the Coattail Inn is open this time of year."

"It's not."

"Then she's likely at the Creekside or the Crosswinds. What I hear from customers is that they're pretty sharp at Creekside but that the front-desk people at Crosswinds are out to lunch."

Sheryl was a reputable source of information. Almost every traveler who stayed in Knoware had one or more meals at Gertie's. And Sheryl listened more than she talked.

Was it worth going back to the two open hotels, asking all the same questions? Was that pathetic? The young man behind the registration desk at Crosswinds had been polite. Had seemed certain that he hadn't seen a blonde woman or that there hadn't been any deliveries that morning.

But Jamie had always been a believer that things happened for a reason. And there was a reason that Sheryl had casually made that comment about Crosswinds. A reason that it suddenly seemed like a good idea to double-check the information he'd gotten yesterday.

He ate quickly, got a coffee to go, paid the bill and left Sheryl a generous tip. If anything panned out from this, he was buying her a steak dinner. Hell, he'd buy her whole family a steak dinner.

He parked across the street from the Crosswinds Hotel. When he went inside, the same young man was behind the desk. "Good morning," Jamie said. "I was in here yesterday, looking for a blonde-haired woman."

"Oh, yeah. Hey, this is great that you came back," the young man said. "I felt bad because you'd also asked about deliveries and I told you that we hadn't had any. But we did get a linen delivery yesterday. I think they

came when I was on break. I didn't realize it until I saw the invoice on the desk in the office."

Yes! He resisted the urge to do a fist bump into the air. First of all, it did not mean that Regan had gotten a ride on the delivery truck. But it was a lead. Something tangible. "Do you have a name and number?"

"Let me go grab the invoice," the young man said. He walked through a door behind him and reemerged seconds later carrying a piece of paper. It was tri-folded, and he unfolded the top flap to show the company name and contact information. "You can snap a photo of that if you want."

Jamie did exactly that. It was a company out of Olympia, Washington. "Thank you," he said. He practically ran back to his car.

He punched the number in. "Fresh and Tidy," a woman answered. "How may I help you?"

"My name is Dr. Jamie Weathers. I run the emergency medicine program in Knoware. I need to speak with one of your drivers who made a delivery yesterday at the Crosswinds Hotel in Knoware."

There was a pause. "Do you know the driver's name?"

"I do not," he said as pleasantly as he could. How many drivers could Fresh and Tidy have delivering to Knoware?

"I'm not sure I understand your call, sir. Are you interested in linen services?"

"No. This is an urgent matter. Health-care privacy laws prevent me from providing any more information." *If all else fails, invoke HIPAA.* "It's just very important that I speak with your driver. Please."

He could hear her typing. "Mickey Spoke has re-

sponsibility for that route. He did make a delivery at the Crosswinds Hotel around nine o'clock yesterday."

Yes! "And Mr. Spoke's number?"

She rattled it off, and Jamie read it back to her. "Thank you very much," he said.

"You're welcome," she said, not sounding at all convinced.

He suspected that she was going to follow up with her driver just to make sure everything was okay. He was going to get to him first. He dialed. The phone rang three times before it was answered.

"Fresh and Tidy. Mickey Spoke."

"Mr. Spoke, my name is Dr. Jamie Weathers from Bigelow Memorial Hospital in Knoware. I am trying to locate a patient who might have been at or near the Crosswinds Hotel yesterday when you were making a delivery there. It is a woman in her late twenties, early thirties, and she was likely wearing a dark coat and a gray stocking cap. She was on crutches. Did you see her?"

"Oh man," Mickey said. "She's not like a psych patient or something, is she?"

"No, sir. We simply just need to make contact with her about an ongoing medical issue."

"I gave her a ride."

Jamie gripped his phone tighter. "Where to, sir?"

"Widow's Peak."

He knew where that was. Everybody in a hundred miles knew where that was. It was less than a year ago that he'd flown in for a charity golf event to benefit the small airfield there that was offering free flying lessons to underserved populations. "Why Widow's Peak?" he asked.

"She said she was headed north and that's all the far-

ther I was going," the man said. "She's a real nice lady. I felt sorry for her on those crutches."

Another member of the Regan Jones fan club. Was she duping everyone? "Do you know, sir, did she get a room there?"

"I'm not sure. She mentioned that a friend was going to pick her up. I left her at the front door and then went around the back to do my delivery. Then I came home and didn't give it another thought. I hope I didn't do anything wrong."

"No, sir. This has been very helpful. Goodbye."

Jamie considered calling Widow's Peak but swiftly discarded the idea. She was there. He could just feel it. He searched for the property in his GPS, found the address and hit Start.

He would find her now—he was sure of it.

Layla was not doing well. After nailing the plywood on the windows, she'd managed to get inside. Had forced herself to eat the remaining portion of her cinnamon roll. Then she'd opened the plastic tote full of bed linens and put a sheet and blanket on the bed. Hadn't had the strength to tuck anything in. She collapsed again and had slept fitfully through the night, getting up once to take more pain reliever.

Now, she felt achy and warm and off-center. And it was an effort to make it to the bathroom. Her travels yesterday had taken more out of her than she'd ever anticipated. She sat on the bed and carefully unwrapped the bandage on her leg. It looked about the same. The stitches all seemed intact, and there was no bleeding. That had to be a good sign.

She should sleep. That had to be what her body

needed. But first, there was something she had to do. She got her coat from the closet and carried it over to the bed. Then she opened her go-bag and found the sewing kit. In it was a small pair of scissors. She used the scissors to very carefully snip the threads of the bottom hem of the lining. Then she transferred hundreds of dollars from her go-bag into the lining of her coat. She resewed the hem with swift, sure stitches.

Then she pulled the right pocket inside out. She placed a phone at the very bottom and then carefully restitched the pocket so that the phone was hidden. If someone looked very closely, they might wonder why the pockets were different depths. But the odds that someone would look that closely were slim. More likely, they might quickly search the pockets. Her phone would be safe. Hidden.

She knew she was going to extremes, but she now realized that it wasn't impossible that she might get separated from her bag. She would do whatever she could to avoid that, but just in case, as long as she had her coat, she'd have access to money and a way to communicate.

Exhausted, she tossed her coat onto the floor and lay back in her bed. That small amount of work had taken everything she had.

She was in trouble.

Jamie walked into Widow's Peak, feeling optimistic. He approached the desk. "Good morning," he said to the middle-aged woman in a blue suit.

"Good morning. Checking in?" she asked.

"No. Actually, I'm meeting one of your guests," he said. Not exactly true, but he didn't want to immedi-

ately come off as a stalker. "Her name is Regan Jones. Could you ring her room?"

"Certainly." The woman tapped on computer keys. "What was the name again?"

"Regan Jones," he said.

She did some more typing. "I'm sorry. We don't have a guest staying here by that name."

He'd been so sure. He pulled out a business card and slid it across the counter. If his friends could see him now. He'd known people for years before they realized that he was a physician who ran the emergency medicine program at Bigelow Memorial. Now he was flashing his card and title around like he was king. But he knew that most people were basically helpful by nature. If they thought they could assist in times of a medical emergency, they wanted to. "I need to speak to Ms. Jones urgently about a medical matter. She would have checked in yesterday. Can you look to see if anybody else checked in? Maybe she's using a different name."

More keyboard clicking. "No one checked in yesterday. We had two male guests who checked out. This is a very slow time of year for us."

Of course. Was it possible that she'd met up with one of the male guests? Had that been the friend she'd told the linen driver she was meeting? "Do you have security cameras in this lobby?"

"Yes."

"I think she arrived around ten yesterday, give or take fifteen minutes on either side. Would you be willing to look at that footage and tell me if you see a blonde woman in her early thirties on crutches?"

She glanced again at his business card.

"It's really terribly urgent," he said. "I have infor-

mation that she needs." The lies were coming really easily now.

The woman nodded. "I'll look."

And ten minutes later, Jamie knew that Regan Jones had indeed walked into the lobby of Widow's Peak, had gone into the restaurant, eaten and then left by the back door of the restaurant. That's where the camera feed ended. "There's no cameras there?" he asked.

She shook her head. "I'm sorry."

She could not have gone far. Unless, of course, she had gotten a ride with someone else. He needed to simply admit defeat. She'd run from the hospital, run from him. Maybe had run because she'd been afraid the police wanted to talk to her. She was trouble.

"Is there anything else I can help you with?" the woman asked.

She was probably thinking he was simply going to stand in the lobby all day, looking perplexed. Looking foolish. "No. Thank you."

He walked out the front door and got in his vehicle, intending to head south. He started the car, checked his mirrors, put the car in Drive. But didn't take his foot off the brake.

He pressed it so hard it was a miracle that pedal, foot and half his leg didn't go through the floorboard of the vehicle.

If she'd had a planned meeting with someone or simply managed to talk her way into a ride, like she'd done with the Fresh and Tidy Linens' driver, she could be a thousand miles away by now.

But she wasn't. That's what his gut was telling him. She was close. And she needed him.

He put his vehicle back in Park and shut it off. Then

it was out of the car and around the big brick exterior of Widow's Peak. He could walk the golf course. See if there was any sign of her. Could walk the rest of the property, too. There were at least five acres here, maybe ten. He was pretty confident the property stretched all the way to the road.

Three hours later, he was sure that she wasn't on the grounds of Widow's Peak. He walked down the hill, toward the road, realizing that it was going to be a long walk up again. But he wasn't leaving until he'd checked everything.

When he got to the bottom of the hill, he saw the houses across the road, on the beach side. Eight of them, all identical in shape, all different in color. He picked up his pace, practically running to knock on the first door.

Nobody answered. Same thing at the second house. And, quite frankly, he was pretty sure they were all deserted, likely closed for the season. There was no sign of activity anywhere. But he kept going.

When he got to the purple house, he saw that the two main windows were boarded up. He still knocked.

Chapter 8

Layla was dozing, not quite awake, not quite asleep, when she heard the knock on the door. Immediately her heart kicked into overdrive. What should she do?

What *could* she do was the better question.

Running wasn't an option. She'd never been a fighter. And even if she suddenly felt inclined, she had the strength of a kitten. The only choice was to hunker down and hope like hell that whoever had come to the door would move on.

There was no second knock. Still, she waited. Finally, she reached for her crutches and got off the bed and to the bedroom window that was on the side of the cottage. With one finger, she moved the shade aside.

And her heart almost stopped.

It was Jamie Weathers. He was on the porch of the cottage next door.

The enormity of the situation had her gripping her crutches as if she meant to squeeze them to death. He'd somehow followed her here. Which meant that he'd tracked her from the hospital, to the hotel, to the linen truck, to Widow's Peak.

It made her feel vulnerable. And so very sad.

She'd thought he was genuinely a nice guy. And this proved it. He'd clearly gone out of his way. He couldn't do this for every patient, could he?

And as flattering as the answer might be, it just didn't matter. Her ability to stay alive depended on her ability to get to Seattle and quietly settle in as Regan Jones. It was a fantasy that she could somehow reunite with Jamie Weathers. Living in a small community like Knoware, where everybody knew everybody, hanging on the arm of the town's most eligible bachelor was not the way to stay under the radar.

She'd had this same conversation with herself since meeting Regan Jones a hundred times. If she was willing to leave her life behind, to forge a new life, then she had to be all in. There was no room for prevaricating. No room even for regrets. Because regrets sapped energy and focus and, right now, she needed both.

She should eat something, have something to drink.

Maybe later. She'd surely feel better later. She made it back to the bed and collapsed.

No answer.

He kept going until he'd knocked on every door. She wasn't there. Nobody was there. The disappointment was so overwhelming that it seemed to sap his strength.

She'd been at Widow's Peak, but he'd missed her.

The logical conclusion was that she'd gotten a ride with someone. But whom? And to where?

He walked back to the road. What did it matter? It was over. The fat lady had been called back for two encores, and now the orchestra was folding up their music stands.

He walked back to his car, got in and this time, when he started it, he didn't even look back as he pulled out of the parking lot. He pointed the nose of the car south and drove on autopilot.

An hour later, he pulled into the garage at his condo. He went inside, thought about lunch and then decided he'd rather just take a nap. But that ended up being a mistake, because he dreamed that a blonde-haired, gray-blue-eyed woman's body had been washed up against rocks that looked suspiciously like the ones he'd seen earlier that day along the coast. She was badly injured but conscious. And she kept crying out his name. Begging for help. And he'd tried. But he couldn't reach her. It was like he was going backward. The harder he worked at it, the farther away he got. Her cries were getting weaker.

He'd awakened in a sweat, feeling sick to his stomach. He looked at his watch. Midafternoon. He needed to do something. He couldn't just sit here…and think.

Maybe he should cut his vacation short and simply go back to work. Or buy a plane ticket and go to Europe for a week. Or—

His phone rang, interrupting his thoughts. "Hey, Marcus," he said.

"How's it going?" his friend asked.

"It's going," he said. He wasn't about to tell Marcus about his morning.

"I found a Regan Jones," Marcus said.

Jamie about dropped the phone. "How—"

"Not your Regan Jones," Marcus said. "*A* Regan Jones. Who physically matches the driver's license photo that your Regan Jones is passing off as her own."

Jamie sat up in bed. He really should have eaten lunch, because his head felt as if it was spinning. "Make sense," he said.

"I got to thinking about your comment that while the photo was a close resemblance, it wasn't her. I could tell you weren't going to let it go. So I started trying to find every other Regan Jones in California. And I think I found the right one in Oakland. I haven't talked to her yet. I thought about doing that without you, but then I figured you'd be pissed about that."

"You figured right. Why do you think she's the right one?"

"I saw her booking photo. I know I said that she didn't have any criminal record, but I was looking at convictions. She was arrested for misdemeanor theft several years ago, but the charges were dropped. Still, there was a photo."

Jamie got out of bed and walked over to the window. It was a clear day, light winds. "I'm going to Oakland," he said.

"It's a twelve-hour drive," Marcus said. "Maybe a phone call?"

"No. And I'm not driving. I'm taking my plane."

"I need to be back by tomorrow night," Marcus said. "Erin has an event at the store."

"On Sunday?"

"It's the only night that the store isn't regularly open for business. It's an invitation-only art show with a new

artist that the store is featuring. All proceeds to go to charity."

"Your wife is a good person," Jamie said. "But who asked you to go, anyway?" Jamie pulled an overnight bag from his closet.

"I asked myself. What time are we wheels up?"

Marcus was a good person and a great friend. "I'll pick you up in a half hour," Jamie said. He would call ahead to Rainbow Field and have them fuel his plane. Door to door it was probably about a three-hour trip.

If their luck was good, they'd be talking with Regan Jones tonight.

Five hours later, Jamie had to admit that they weren't having much luck. He and Marcus had finally stopped to have a bite to eat. At eight fifteen, it was late for dinner, and late to be knocking on strangers' doors in a strange city. The flight down had been good. No problems there. The rental car was fine. That's about where things went haywire.

The address that Marcus had for Regan Jones, the Regan Jones who supposedly matched the license photo that his Regan Jones had been offering up, proved to be a dead end. Yes, a Regan Jones had lived there. The current renters did not know when she'd moved out, but sometimes an odd piece of mail still arrived for her, which was why they recognized the name. They knew there was no forwarding address on file, because when they'd attempted to return the mail to the mail carrier so that could happen, she'd told them exactly that and explained the only option was a return to sender.

Fortunately, Marcus, in his usual thorough manner, had not simply gotten her last known address. He'd

also gotten two previous employers. One had been an off-brand dollar store. The manager on duty had only been there two months and definitely had never worked with a Regan Jones. The other was a small bar in a lower-level walkout where the servers were all young women dressed in shorts and tank tops and the clientele was mostly men who probably enjoyed the view as much as the alcohol. The bartender there knew Regan Jones. When Jamie showed him the photo, he'd nodded. Jamie had hardly been able to contain his excitement. It had taken a dive when the older man had said, "She was a train wreck. I was glad when she finally got the boot." And no, he didn't know where she'd landed and he didn't much care. Then he'd told them to order a drink or move aside for the paying customers. They'd moved. And found a little restaurant down the street.

"Good burger," Marcus said, holding up his half-eaten sandwich.

They hadn't come all this way for dinner. "Yeah. Now what?"

"We go back to the bar tomorrow, try to talk to some of the other employees. Hopefully it's a different bartender, one who isn't quite so touchy. I'm not much interested in a bar fight."

Jamie shrugged. "We've always done okay in those." In their much younger days, he, Marcus and Blade had occasionally mixed it up in a local drinking establishment. Luckily, no one had ever been seriously hurt—and nobody ever pulled any weapons besides an overactive fist.

Marcus smiled. "The good old days."

"Now you and Blade are settled, responsible, law abiding."

"That's kind of a requirement for the chief of police. And the director of emergency medicine at Bigelow Memorial isn't exactly a summer job."

"True. Let's get out of here and grab some shut-eye."

At the hotel where they'd checked in earlier, Marcus parked and they both got out. "You go ahead," he said to Jamie. "I'm going to call Erin before I turn in."

Jamie nodded and walked through the automatic doors. Damn, but he wished he had someone to call. Not just someone, he thought. Her.

The bar didn't open until eleven, but the next morning they were in the alley, outside the back door, by ten thirty. When two young women, maybe midtwenties, approached, Jamie turned to Marcus. "Let me."

"I'm the cop," Marcus reminded him.

"Exactly. You'll scare them. Try to look like an insurance guy." He took two steps toward them and stopped. He offered his best smile. "Good morning," he said.

"Morning," the redhead replied. Her eyes were darting around, likely trying to figure out if they were in danger.

Jamie didn't move toward them. Instead, he put his hands in the air. "I'm Jamie, and this is my friend Marcus. We're trying to find a Regan Jones who used to work here. We were hoping that you might have known her."

The redhead shook her head.

"Why are you looking for her?" the woman with the very black hair and multiple piercings asked.

She hadn't said that she didn't know her. Jamie took a chance. He reached into his shirt pocket and pulled a business card. He didn't want to step closer, didn't want

to intimidate in any way. He tossed it in their direction. It fell short by a foot, but the dark-haired woman picked it up.

"I'm her physician," Jamie said. "It's critically important that I reach her. I have information that she needs."

The woman studied his card. Finally, looked up. "I don't know where she lives, but she's working at the Front Porch." The woman dropped his card in her purse.

"Is that in Oakland?" Marcus asked.

"Yeah. On Paris Street."

"Thank you," Jamie said. "You've been very helpful."

The dark-haired woman shrugged. "She was always nice to me. I hope she isn't sick."

It took them twenty-five minutes to get to the Front Porch. It was a cute little restaurant on what appeared to be a decent street. They were open for lunch.

Please, please, let her be working today, Jamie prayed as they walked in.

She was. He didn't need any introduction, because he could see her across the room, wearing black pants and a white shirt, chatting with a table of four guests. She looked very much like his Regan Jones. They wouldn't pass for twins but maybe as sisters, definitely as distant family. Similar height and weight. Same fine bone structure. Her hair was cut much the same but was darker. "That's her," he said to Marcus.

His friend nodded. "Stay calm."

Now that she was literally within arm's reach, he wasn't exactly sure what to say to her. But even if he had to blunder his way through this, there was no way he was leaving without some answers.

The hostess led them to a table, and luckily enough, Regan was their server. "Good afternoon, gentlemen," she said, setting down two glasses of water. "My name is Regan, and I'll be your server. Can I start you with a drink or a cocktail?"

"Just water," Jamie said.

"Same," Marcus said.

She rattled off the lunch specials, and Jamie heard none of it. He waited until she finished and leaned forward. "We came here looking for you," he said.

Her eyes widened. But she held her ground. "Why? Who are you?"

"My name is Jamie Weathers, and this is Marcus Price. We live in Knoware, Washington, and we're searching for a woman who has disappeared from there. She looks very much like you, and she said her name was Regan Jones."

He watched her face. She did not look all that surprised. "Regan Jones isn't that unusual a name," she said.

He was going to take a chance. "I think she's using your identity, and I think you know all about it. This is a matter of life and death." He pulled his business card and held it out to her. "I have important medical information that she needs. Listen, I don't care why she's doing it and what deal the two of you had, I just need to find her. Can you please help me?"

Regan took his card and then stuffed it quickly into her shirt pocket. "I don't have any information that I can give you."

"Please, please, just give me five minutes of your time."

Regan glanced over her shoulder at the hostess. "Listen, I've got tables to wait on."

Jamie opened his menu and pointed at the first item he saw. "I'll take the turkey and avocado club," he said.

"Same," Marcus said without even opening his. "And two beers. Whatever you got on tap."

She walked away without saying if she'd talk to them later. Jamie wanted to race after her, to make her commit, but he knew that kind of behavior could easily get him tossed and he'd have blown any chance of convincing her that he wasn't a threat.

She brought the beers, and both he and Marcus stayed quiet. As did she. Repeat performance by all when she set down their food. She cleared their dishes when they were done. She didn't offer dessert. But they lingered and watched as the other tables she was waiting on paid their checks and left. Every time she disappeared into the kitchen, Jamie held his breath until she came back into view.

Marcus was evidently tracking along the same path when he suddenly pushed back his chair. "I'm going to go watch the back door," he said.

"You think she's going to make a run for it?" Jamie asked.

"I don't know. But we need to get this wrapped up, and I'm not inclined to chase her around Oakland."

In the end, she didn't run. She came up to the table, pulled out the chair Marcus had been sitting in and sat down. "I guess you're not leaving," she said.

"Nope. And I'll be back every day until I get some answers."

"I really don't know much."

"Whatever you can tell me will be appreciated,"

Jamie said, meaning every word. "I mean neither of you any harm."

"I looked you up on my phone. You're really a doctor."

He smiled. It was smart to check him out before talking to him.

"I met her when I attempted to volunteer for a clinical trial. I needed the money. She worked at the lab. She's some kind of scientist."

All that was fascinating, but he kept his inquiries focused, knowing that she could bolt at any moment. "What's her name?"

"Layla. Layla Morant."

Jamie silently repeated it to make sure he had it. "Why is she using your identification?"

"I have no idea. She never said. But she paid me enough that I was able to get out of a bad situation with an ex-boyfriend and find a better apartment and a better job. And open a savings account. I've never had a savings account before."

"The address on the license she's carrying is Los Angeles. Same for the vehicle registration for the car she was driving."

The woman nodded. "I lived there a few years ago. I never changed my address."

"What's the name of the lab where Layla Morant worked?"

She shook her head. "I don't remember. But it was in San Francisco. Not too far away from the Golden Gate Bridge. Kind of a small place. I was sort of mad at first, because I got rejected for the clinical trial but overall, I made out better. Now, look, I need to get going."

"Thank you, Regan," he said. It felt odd calling her

that. It was a name he associated with another woman. He was going to have to start thinking of his Regan as Layla.

He paid the bill, leaving a tip in the two hundred percent range. She looked at it and smiled. "I guess Layla is the gift that keeps on giving," she said. She hesitated. "She was nice. Kind of wired tight, if you know what I mean, but nice."

It was a similar sentiment to what the black-haired waitress had said about her. He wondered if that was what had attracted Layla Morant to the real Regan Jones. Had she sensed that they were both kindred spirits? Or was it the physical resemblance? Both had wide-set, pretty eyes, although he'd realized quickly after Regan Jones had come up to wait on him and Marcus that he'd not gotten the same feeling from her blue eyes that he'd gotten from Layla's. From the first moment he'd locked eyes with her at the accident scene, he'd felt as if he was drowning in the turbulent depths of her gray-blue gaze.

He went to find Marcus, who was still by the back door. "Layla Morant is her name," he said. "She worked at a lab that did clinical trials somewhere close to the Golden Gate Bridge."

Marcus nodded. "Well done."

"We still don't have the name of the lab," Marcus said.

"Child's play," Marcus said. "Now that we have her real name."

Marcus was right. They went back to their rental car, and it took them less than ten minutes on social media to find her. She was listed in the credits of a group photograph for Weber Clinical Laboratories. "What are you

waiting for?" Marcus asked, sitting in the passenger seat. Jamie had started the vehicle but had yet to pull away from the curb.

"It's a Sunday. There's probably nobody working."

"Maybe not. We won't know if we don't knock on the door."

Still, Jamie didn't put the vehicle in gear.

"There's something else," Marcus said.

"I think I may be a little afraid of what I'll find," Jamie said.

"We're not giving up now," Marcus said.

Jamie didn't want to give up. But since the minute his hand had connected with hers, he'd had a feeling that she was special. Now, given that he'd had confirmation that she was living a lie, using another woman's identity, it was daunting to think that he was going to get confirmation that she wasn't a good person.

It was a forty-five-minute drive to the three-story, tan brick building. It was nondescript on the outside. Inside, it appeared much more high-tech, with sleek gray walls and shiny granite-tiled floor. They didn't get more than five feet inside the door before a security guard and a glass wall stopped them. Jamie wasn't surprised by that. Vaccine development was super competitive, and the security of both premises and proprietary information was taken very seriously.

"You take this," Jamie whispered to Marcus.

Marcus pulled out a business card and slid it through the slot in the Plexiglas window. "My name is Marcus Price, and I'm the chief of police in Knoware, Washington. I need to speak with the person in charge."

The man at the desk inspected the card and reached for his phone. Jamie couldn't hear the conversation,

but it was fairly short. "Dr. Stedlight will be down in a few minutes."

It took him ten. When he arrived, Dr. Stedlight was wearing faded blue jeans and an old Jimmy Buffett T-shirt. "We don't have a dress code on weekends," he said self-consciously.

Jamie didn't care if the man wore tights and a cape if he could provide some answers. When he led them to a first-floor conference room, they took chairs. Dr. Stedlight held Marcus's business card in his hand and Jamie handed over his.

"What can I do for you, gentlemen?"

"We understand that Layla Morant is employed here," Marcus said. "We're attempting to locate her and hope that you can help us."

"Why do you need to find her? Has something happened?"

"It's a confidential medical situation," Jamie said.

"With her mother," Dr. Stedlight said knowingly.

"Uh...no."

Now Dr. Stedlight looked concerned.

"I'm sure you understand that I can't say much more than that," Jamie said.

"Of course. We take confidentiality very seriously here at Weber."

"I'm sure you do. And we'd be happy to wait a few minutes to give you a chance to verify our credentials," Jamie said. If it was good enough for the real Regan Jones, then perhaps it would fly here as well.

Marcus caught up fast. "You can look at the website for the town of Knoware, Washington, and my photo shows as the chief of police. Similarly, if you check the website for the Bigelow Memorial Hospital and click

on medical staff, you'll see Jamie's photo as the director of emergency medicine."

Dr. Stedlight pulled a cell phone from his lab coat and started keying in information as Marcus and Jamie waited. This was what it must feel like to be in the chair while the doctor types, thought Jamie. You can't see the information. All you can do is wait.

Impotent. That was how it made him feel.

Finally, Dr. Stedlight put down his phone. "Your credentials check out."

"Very good," Marcus said smoothly. "Now tell us about Layla Morant."

"I can verify that Layla Morant is employed by Weber Clinical Laboratories. Without looking at her file, I'd estimate that it's been at least eighteen months, probably going on two years. She's a senior developmental scientist."

"What's a senior developmental scientist do?" Jamie asked.

"Well, here at Weber, they work on product development. Specifically vaccine development. She's an excellent employee. I wish I had fifty more just like her, and when she's not here, we miss her." He glanced at his watch. "I'm sorry to be abrupt, but I told my wife that I'd only be here for a few hours this afternoon. We're having people over for dinner. If you need anything else, we'll need to do this at a later time."

"So Ms. Morant is not currently at work," Marcus questioned.

Dr. Stedlight shook his head. "Her mother is ill. Back east, I believe. She's needed there, so we've granted her a leave of absence." He stood up.

"Just one more thing," Jamie said. "Can we have her address and cell number?"

"I've got it in a file in my office. You can wait in the lobby and I'll call down to security with the information."

The three of them parted at the elevators, and Jamie and Marcus stood in the lobby, not talking. Seven minutes later, the security officer's phone rang. He wrote something down and then ripped the information off a pad of paper. "For you," he said.

Jamie took it. It was an address and a phone number. "Thank you," he said.

They walked out the door and back to their car. "What do you think?" Jamie asked once they were inside.

"He's a fan," Marcus said. "I wonder if he still will be after he learns the truth about her, that she's not really taking care of an ill parent but rather living somebody else's life."

"Maybe she's intending to return to work."

"Maybe. We can try her phone," Marcus said.

Jamie shook his head. He doubted that she'd answer it, and he wasn't at all sure what kind of message to leave.

"I can ping it," Marcus said. "Maybe get a location."

He was interested in that. "Try it," he said.

It wasn't too much later that they knew that there'd been absolutely no recent activity on Layla Morant's cell phone. "There was no cell at the accident scene. I guess I figured it was probably in her gym bag," Jamie said. "We need to get you back to Knoware. I'd just like to see her house before we go."

She lived in a condo building not unlike his own.

A little bigger. Hers was five stories, while his was three. Her condo was on the ground floor; his was on the second. He parked, and they walked up to the door. Knocked. There was no answer. The blinds were down, so it was impossible to see in the window.

"Want to try to talk to some neighbors?" Marcus asked.

They needed to get back so that Marcus could attend the event at Erin's store, Tiddle's Tidbits and Treasures. "Nope. Let's head back."

Jamie plugged the address for the airfield into his GPS. The trip hadn't been a waste of time. He knew her real name, knew where she worked, where she lived. That was substantially more than he'd known twenty-four hours earlier. He was getting closer.

Who were the two men knocking on Layla's door? Douglas Glass shifted in his seat. He'd been here most of the previous day and this morning since eight, and it was the first activity that he'd seen. They were driving a rental.

When they pulled away from the curb, he was behind them. He'd honed this skill earlier in his hunting days. Young women, especially those with a few drinks in them, were generally ridiculously easy to tail. These two might be more aware, so he was careful to keep his distance.

He was surprised when they turned off on the road leading to a small private airfield. He kept going, thinking it was too big of a risk to follow. But then, ten minutes later, when he thought it safe, he drove toward the airfield.

He got there in time to see them walking toward a

small airplane. One got in the passenger side and the other walked around the plane, doing a visual inspection. Then he climbed into the pilot's seat, and within minutes, they were in the sky.

Very interesting.

He noted the description of the plane and the time of takeoff. It shouldn't be that difficult to find out who was flying the plane. If that person could somehow lead him to Layla, any amount of effort would be worth it.

Chapter 9

By Sunday evening, Layla's hope to feel better had not materialized. She was hot and uncomfortable sleeping, even though the cottage was cool. Now that she'd checked her temperature, she understood why—102.6. Not good.

But not necessarily horrible, she argued with herself. Sometimes a temperature could be a sign that the body was fighting an infection. Maybe that's what was going on. She'd take more acetaminophen and drink plenty of water.

She got the pills down and managed four sips of water before collapsing back onto the bed. What the hell was she going to do if she couldn't pull herself out of this?

She had a phone. She could call 911. They'd want to know her name. If she told them Layla Morant, she had no identification with her to prove that true. And

no way was she risking her real name suddenly appearing in some record that Douglas Glass could trace. She could tell them she was Regan Jones. She could offer proof of that, but then she had the very real worry that somehow the 911 call and subsequent treatment would get linked to her very recent stay at Bigelow Memorial. She'd walked away from a hospital bill. Would they be inclined to find her and collect? Surely the hospital experienced that situation with multiple patients. They had to be inclined to simply write it off as bad debt. But what about Jamie Weathers?

He was part of the hospital. A somebody there. It did not go beyond the stretch of imagination to think that somehow, he might learn that she was once again seeking medical treatment. She'd gotten away but hadn't traveled that far.

Would he come looking for her?

That had a Cinderella-and-glass-slipper feel to it. And she'd stopped believing in fairy tales a while ago. Certainly her experience with Douglas Glass had cured her of believing in happy endings or even that right won out in the end. Justice was definitely not always served.

The truth of the matter was that she couldn't afford to have anybody looking for her. Which brought up the final reason why it wasn't a good idea to seek medical treatment as Regan Jones. Every time she did that, she ran the risk that the real Regan Jones would somehow be pulled into all of it. She didn't trust that the woman would stay silent if pushed. And once she told the story, it was hard to say who might search for Layla. Her boss. Her colleagues. Her friends. The police.

Best to avoid any chance of that happening.

She'd wait another day.
She closed her eyes and slept.

They made the flight back without incident. It had been a quiet ride, as if each of them had tacitly agreed to take the time in the air to process their thoughts. Jamie had landed the plane and was taxiing to the hangar before Marcus finally said, "We need to talk about this."

"Okay."

"We now have confirmation that the person we knew as Regan Jones is not, in fact, Regan Jones but rather Layla Morant. She is using another woman's identity. She *paid* to use another woman's identity. She *received medical care* under another woman's identity."

Marcus was simply trying to make his point, but it irritated Jamie. "I get it. She's doing a bad thing. But maybe she has a good reason."

"She might. But I'm an officer of the law, and you're the medical director of the ED where she received services under false pretenses. That's fraud. We can't simply ignore this. That's not the right thing to do."

That was the real reason he was irritated with Marcus. Because he knew what he was saying was true. "You are suggesting what, exactly?"

"I'm suggesting that I need to make a report through official channels. We need to flag both Layla Morant and Regan Jones. You said that she was going to Canada. If that's true, if she attempts to book travel, or cross a border, or even pay for an item with a credit card, law enforcement will be notified. If she's got a legitimate reason for what she did, she can explain it then."

Ultimately, it would be a good thing for her to get caught. She could get the medical care she needed. Still,

he couldn't help feeling bad about it. They were setting a trap for her. "You're sure we need to do this?" he asked.

"I am. And I think you know it's the right thing to do as well."

Yeah. But that didn't mean he liked it. "Fine. Do it."

"What are your plans for tonight?" Marcus asked.

Jamie shrugged. "Go home. Eat. Go to bed."

"Come to the thing at Tiddle's. It will give you something else to think about. I think Blade and Daisy are coming, and I know Erin always loves to see you."

He always liked hanging out with his friends and their wives. But tonight, he just wasn't in the mood. Especially after hearing Marcus's arguments in favor of officially reporting Layla Morant.

It was really difficult sometimes to do the right thing.

"Thanks. But I'm just going to go home. Tell Erin I hope the night is a fabulous success." He knew that he was going to be a topic of conversation tonight. It wouldn't go beyond Blade and Daisy and Marcus and Erin, but between the four of them, there'd likely be plenty of discussion about how Jamie had fallen for a… con artist, liar, criminal. None of the descriptors were very flattering.

Jamie didn't fault them. If positions were reversed, he might be saying the same thing. But they hadn't been in the room. He had been. And he felt changed by it.

As he walked to his vehicle, he gave Marcus a final wave. He was grateful to his friend for dropping everything to go with him. But because he had, Layla was now in more trouble. That was going to keep him up tonight.

The next morning, Jamie felt no satisfaction in having been right. He hadn't slept well. But that did not stop

him from running four miles. Afterward, while he was showering, he reflected upon the previous day. There'd been several ups and downs, but the biggest and most interesting surprise had been learning that Layla Morant was a highly respected scientist.

She wasn't a crazy person. But she was running a hell of a scam. There could be all kinds of reasons. Bad ones.

Or was it not a scam but truly a legitimate attempt to disappear? Was someone hunting her?

That was a chilling thought. But the more he considered it, the more legitimacy it gained in his head. He got out of the shower, dried off and dressed. Then he booted up his laptop and searched the web, looking for mentions of Layla Morant. There were a few, all related to her work at Weber Clinical Laboratories.

He pushed his laptop aside, feeling as unsettled as he'd ever felt. Something was terribly wrong. He could feel it in his bones. And he didn't intend to sit here in his condo all day letting it eat at him.

Fifteen minutes later, he was on his way to Rainbow Field. In his daily work, he'd often had to search for victims from the air. He knew the downsides. Small objects were tough to see, faces hard to distinguish. But he knew the benefits, too. Could sometimes see into more heavily wooded areas that were impossible to access by a vehicle. Could cover more geographical area in one day.

It was worth a try.

He repeated that more than once as he got in the air and headed north. Layla's last known location had been at Widow's Peak. She could be a thousand miles from there by now, but it was really all he had to go on.

He'd start there. Maybe there was something beyond the golf course that he'd not been able to discern from the ground. There were a few small coastal towns within twenty miles that were likely pretty quiet this time of year, but he'd buzz them just in case she'd somehow made her way there.

He'd been in the air for more than two hours, going farther north than he'd originally intended, when he finally decided to head back south. It was a good day for flying, very clear, with more sun then they usually had in late November, but still, he'd seen nothing of interest. He'd flown a bit inland on the way, but now he stayed along the coast. It was beautiful. Rugged. Rocky. Lots of spray from the ocean that was never very calm in this area.

He saw the painted cottages that lined the coast near Widow's Peak. Was almost past them when he caught a glimpse of someone on a porch.

Someone in a chair. Wrapped in a blanket.

He made a big sweeping turn and came back.

He or she was gone. But what appeared to be a wooden kitchen chair remained.

There'd been no chair there the day before. He was confident of it.

He increased his altitude and didn't make another pass. Whoever had been on the porch had made a hasty exit. Maybe they were simply done sunning. Or maybe they hadn't wanted to be seen from the air. That was enough for him.

He was coming back.

She'd been dozing when she'd heard the plane. Had moved as quickly as she could, but since that involved

getting her crutches out from underneath the blanket, getting them underneath her and moving inside, it had taken too long. She'd glanced over her shoulder, watched the plane turn and had known there was no time to retrieve the chair.

And now she stood inside the door, her strength so tenuous that it was a supreme effort to stay upright, and listened to the plane pass overhead. Would it come back? Make yet a third pass?

She waited. And waited.

She could not stand much longer. She took a deep breath and tried to flood her brain with oxygen. If it hadn't come back by now, it surely was not.

Going outside had been a bad idea, born of her tossing and turning on the bed. The sun, which had not been visible for days, it seemed, was bright and high in the sky. The vitamin D would do her good, she'd reasoned. She'd known it was a risk, but she'd seen no one walking the beach yet. And it would only be for a short while.

All that, along with the very real concern that perhaps she was really ill and wouldn't live to see many more sunny days, had her slowly pushing a kitchen chair to and through the doorway. Then sitting, the light blanket covering her and her crutches. She'd raised her face to the sun and closed her eyes.

Now, she made her way back to the bedroom and collapsed on the bed. Tears gathered in her eyes. She'd grasped for a sliver of pleasure, and even that was too risky. This was her life going forward. It was more awful than she'd imagined.

Her new normal.

How many times would she say that to herself in the

coming days? How many times would she try to convince herself that she was okay with it?

She should drink some water, try to keep hydrated. And take her temperature, see if it was higher.

She did neither.

Maybe it would just be easier when the end came.

Jamie landed and taxied toward the hangar. Twenty minutes later, he was finished up and in his SUV. It was early afternoon, and he'd missed lunch. He needed to eat, and just in case, he should probably stop at home for a quick change of clothes, some toiletries. *Don't get caught without a toothbrush.* His mother had raised three boys, and once they'd been in college and had a bit more freedom, that had been her way of warning them to be safe if circumstances resulted in them not coming home that night. She wouldn't say *condom*, but having a toothbrush meant a lot more than simply keeping your teeth clean.

Thirty minutes later, he'd swung by Gertie's Café and gotten himself a grilled ham and cheese to go. He ate it as he drove to his condo. There, he packed his overnight bag. He thought about calling Marcus or Blade to give them an update, but decided against it. If they came by and he wasn't home, they'd call. It wasn't like he was going to be out of reach, and this way, he could avoid hearing them caution against being too hopeful.

He was hopeful, he realized when he caught himself singing along with a tune on the radio as he backed out of his driveway. He drove fast and got there in under forty-five minutes. He parked in the driveway and

walked around the side of the cottage to the door that faced the rugged shore. The chair was still there.

He knocked. Nobody answered. He knocked again, harder.

He wasn't leaving. Not until he had some answers. His gut told him he wasn't wrong, and he was going with it, even if it meant that he looked like a fool.

"It's Jamie Weathers," he yelled. "Open the door, Regan." No need to spill the beans that he knew her secret. "I'm not leaving until you open the door. I'll stand here all night. In fact, I'll call all my friends and have them stand here all night with me. And we'll play music and dance and maybe have a hell of a big campfire. We're going to attract some attention. If that's what you want, then great. That's what you'll get."

He stopped. Listened. Heard nothing from inside.

He kicked the door with his foot. It was solid, but he thought a few well-placed kicks in the right place might get him inside.

"I'm about to break the door down, Regan."

It sounded tough, but he probably wouldn't do that, truly. There were easier ways to get inside. These two big windows were boarded up, but not every window was.

"On the count of three. One." He paused. "Two." Damn. Would he really break into somebody's home just to see if his gut was right? "Th—" he began. And stopped. Because he was pretty sure he heard the telltale thump of crutches.

He heard the lock click, and the door swung open. It was her.

"Why?" she whispered. "Why are you here?"

He stared at her. She looked whipped, like she was

barely standing. Her hair was dirty, there were dark circles under her eyes and her shirt was stained with dried sweat. "Because you need me, darling. You need me."

Layla didn't protest when Jamie came in. She didn't have the strength. It had taken everything she had to get to the door. "It's too late," she said. "I'm too sick."

"Well, now that's a challenge if I ever heard one," he said smoothly. "Let's get you horizontal."

"I'll bet you say that to all the girls."

He smiled, but it didn't reach his eyes. "Only the really pretty ones." He was looking around while he was talking. "Where are you sleeping?"

"In one of the bedrooms."

"Can you walk or should I carry you?"

"I can walk." Maybe.

She made it, with him at her side the whole way. When they got close to the bed, he reached for her go-bag, which was at the far side of the bed.

"No," she said, using every bit of her energy. She needed her stuff close.

"Fine," he muttered.

Then she collapsed on the bed, with her go-bag at the side of her right leg. He immediately unwrapped the bandage on her leg. He said nothing. Just wrapped it up again. "I keep some basic medical supplies in my vehicle. I'm going out to get them. If you have any bright ideas about locking the door again, forget it."

"Out of bright ideas," she said. Her throat was dry, and it took effort to talk.

"Lucky for you, I'm not. Be right back."

She closed her eyes.

* * *

Her temp was too high and her respiration too fast and too shallow. On the positive side, her lungs sounded clear, and while she appeared drained, she was coherent and her motor movements coordinated. Her stitches had held and there was little drainage. Swelling was down. Still.

"We need to get you back to Bigelow Memorial," he said. "Run some labs. Do an ultrasound." He was still worried about the possibility of internal bleeding.

She shook her head. "No."

He could easily overpower her. Simply carry her out to his vehicle, strap her in and take her wherever he damn well pleased. But force wasn't his way, had never been his way. "You're running too high a temperature. Best circumstance is an infection that could be treated effectively with antibiotics. Worst case is something... else. There's a range of possibilities that we can't possibly rule out without more testing."

"How did you find me?" she asked.

He wasn't done talking about her health, but he was willing to answer a few questions. "Some detective work. A lot of luck. I followed your movements from the hospital to the Creekside Hotel to Widow's Peak. Then I saw you outside, on the porch. From the air."

"You were in that plane," she said, some awe in her voice.

"I was flying that plane," he said. "It's mine."

She shook her head. "Dr. Weathers, since that very first turkey dinner, you continue to surprise me."

Yeah, well, she surprised him, too. He hadn't expected her to become this important to him in just a few

days. Her voice was weak, strained. He offered her the bottle of water on the bedside table. "Small sip," he said.

She took it. "I'm glad you came back. I didn't want to die alone."

"Nobody is dying on my watch," he said. "That's why we're going back to Bigelow Memorial."

She shook her head. "No."

"Why?" he asked. He had a pretty good idea, but he wanted to test whether she would finally be honest with him. If she chose not to be, well, that was going to be somewhat crushing. How could he ever hope that they could move forward together if one of them was lying about most everything?

"I can't say."

He'd gotten secrets from patients before. Sometimes it was as simple as they found the information embarrassing. Most times that had something to do with bowel or bladder functions or, with men, difficulty in the bedroom. This was different, of course, but he forced himself not to dwell on the disappointment he felt but rather, on tried and true techniques. "As a physician, I hear all kinds of things," he said. "It would be hard to surprise me. And I can't provide you the best care and we cannot even hope for the best outcomes if you're not a hundred percent truthful with me."

She didn't answer. She simply closed her eyes.

Again, he considered forcing the issue. And he'd simply live with however mad she got with him. But there was probably a middle ground here. Yes, she was ill. Yes, he suspected she was suffering from some kind of infection and likely dehydrated. But he could try treating her here. "How are the ribs?" he asked.

"Pretty sure they're still there."

Cracked ribs hurt like hell. Breathing, talking, moving. She was definitely not the complaining type. Really pretty brave and capable to have gotten this far with her injuries. He made his decision. "There's one alternative to the hospital that we can try. It requires me to return to Knoware and get more supplies. Then I'll start an IV of antibiotics and fluids."

She opened her eyes. "No hospital?"

"Not yet."

"No police?"

There it was. She was afraid of the police. Was she a criminal? Ultimately, that decision didn't dictate the care she got. Criminals were entitled to medical care. He frequently provided care to people from the county jail. Once she was well, he'd have to wrestle with the decision of whether or not to enlist the help of police. "No police," he said firmly. While it did not matter in regard to her care, he knew it mattered very much to him personally. He believed in the law, believed that most police were decent people wanting to do a decent job, knew for sure that there were some like Marcus who were extraordinary.

Her eyes locked with his. He could not have looked away.

"Thank you," she said. "I haven't been all that lucky in the past couple of years, and I was very lucky that you were the one who responded to the accident. I appreciate everything you're doing. I really do." She paused. "I just have one request. Be honest with me, straight up. Factual. I can handle it."

He was pretty confident she could. He stood up. "I'll be back in two hours. Try to sleep until then."

She nodded. "Lock the door, please. There's an extra set of keys in the kitchen drawer next to the sink. You'll be able to get back in."

"You're going to be here when I get back?" he asked, suddenly unsure of leaving her once again.

"I promise," she said.

The muscles in his chest relaxed. It was the first time he'd heard her say those words. He didn't know this woman, but he had a feeling that her promises meant something to her.

Before he left, he tested the keys on the door lock, and they worked like a charm. He stuffed them in his pocket and got into his SUV. On his drive back, he debated calling Marcus and Blade and giving them an update now that he'd actually seen her. But in the end, he decided against it. They would support him, like always, but they would also likely insist upon understanding his mind-set about the situation. And he wasn't so sure he was ready to explain that to somebody else. It was sort of muddled in his head. All he knew was that it felt right to help her.

He drove to the hospital first and pulled into the underground garage where they parked Mobile One. There were three storage bins in the garage where they kept the medication stock and equipment for the vehicle. It took him less than fifteen minutes to find everything he thought he might possibly need. He did not sign it out as was protocol—he simply removed it from the shelves. He did take a photo of everything and jotted down a quick log so that he could account for the supplies later. Right now, he didn't want anybody wondering why he needed medical supplies when he was supposed to be on vacation.

Caitlin Rose made sure actual inventory matched the electronic records once a month on the fifteenth. By the middle of December, he'd have fixed this.

He left the garage and drove to the grocery store. He'd taken a quick look in the kitchen of the cottage, and all he'd seen was a loaf of bread and a jar each of peanut butter and jelly. He didn't intend to live on that. At the store, he picked up enough food to last at least a week. Fruit and vegetables. Cheese. Meat. Ice cream. All the necessities of life.

He drove to his house next. There, he got a big cooler for the food so things wouldn't melt or get hot on the way back. And a few more clothes and toiletries. He got back in his vehicle and glanced at his watch. If he hurried, he'd make his promise of two hours.

He did not notice the strange car parked across from his condo.

Douglas Glass watched the man drive away. He'd been home for less than ten minutes. Douglas started his car and eased into traffic. In minutes, the man had left the small community of Knoware behind and was headed north on the highway. He drove fast, as if he had someplace to be.

Did any of this have anything to do with Layla Morant? That was the big question. And until Douglas knew for sure, he wasn't going to give up this opportunity to follow him. However, twenty minutes later, when the needle on the gas gauge hovered on empty, he realized that he should have been better prepared. He continued following for another fifteen miles, but the man ahead of him gave no indication that he was stopping or slowing down. Douglas was very concerned

that he might truly run out of gas. If that happened and he called someone for help, there would be a record of that. If he called his mother, she'd be full of questions. If a stranger stopped to help, it would be a loose end that would interrupt his sleep. A loose end named Layla Morant had sent him to prison once before. He couldn't let that happen again.

He saw a sign for a gas station five miles ahead. He pulled in, filled his tank half-full as quickly as he could and was on his way. He drove fast, even faster than before. But then he got behind a semi that fairly chugged up the hills, and there was enough traffic coming toward him that he wasn't able to pass for many miles. When he finally did, he realized that he'd lost the man.

He knew his name, of course. Jamie Weathers. It had been relatively easy to get, because he'd had information on the plane he was flying. From there, he'd easily discovered online where he lived. Knoware, Washington. Douglas wasn't unfamiliar with the place. He thought he'd been there once as a kid, when the family was visiting his great-uncle's farm that was somewhere within thirty miles or so.

Of course, by that time, it no longer belonged to his great-uncle. Some twenty years earlier, his grandfather, his mother's father, had been in business with his brother, and there had been a falling-out. His great-uncle lost his house and farm to Douglas's grandfather. Through inheritance, it had passed to his mother, and that's what had prompted the trip for her and Douglas. She wanted to see the property for herself. He barely remembered the place and wasn't confident that his mother still had ownership. They'd only visited the one time that he could recall.

He learned, too, that Jamie Weathers was a doctor. Interesting. He wished he knew more about Layla to know if Dr. Weathers was an old or new friend. Or perhaps even more than that? He needed more information on both Layla and the doctor. He'd have to be careful to hide his searches, but there were ways to do that. Ways that he'd learned in prison.

Reluctantly he turned his vehicle around and started for home. The trip to Knoware had been risky to begin with. He'd wanted to fly but hadn't wanted the paper trail. Instead, had borrowed his mother's old Mustang. It was a second vehicle for her, she rarely drove it and it was too old to have GPS technology. She'd had the car since she was a teenager. Now, it was proving to be invaluable to Douglas.

He'd told her he was visiting an old friend. She'd seemed to accept his explanation, but he'd known that she was worried that he might do something that was going to end badly for him.

That wasn't going to happen. This time, there wouldn't be any loose ends. Nobody to run their mouth to a grand jury. He was going to make sure of that.

Chapter 10

Layla woke to sounds coming from the kitchen. Soft banging. Metal clanging. She checked her watch. Jamie had said he'd be back in two hours, and it appeared that he'd made it. She wondered if she should get up, put on a good show, attempt to convince him that she wasn't as sick as he thought. But the effort that would take was, quite frankly, well beyond her at this point.

She didn't have long to wait to see what he was up to, because he entered the room minutes later, pushing an IV pole on wheels with one hand and carrying a white plastic tray in the other. "You came back," she said, her mouth feeling so dry.

He smiled at her. "Of course. Any change while I was gone?"

She shook her head. "You can't park outside."

He looked surprised at her change of topic. "I have things to carry inside," he said.

"You can't park outside," she repeated. Before she'd gone to sleep, it had dawned on her what he'd said about seeing her from his plane. That had been a stupid mistake on her part. She had not anticipated the possibility that someone would be searching for her by air, and she should have. She needed to stop making mistakes. She did not want somebody driving down the highway to see his vehicle and think it odd that cottages that were usually vacant in the winter suddenly had an inhabitant.

"I'll move it once I've started your IVs and have carried everything inside."

"Where?"

"I'm going to hang two bags, one a saline solution for dehydration and the other an antibiotic for infection," he said, ignoring her question. He slipped gloves on while he talked and moved fast. "Going to feel a slight pinch," he said as he tapped a vein in her arm and inserted a needle. In seconds, she could feel the slight burn as fluid dripped through the tubing connected to the fluids that he thought were going to save her.

Man, she hoped so.

"Doing okay so far?" he asked.

Okay was a relative term. She felt weak, slightly nauseous and warm. But it was good to not be alone. That had been pretty scary, if she was being honest. "Where will you move your vehicle to?" she asked, not willing to let it go.

He picked up a thermometer. Stuck it in her mouth. It beeped, and he checked it. "Up three-tenths of a degree since last time," he said. He pulled a small notebook and pen from his shirt pocket. He opened to a page and wrote the time and the temperature down.

"Rudimentary charting," she said.

He shrugged. "In medicine, there's an old saying. If it's not documented, then it didn't happen."

That was sort of how it worked in the world of vaccine development, too. Data ruled. Everything was measured and recorded. Variation required investigation and resolution. "My temp isn't spiking," she said, determined to focus on the positive.

"No. But I would have expected the meds you took two hours ago to mitigate it somewhat."

Well, there was that. He hadn't said it harshly but rather more matter-of-factly. She appreciated that he'd listened to her request not to sugarcoat anything. Maybe she should try to make a joke, lighten the mood. Something along the lines of *Looking at you, Doc, makes me kind of hot.*

Would he laugh? Or roll his eyes? Or simply ignore her? Probably none of the above. He would likely chart in his little notebook that patient appeared to be delirious and filters had been abandoned.

"You should eat something," he said. "I brought some cans of chicken noodle soup. Not as good as homemade but will do in a pinch."

It would take energy to sit up and eat, but she understood the need. And he was doing everything he could to help her get better, so she could do the same. "I'll try," she said. "Your vehicle?"

He sighed. "I'll park it in Widow's Peak parking lot. There's enough cars there that I don't think they'll notice one more."

"Okay."

"But first, you eat." He left the room and returned

with a coffee cup filled with soup. There was a spoon in it. "Easier to hold than a bowl," he said.

She took a bite.

He reached for the wrist that wasn't holding the cup and took her pulse. He looked up from his watch.

"Verdict?" she asked, taking another sip of soup.

"Not bad."

"You're a real confidence booster," she said. She took a third sip and then reached to set the cup on the nightstand. "I'll have some more later."

"I'm going to change the dressing on your leg," he said. "And then, yes, before you ask, I will move my vehicle."

"Fine." She was so tired. She could not keep her eyes open.

It was dark by the time Jamie finished unloading his vehicle and then drove it to the parking lot, where there were at least thirty other vehicles. He didn't like having his transportation this far away from him, but he'd sensed that he was going to get little cooperation from his patient until he agreed. As sick as she was, her primary worry had been about detection. That said a lot. Exactly what, he wasn't sure, but he knew it wasn't good. He knew what Marcus would say—that the warning signs were blinking bright and Jamie should open his eyes.

He wouldn't turn a blind eye, he told himself as he walked back to the cottage and quietly let himself in. He checked her. She was asleep. It was the best thing for her, really. She would wake more hydrated and the antibiotics should begin to work fast.

If she had an infection, it should respond to the an-

tibiotic. But if he didn't see that improvement, he was taking her back to the hospital, even if he had to drug her to get her to cooperate.

If she rallied, that would be the best situation. He'd have gained her trust. In return, he'd make it clear to her that he had questions. Her identity, sure. But simpler ones, too. Was she really headed to Canada? Or was that also a lie? How had she chosen this place as her hidey-hole? How had she gotten in? How long had she been planning to stay before moving on? She'd told the linen truck driver that she was meeting a friend. Was any of that real, or should he expect somebody to show up?

What was he going to do if it was a love interest?

He realized he was borrowing a fair amount of trouble and decided to do something a little more practical with his time: he would figure out who owned this cottage, because one thing he was confident of—especially after her insistence that he move his vehicle—was that they were squatting here without permission. That put them on the wrong side of law, and that wasn't something he was comfortable with.

He used his smartphone to find the information he needed. Benjamin and Jenny White had owned the property for fourteen years. A few more clicks and he was confident that he'd found the couple in Seattle. This was probably their summer home.

Now that he had the information, he wasn't quite sure what to do with it. Contact them, apologize for using the property without permission and ask to stay on for some undetermined time while Regan—or Layla or whatever her real name was—healed? Boy, that didn't sound like a conversation he wanted to have. Or wait

for the police to show up and arrest them for breaking and entering? That sounded worse.

They needed to leave.

His condo would be a perfectly good place for her to rest and recover. But he had a feeling it was going to be a fight.

He walked back into the bedroom and was surprised to see that her eyes were open. "Hey," he said. "I didn't know you were awake."

"Contemplating how to get to the bathroom with this," she said, looking at the IV tubing.

"I'll unhook it," he said. It was a good sign that she felt strong enough to go to the bathroom. He got her free and handed her the crutches. "Need any other help?" he asked.

"Nope. Been doing this by myself for quite a few years," she said. "Your vehicle?"

"In the parking lot."

"Thank you," she said, sounding very relieved.

He nodded. He watched her move toward the small bathroom, ready to spring into action if she looked unsteady. But she made slow progress and closed the door tightly. After a few minutes, he heard the toilet flush and the sound of running water in the sink. Finally the door opened, and he could see the edges of her hair around her face were wet. It had probably felt good to splash some water on her face.

He pulled new IV bags from the equipment stash he'd commandeered and hung new fluid. Then he took her crutches from her and she got herself back onto the bed.

"More?" she asked.

"Definitely," he said. "I want to listen to your lungs and heart."

She nodded.

He hung his stethoscope around his neck. Then he helped her sit forward and listened to all four quadrants. Lungs still very clear. That was excellent. Then he let her sit back, and he listened to her heart. He'd done this same procedure on a thousand patients, but suddenly it felt very personal to be leaning over her in bed, his fingers lightly pressing into the rise of her soft breasts.

Focus. Focus.

"Now your abdomen," he said. "Can you raise your shirt?"

She didn't nod or speak, simply pulled her shirt up. God, her skin was smooth. And tanned still from summer. He listened. Heard the normal gurgles and murmurs. Abdomens were very noisy. "Any pain?" he asked.

"No. I mean, I'm still sore, but mostly all over. Not substantially worse in my stomach."

Again, good news.

"Am I going to live?" she asked, her tone light. But he remembered her comment from earlier that day, that she hadn't wanted to die alone.

"Of course," he said easily. "I told you. Nobody's dying on my watch." He took off his stethoscope and laid it aside. "Feel up to eating the rest of your soup?"

"Sure," she said.

"And maybe part of a sandwich?"

"Half a PB&J," she said.

"Dinner of champions," he said.

"Dinner?" she asked, looking toward the window. "I guess it is dark outside. Did you eat?"

"I'll get something now," he said. He walked back out to the kitchen, heated up the remainder of her soup and

made her sandwich. Then he quickly threw together a ham and cheese on rye for himself along with a generous bunch of grapes. He added a glass of milk for himself and a glass of water for her.

He put everything on a tray that he found in the cupboard and carried it into her room. He distributed their dinners and then took a seat in the corner chair. The cushions were spent, and he sank deep. No matter. There was not a position that he couldn't eat or sleep in. That was a by-product of both medical school and his stint as an army doctor.

She eyed his food. "I imagine you're very grateful that you went to the grocery store."

"Your choices were not…significant," he allowed.

"I was…traveling," she said.

"Of course." He chewed, debating which of the thousand questions he had should be asked first. "To Canada, as I recall."

"Yes."

"Yet, oddly, when I spoke to the driver of the linen truck that dropped you off at Widow's Peak, he mentioned that a friend was coming there to pick you up."

She stared at him. "I didn't want him to be worried about me. He was a nice man, and it would have bothered him to think that I was…stranded."

"Why here? Why not stay at Widow's Peak?"

"It looked expensive."

"Did you walk from Widow's Peak to here?"

She shook her head. "Golf cart."

He smiled. "And how did you get in?"

"Cut a hole in the glass on the front window so I could open the latch and push it up. Then I crawled in."

There was no way. She could not have put any weight on her leg. "I don't—"

"I leaned in, braced my hands on the floor and turned my body over while I was balanced on the sill."

She said it like it was no big deal. "There's this movie, where the main character is a superhero and is elastic. That's not you, right?"

It was her turn to smile. "The thousands of dollars I have spent on yoga classes finally paid off."

"Indeed." Another question dawned on him. "How did you cut a hole in the window? There's plywood covering the two windows."

"Not when I started. Just glass. And I had a…small tool in my bag."

Her bag of tricks. He wouldn't be surprised to see white rabbits jumping out any minute. She'd gotten herself inside and then had the foresight to repair the damage she'd done to the window in the best way possible. "Why, you're sort of amazing. I don't think I'll ever underestimate you again," he said. If he did, it would be at his own peril. She was resourceful and had grit and determination to spare.

He'd finished his food. She'd eaten most of her cup of soup and about half of the half a sandwich he'd given her. "Done?"

She nodded. "Do you need to drive back to Knoware? I imagine you have to work tomorrow."

"Not tomorrow." There was no need to tell her that he had a whole week of vacation. "I'm planning on spending the night." He studied her. It dawned on him that perhaps she didn't feel safe. "Is that okay with you?"

"It's very kind of you," she said.

He wasn't being kind. Not really. Kind people did

things for no reason. He had motive—he wanted to spend more time with her. Learn the truth. "You should sleep," he said. "I'll check you in the middle of the night, replace the bags. By morning, I'm hoping you'll start to feel better." If her temperature wasn't down, they were headed back to Bigelow Memorial.

"I will be better," she said, her tone resolute.

Grit and determination to spare, he thought as he carried the dirty dishes to the kitchen. On the way he made a detour to the living room and lifted the shade of the window. There was her hole. Big enough that she could stick her hand and arm through and unlatch the window.

She'd done all this while putting weight only on one leg.

Magician. Superhero. Supremely motivated and a little lucky. He wasn't sure which descriptor to assign. He was simply grateful that he'd managed to find her. He had a feeling that if she'd managed to elude him this time, he'd never have seen her again.

And then, he thought, letting the shade fall back into place, there would have been a hole in his life.

She hated lying to him. It seemed that honesty was the very least she could offer in exchange for him saving her life. But if she said the words, even if they were spoken with the best of intent, she would be undoing everything, absolutely everything, that she'd done to ensure her safety. It was too big of a risk.

She knew next to nothing about Jamie Weathers. Other than the fact that he was a decent, caring physician who was going above and beyond to care for a

patient. Other than he'd done everything he could to make her feel safe and confident that she was going to recover. Other than that he'd made her laugh and was constantly trying to feed her.

She guessed she did know a few things. Nice things.

He was a pilot. That had come as a surprise. She suspected he had a few more aces up his sleeve, and quite frankly, clichés aside, she wanted to roll up his cuffs and fish 'em out. One by one, until she understood the whole man.

To what purpose, she argued with herself. Was she so interested in self-torture? Because that's what it would amount to when she had to leave him again. She would know more, miss more, regret more. Ugh.

It wasn't as if she'd not considered the more intimate aspects of her situation when she'd first contemplated her arrangement with Regan Jones. She was thirty-two years old. She was going to want to have sex again. Want to feel the warmth of a man's body next to her in bed. Maybe, just maybe, even have a child.

And throughout the months of deliberation and finally preparation to become Regan Jones, she'd decided that with the right guy, that could happen. If she found somebody who was really a nobody, somebody who was happy living a low-visibility life. Marriage was out of the question. That was a legal relationship and, like all legal relationships, would invite scrutiny that she wanted to avoid. But if she connected with the right person, who was happy sharing a life in a less formal setting, just maybe it could work. Just maybe she could still have some semblance of what she wanted.

It would not be easy but she'd told herself that it

would be years before she was ready to embark upon a relationship. By then, she'd have been living as Regan Jones for so long that she'd really think of herself that way. Layla Morant and the life she'd left behind would simply be a distant memory. She'd have settled into her new life, gotten comfortable with it. Only then would she be ready to handle navigating a relationship built upon half-truths.

She certainly wasn't ready to do that less than a week into her new life.

Not when she was ill and her wits felt scattered, not laser-focused on keeping her story straight.

Not with Jamie Weathers, local hero. The antithesis of a nobody.

So it was really impossible to share secrets. She simply could not take the risk that he'd either maliciously or completely innocently disclose her situation to the wrong person and somehow Douglas Glass would find her.

She closed her eyes. She needed to recover quickly and move on. That was the goal.

Douglas called his mother from his hotel room. It was late, almost ten, but he knew she wouldn't be in bed. She'd be waiting for him. He'd promised her that he'd be back at the house. It was a requirement of his parole that he remain in the state of California and be home by 10:00 p.m. unless he had prior permission from his parole officer. He'd spent too much time watching Dr. Weathers's condo. He'd been rewarded with a sighting of him and had desperately wanted to know where he was going and if it had anything to do with Layla. He'd been frustrated after losing him and had returned to the condo, hoping the man would come back. He'd

intended to talk to him, to demand to know why the man had been watching Layla's condo.

But he hadn't come back. Finally, Douglas had started the long trip home, thinking he would simply drive through the night and be back in San Francisco by morning. Certainly before anybody would be looking for him. But he'd gotten so tired. Had almost run his car off the road twice before he'd finally admitted that there was no way he could continue.

"Dougie, where are you?" his mother answered.

He'd lied to her about his trip. She thought he was headed to Northern California to visit an old friend. Right now, he was still in Oregon. California was at least an hour south still. But he wasn't telling her that. "Mother, I'm at my friend's house. We had the nicest dinner and time just got away from us. I'm going to spend the night."

She was silent. She knew about the terms of the parole.

He waited. She would have something to say. She always did.

"This is not good, Dougie."

"Don't worry, Mother." She would, but she simply didn't understand. "I'll be home before anyone even knows I was gone. Very early." She would lie for him if it came to that. He had no doubt about it.

"Don't truffle this up, Dougie," she said.

His mother decried vulgarity and frequently spoke out about the limited vocabulary of those, especially women, who uttered profanity. That had not stopped her from inventing her own words. As a child, when he'd heard his mother's soft "Truffle you" when another

mom had beaten her to a parking spot in the schoolyard, he'd soon discerned what it really meant.

"I won't." *Truffling up* could mean a return to prison. So he was going to be very careful. Confident with the knowledge that as soon as he found Layla Morant, everything would be just fine. Settled.

Chapter 11

On Tuesday morning, Layla felt well enough to sit up in bed to eat her scrambled eggs and toast. "You're a good cook," she said. Jamie sat in the corner chair, eating his own breakfast. They'd already gone through the rigmarole of checking vitals and unhooking tubing so that she could go to the bathroom. Her temperature was down a full degree. That seemed to rather delight Jamie.

"I'm a decent cook," he said. "My friend Marcus is a really good cook. He's got a kitchen in his house that could be on television."

"Your friend Marcus the police chief?" she asked. It was a stark reminder that Jamie's loyalties could be easily influenced.

"Yes. He's a good guy. Trustworthy."

Were his words deliberate? Did he think that she needed to put her trust in the police? "I intend to leave

money here to pay for the repair of the window and for the use of the property," she said. Yes, what she was doing was technically wrong, but she'd do her best to make it right.

"There's that and, I guess, anything else you might want to talk to the police about. Like the accident, I suppose," he added.

"Right. Not much to say," she said. "I already told you. I saw a deer. Tried to avoid it. Came out on the short end of the stick since the deer got away. Was likely watching the whole event from the nearby forest."

That seemed to amuse him. "You think? Laughing with all his deer buddies. Maybe some front hoof slaps. A high two." He drew a two-pronged hoof in the air. "Get it? Two."

"Got it." His slightly curly hair was sticking up in the back of his head, making him look pretty cute. He was wearing an old T-shirt and loose blue gym shorts. She suspected that was what he'd slept in. "You wake up funny?"

"Amusing kicks in after two cups of coffee," he said. "By the time lunch rolls around and I've finished a pot, I'm downright hilarious."

"I imagine you need that in your job," she said. "Lots of sadness. Stress."

"Satisfaction and joy, too," he said. "Some days it's a real pendulum, swinging back and forth pretty fast. Can make a sane person's head swim."

"Speaking of your work, how is that you can be here with me? You seemed to practically live at the hospital."

"Vacation. I was scheduled to be off the week after Thanksgiving."

"To get an early start on your Christmas shopping?" she asked.

"That's exactly right," he said with a straight face. "Given that I generally give gift cards or alcohol, it doesn't really require that much shopping."

"Widow's Peak was all decorated," she said. "They have a huge tree in their lobby. I swear it's twelve feet tall."

"I saw it," he said. "What about your shopping this year?"

"I did it early," she said. After her parents had died, her shopping had been greatly diminished. She had already bought her friend Becky's gift. It would be delivered in mid-December. And she would have picked up a few small gifts for coworkers. But with her final note to them before she'd booked it out of town, she'd likely bought herself some grace for this year. Her plan was to send a letter to her boss in a couple months, resigning her position, saying that her mother was going to continue to need her for the foreseeable future. When that news made its way to her coworkers, they would quickly forget her. Maybe they'd try to send an email. But when it wasn't answered, they'd assume she'd moved on.

"Early shopping is definitely going to pay off for you this year," Jamie said. "And as your doctor, I'd suggest no climbing on the ladder to decorate a tree once you get to Canada."

"Good advice," she said. "Will you have to work over Christmas?"

"I might get a couple days off. Enough time that I can visit my family in Florida."

She wanted to know about his family but was afraid that her questions would be seen as permission to ask

about her own family. "Medicine is an all-consuming career, isn't it?"

"Definitely."

"But you wouldn't do anything else," she said.

He shook his head. "You know, I don't think we ever talked about your work. What is it that you do, Regan?"

Layla would have loved to tell him about her work at the lab, how rewarding it had been to be on the front lines of vaccine development in the last couple of years. But Regan Jones was not a scientist. "I've had a bunch of jobs," she lied. "Usually in restaurants."

"Fancy restaurants?" he asked.

She shook her head. "Nice places but not fancy. Decent tips."

"In Los Angeles?"

She nodded.

"Marcus Price worked there for ten years and I visited from time to time, so I know a few places. Maybe I know the ones you worked at."

She shook her head. "Los Angeles is a pretty big place."

"Sure. But…"

She considered her options. "There was an Italian place called Maria's." She'd just bet there was.

"Hmm…" he considered. "Not sure. Where was it located?"

"North," she said.

"Anyplace else?" he asked.

She yawned. "I think I'm going to take a nap." She closed her eyes.

She did not hear him move from the chair. She kept her eyes shut.

"Sleep well, Regan," he said finally. Then she heard him get up and leave the room.

* * *

Jamie wanted to kick something. The refrigerator seemed like a good target, but he resisted. She was going to keep up the pretense of being Regan Jones. Even now, she didn't trust him enough to tell him the truth.

Marcus would tell him to run fast and not let the door hit him on the butt on his way out. Blade would likely be more diplomatic but no less emphatic. He, after all, had had a bad marriage before he'd found Daisy. His first wife had told the ultimate lie and hidden an affair for months.

The only good news was that healthwise, Layla was better. Temp was down. She was eating and drinking, and based on her trips to the bathroom, those systems were working fine. She had no pain in her midsection, and that made him fairly confident that there was no need to worry about internal bleeding. She'd responded well to the IVs.

He could probably leave in a day or so and feel pretty good about it. Well, feel good about her prognosis, that was. He wasn't going to feel great about leaving her.

He heard his cell phone buzz, and he picked it up. Marcus. "Hello," he said.

"How's the vacation?" Marcus asked.

"Not bad," Jamie said.

"What are you doing?"

Oh, this was hard. He couldn't remember the last time he'd lied to Marcus. Maybe fifth grade. "Hanging out. Getting some projects done." Layla was sort of a project. He was definitely in the not-so-sure-how-it's-going-to-turn-out phase.

"You want to grab breakfast at Gertie's with Blade tomorrow?"

Would he be ready to leave by tomorrow? He wasn't confident of that. "I think I'm going to pass. I might take my plane up and get some flying time in."

"Okay," Marcus said. "Well, there was something I wanted to tell you," he added, his tone thoughtful. "I wasn't sure you'd care, but I did get a little more information on Layla Morant."

Jamie could feel his heart start to race. Great. He was going to have a myocardial event. That was going to betray the apparent lack of interest he was attempting to project. "Oh, yeah. What's that?"

"She filed a complaint with the San Francisco Police Department that her life had been threatened by Douglas Glass."

"Who the hell is Douglas Glass?"

"Don't know much about him other than his family is filthy rich and he's spent the last twenty months in prison. He got released just a few days ago."

Jamie's mind was working fast. "As in about the same time Layla supposedly abruptly left her job to take care of her ill mother."

"Uh-huh."

"She's running from him," Jamie said.

"She could be," Marcus allowed. "It does explain her using the identity of Regan Jones. I just thought you'd want to know. You thought she was probably a good person, and while this doesn't prove that, it also suggests that she's maybe not a bad person."

Now was the time to tell Marcus the truth. But he felt an overwhelming need to keep Layla's secret. If she'd thought it important enough to leave her job, her home,

her identity behind, then he owed her the chance to tell her version of the story before he started spewing out information to others. Marcus had made his position clear—she should be stopped by authorities and then she'd have her chance to explain. But they'd made that decision before this new information had come to light.

"Sounds complex," Jamie said. "Are you compelled to do anything with this information other than what you've already done?"

"I don't think so."

That was good. But he did feel rather sick. Because of his insistence in finding her, he'd put her at risk. Both her real identity and her assumed identity had been flagged by law enforcement. The minute she used a credit card or took any action that could be easily traced, she was going to be discovered.

His heart was no longer racing. It just felt heavy in his chest.

"Yeah, well, let me know if you want to grab a beer later on in the week," Marcus said.

"Sure. Will do." He hung up. He hadn't been honest with Marcus, but he was going to man up and tell Regan/Layla the truth before he left. She had to know that her cover was blown. That she needed to be cautious about any further action she took. She wouldn't want to dig an even bigger hole for herself.

She was going to be really angry with him. Deservedly so, if she'd done all this because she'd been afraid of some guy. He'd help her. If she'd let him. Hell, he'd hire a bodyguard for her if she needed it.

He wanted information on Douglas Glass.

He typed Douglas Glass San Francisco into the search field of his smartphone. Multiple pages of hits

came up. Douglas Glass had been the chairman of the board of a clinical lab in San Francisco. Not Weber Clinical Labs, where they'd spoken to Layla's boss. It was another place he'd never heard of.

Jamie kept reading. Glass had been tried and convicted on multiple counts, including wire fraud and falsification of government documents resulting in the overpayment of—*oh my*, thought Jamie—millions of dollars earmarked for vaccine development.

He sounded like a bad guy. But there was nothing to indicate that he was a threat to Layla. More curious than ever, he wanted to go into her bedroom and demand answers about Douglas Glass. But he couldn't do that. Regan Jones had no history with Douglas Glass. The question would come out of nowhere.

He sank down on the couch and stared at the bookshelf in the corner. There were ten or fifteen titles. Mostly biographies of former presidents. Not exactly his cup of tea. What was it he'd told Caitlin Rose? That he intended to use his vacation time to read crime fiction.

It dawned on him, and not in an amusing way, that he was perhaps in the midst of *true crime*. Maybe he should be making some notes. Turn it into a blockbuster novel one day. Quit his day job.

Except that he loved his day job. And if he in any way helped or assisted someone else in criminal activity, he ran the risk that his license as a physician could be at risk. And what Layla was doing certainly wasn't passing the smell test right now.

But maybe she had good reason.

It was a hell of a situation.

He quietly walked down the hall to check his patient. Carefully he opened the door. She was sleeping. It gave

him a chance to study her face. She was a beauty. But he didn't think she let herself be defined by that. He thought back to the accident scene. Not once had she asked about her face, whether it was damaged. And, as far as he knew, there'd been no requests in the hospital for a mirror to inspect any damage. When he'd knocked on the cottage door that first time and demanded entrance, she'd answered looking, quite frankly, pretty bad. But she hadn't apologized or seemed embarrassed.

As always, her duffel bag was on the bed, next to her. She'd been adamant from the first moment he'd gotten here that she wanted her bag close. He really wanted a closer look at the contents. But thus far, he had restrained his curiosity. If she woke up when he was looking in it, all the trust that he'd worked to earn would immediately vanish.

Maybe he should just ask her. She wanted him to be forthright. He could expect the same. He opened the notebook where he was tracking her vitals. It was time for a recheck.

"Regan," he said softly, not wanting to startle her.

Her eyelashes fluttered. Her incredibly long eyelashes. Her eyes were really spectacular. Such an unusual color, the gray-blue of a turbulent Pacific Northwest sky.

She smiled at him, and he felt as if the whole world was a little better for it. "How long was I sleeping?" she asked.

"A couple hours," he said. "It's time to check vitals."

"Can I use the restroom first?" she asked.

"Of course." He undid her IV tubing and watched her carefully slide out of bed. She was moving better than she had been even a day earlier. Steadier. Quicker.

She was back in a few minutes, and he could smell

the mint from the toothpaste she'd used. Her face was washed, and there was still a spot of moisture on one cheek. On impulse, he took his finger and gently swiped at it. "You missed a spot," he said.

Her now-dry cheeks turned pink. "Don't check behind my ears."

Maybe he'd do some magic tricks of his own and pull out a quarter. "Your ears are safe," he said. "I need your arm," he said, pulling out the blood pressure cuff. "One twenty-five over seventy-three. That's good," he said a couple minutes later. Then he took her temp. "Down another degree. You're just a tad bit above normal now."

He motioned for her to sit up in bed, and he shifted so that he could listen to her lungs. Clear. "How are the ribs?"

"Still letting me know they're there," she said.

"Probably be that way for a couple weeks. I'll get you some ibuprofen. That may help."

"How much longer for the IVs?"

"I think we can discontinue the fluids. I'd like to do one more day on the antibiotics."

She nodded. "It's a big relief to feel better. I can't tell you how thankful I am."

"You need a cast on your leg."

She looked down at it. "What happens if I don't get a cast? Will it heal?"

"It will. Might take longer than if it was in a cast. And you run the risk of reinjuring it."

"Can you cast it?" she asked.

He had put a couple casts on during medical school, maybe one as an intern. Most of the casting was done by cast technicians. It was equal parts art and science, and some cast technicians were better than others. "I

could. But it would be better for you if somebody who applied casts frequently did the work."

"But I trust you."

Wow. That hit him at his core. "We can make that decision in a day or two," he said. "I don't have any materials here right now, anyway."

"Okay. A day or two." She paused. "I think I might go stir-crazy if I have to lie in this bed for another day. Can I sit up, maybe watch some television or play some cards as long as I keep my IV in?"

"I don't see why not. But I have to warn you, the television is strictly for DVDs, and the selection isn't robust." He'd discovered that while she'd been sleeping.

"Westerns?" she said.

It was a good guess, considering the decorating style. He shook his head.

"Scary movies?"

"No."

"Am I close?"

"What do you think of Steve Martin?"

"Love him," she said.

"Well, then, you're probably going to be very happy. And if you're a Julia Roberts fan, you're probably going to be downright ecstatic."

"Be still my heart," she said, patting her chest. "If you can figure out a way I can wash my hair, I'll know the day can't get any better."

He looked at her leg. A shower was pretty much out of the question. But he wanted to make her happy. "There's a kitchen sink. I think we can make something work."

She looked so happy that he figured he'd tear out all the plumbing and put in new if that's what it took. But

in the end, it was simpler than that. She sat on a chair in front of the sink with her broken leg stretched out and balanced on another chair. He stood behind her. She twisted her body and leaned over the sink, allowing him to dump water on her head from one of several pots he'd filled in advance. Then she shampooed, and he repeated the rinse process. When it was all over, they were both laughing, because there was water on both of them, on the counter and on the floor.

"I'd have made a lousy pioneer," she said, accepting the towel that he handed her.

"This is on me," he said, motioning toward the spills. "I got…uh…distracted and didn't have my usual precise aim."

"Distracted by what?"

Her pretty neck, her delicate ears. "Uh, there was a bird outside the window."

"Oh, I love birds."

"Yeah. They're great." He handed her the crutches. "You feel up to a movie?"

"Father of the Bride?"

"Been wanting to see that again."

She smiled. "Where should I sit to make it easy for you to do the IV?"

"Take the couch." He went to get the IV pole and a bag of antibiotic. When she was seated and hooked up, he took the other end. It only made sense. It was a small living room, and the only other place to sit was a chair with no view of the television.

"All we need now is popcorn," she said.

He shook his head. "No popcorn. But I got us some cheese and crackers. Will that work?"

"Sounds good to me. And that's nice to say. I think

I'm actually feeling a little hungry. It will be a pleasure not to have to force food down."

"I'm going to have a soda. You want one?"

"Just water," she said.

"Good answer. Better for you." He got the snack ready. Considered putting it on two separate plates and then decided that they'd share one. It was a good excuse to sit close to her.

He walked back to the living room and casually put the plate on the couch next to her leg. Then he turned on the television and loaded the DVD. When he settled in to watch the movie, he sat on the other side of the plate. He was close enough that if he stretched out his arm, he could put it around her.

But he kept his arms to himself. Being together, doing something so very normal like watching a movie, was enough.

An hour later, about halfway through, she turned to him. "Don't you just love this? It's so fun."

"What's not to love about a corny romantic comedy?"

"Corny romantic comedy," she repeated with distain. Then she punched him on the arm.

The movie was okay. He was pretty sure he'd seen it years ago. But she was right. It was definitely nice, maybe even fun, sitting with her. Her hair had dried, and the silky blond strands swung around her face when she turned her head. She smelled good, like lavender.

When it was over, she yawned. So widely that he could see a few fillings in her back teeth.

"Do they have part two?" she asked.

"You won't make it past the opening credits," he said.

She seemed to consider that. "I suppose you're right.

It is a bit infuriating that I need to take an afternoon nap. What am I, a toddler?"

"You're recovering," he said simply.

"Fine." She slipped her bottom to the edge of the couch and stood on one leg.

He handed her the crutches. "I'll follow you with the IV. We won't need to unhook you."

Halfway down the hallway, she turned to look over her shoulder. "I know how fortunate I am that you brought a mini hospital to me."

"We underpromise and overdeliver." He kept his tone light.

She shook her head. "There's no *we* here. This is you. You're doing this. I'll never forget it. I won't. It's an act of human kindness, and quite frankly, there's not enough of that in the world right now."

His knees felt weak. If she stumbled and fell now, they were both going down. But they managed to get to the bed. He helped her get flat and was close enough that he could feel her breath on his arm as he adjusted her pillows.

"I don't want your appreciation, your gratitude," he said, his tone maybe harsher than necessary. But he was tied in knots over this woman. That had never happened to him before.

"I... I..."

He had confused her. No wonder. He was pretty damn confused himself. "I don't want you to feel as if you're in a position where you owe me anything."

"Okay," she said, her eyes still wary.

It was time to lay it on the line. "Because I very much want to kiss you. And I don't want to do that without your permission and your acknowledgment that this

has nothing to do with our relationship as doctor and patient and everything to do with our relationship as man and woman."

She stared at him, her beautiful gray-blue eyes wide-open. He wasn't sure she was breathing. Sure enough, three seconds later, she sucked in a breath of air. "It is not in your best interest to be…attracted, or interested, or even curious, about me."

He was all those things. "I would like to decide that for myself." He lowered his face another inch. "But not until you say yes." He held the position of power here. He was bigger, stronger, healthier. He controlled her medical care, with no one to intervene on her behalf. He would not ever leverage that kind of power over any person, let alone a woman he was very interested in. It went against everything he believed in.

"It's a mistake," she said softly.

"Mine to make," he countered.

She sighed. "And mine. But I am awfully tired of being so very careful." She tilted her face, bringing her lips a little closer. "Kiss me, Jamie."

Chapter 12

His first kiss was tentative. Soft. Brief. Way too brief. She lifted her arms and wrapped them around his neck, pulling him close. And he settled in and, in a most thorough and most delicious way, kissed her. He tasted sweet, reminiscent of the root beer he'd drunk.

When he lifted his head minutes later, she unwrapped her arms and let them fall to the bed. *Oh my*. "Do not take my vitals right now," she whispered. "My heart feels as if it's going to beat itself right out of my chest."

He smiled and used a hand to push a wayward piece of her hair behind her right ear. "You have the most amazing eyes," he said.

"Was that my eyes you were just examining?" she asked innocently.

He lightly pinched her chin. "I was just getting started.

The most amazing eyes. The cutest, straightest nose, the loveliest heart-shaped mouth and a rather stubborn chin."

"Is that your professional opinion?"

"Nope. That's my I-think-this-woman-is-hot opinion."

He made her feel hot and sexy and wanted, even though she was lying in a bed with cracked ribs and a broken leg. Doing much more than kissing was pretty much out of the question, and maybe that's why it felt safe—maybe that's why she'd thrown caution to the wind and asked him to kiss her.

He was so sexy, so accomplished, so nice. It was hard to imagine that nobody had scooped him up yet. "How is it that you're not married or with someone?"

"Uh… I don't know," he said. "I've worked a lot."

"But you've dated?"

"Of course," he said. "Since I was sixteen. But since that was about twenty years ago, I hope you're not going to ask me all their names."

She had a feeling he remembered. He was the kind of guy who remembered the names of the girls he dated, even if it had been something short and casual. "I was going to ask for the list to be both alphabetical and chronological."

"You're getting feisty. You must really feel better."

"I do. I have to admit, though, if I don't keep up with the pain relievers, both the ribs and the leg get pretty achy."

"Cracked and broken bones hurt. Really hurt. Give it another week," he said.

Since she'd gotten the call from her attorney about Douglas Glass's early release, it seemed that she'd been living in two- to four-hour segments. Sort of like a real-

life movie. Thinking a week out seemed like such a luxury and such a risk. She absolutely couldn't afford to think that everything could be the same in a week as it was today. If she got complacent and let her guard down, it could be bad.

He smoothed her hair back. "You really should sleep."

Time was not on her side. She was either going to have to leave him behind or he was going to have to return to his life way too soon. She needed to carve out the minutes while she had the chance. She patted the side of the double bed where her go-bag rested. "If you put this on the floor, do you think you could lie here with me? And...hold me while I sleep?"

"You'd be comfortable with that?"

She shrugged. "Unless you punch or kick in your sleep."

"I'm a well-behaved sleeper." He didn't waste any time in reaching for her bag. He set it on the floor, near the head of the bed. If she stretched out her left arm, she would feel it.

Then he carefully crawled into bed and slipped an arm underneath her neck, bringing her close but not jostling her.

"Your arm is probably going to fall asleep," she said.

"You let me worry about that."

How nice, since she really couldn't worry about any more than what was already on her plate. "This feels good," she said.

He leaned over and kissed the top of her head. "Yeah. It does."

By the time Douglas Glass got home, his mother was already having a cocktail. He'd intended to arrive

earlier, but once he'd fallen asleep in the hotel, it had been so difficult to get up and get going the next morning. He'd hated being on a schedule in prison, having to get up at a certain time, go to bed at a set time. He was done with that.

But now he was going to have to deal with his mother's disapproval. "Your parole officer can make unannounced visits," she said.

He'd not yet met his parole officer. That was to happen tomorrow. "Perhaps with the right financial incentive, he or she might be willing to be a little lenient with bedtime check-in," he said.

"Don't try it, Dougie. With your luck lately, you'll find the one who won't take a bribe."

The way she said it, it was more a damnation of him than of parole officers. She was irritated with him. He was going to have to do something to get back in her good graces. She was his checkbook. He wasn't sure which one of them hated that dependency more. He'd had the chance to finally make some real money of his own, and Layla Morant had poked her nose in.

And the truth of the matter was that his mother was probably right. He'd have to be careful. He couldn't be running back and forth to Knoware, Washington, to watch over the doctor's house. But perhaps he could hire someone to do it for him. The doctor had been watching Layla's condo for a reason. He was the best available link to that woman, and Douglas didn't intend to ignore it.

"Would you like another?" he asked, eyeing her empty glass.

"Yes," she said grudgingly.

He reached for the cut crystal. She put her own hand

over his. Her skin was cool. "I'm grateful to have you home, Dougie. But there can be no more scandals. You know that would kill me, don't you?"

Jamie's arm did indeed go to sleep. He didn't care. He managed to shift her head enough to ensure an amputation wasn't in his future, and then he simply settled in to enjoy having her this close.

Finally.

Well, that seemed like an odd thing to think, since it was only Tuesday evening and they'd met last Wednesday. But he had a feeling their relationship wasn't going to be measured by time. The connection had been immediate, there was no working up to it over a period of months or years. So he was prepared to fall fast and hard.

When she'd invited him to crawl into her bed, to hold her, his heart had almost burst. It was a step toward trust. Didn't know how big of step, or how many steps were in between "hold me" and truth, but it was something.

She opened her eyes and caught him staring. "Hey," she said. "You stayed."

"I slept a little," he lied. There was no reason to be too forthright. *Simpering fool* was not attractive.

"I should get up. Use the bathroom."

He got out of the bed on his side. "Let me unhook you." The IV was empty. "I think we can take the needle out," he said. "I'm not anticipating that you'll need more. You want me to do that before you use the bathroom?"

"Sure," she said. "Happy to get rid of it. But have to admit that it delivered a wonder drug."

"Just glad it worked."

"Me, too. Otherwise, you'd have had to toss my body into the ocean and hope the tide carried me out."

"Stop," he said. He could tell she was joking, but he knew that without medical intervention, she'd have been in a very bad spot. It was sobering to think of how close she'd come to being sick enough to die. He slipped the needle out. There was no sharps container, so it was going to have to go in the regular garbage. He'd wrap the end in tape to make sure no unsuspecting garbage collector got a needle stick. He cleaned the entry site and put a bandage over it. "Good as new," he said, slapping on some tape to hold the bandage.

"Excellent," she said.

"Hungry?" he asked.

"Yeah." She nodded thoughtfully. "It's my turn to cook."

"Not necessary," he said.

She swung her legs over the side of the bed and reached for her crutches. "Let's go see what we have to work with."

"Careful," he warned, holding up a hand. "You've got the tip of your crutch caught in the strap of your duffel bag."

She looked down, saw that he was right. She used her crutch to push the bag farther under the bed, as if it held no real importance.

Maybe they really were making progress.

When they got to the kitchen, he hoped that she wouldn't be too disappointed. He'd gone for the basics when he'd brought groceries. He opened the cupboard where he'd stored the items. "That's our cereal

and bread. For drinks, I brought some soda, some hot chocolate mix and coffee."

There were also some canned goods and pasta that the homeowner had left behind. She inspected them closer. "You think they'd mind if we used a few of their canned goods?"

They were probably going to care more that they were sleeping in their beds and that she'd broken a window to get in. "We can replace them or leave money." He walked over to the refrigerator. There were more choices here. "Milk, eggs, couple kinds of cheese, butter, assorted fruit and veggies."

"Hmm," she said, studying the contents. "I'll take the asparagus, the mushrooms and the yellow pepper."

"What can I do?"

"Preheat the oven to three seventy-five and then wash and cut the veggies into bite-size pieces."

He did that. He could hear her in the cupboard behind him. Then she was opening drawers until she found a can opener. "Now what?" he asked.

She had pulled a well-used cookie sheet from a cupboard. He watched as she poured some oil olive on the veggies and then added salt and pepper. "These can go in the oven. And can you fill that pot with water for me? About half-full."

He sat the now-filled pot on the stove, and she turned the burner on high. Then she was pouring cans of tomato sauce and stewed tomatoes in the pan. She started opening cupboards until she found the spices. "Spices are communal, right?"

"Hard to miss a sprinkle or two."

"Exactly," she said and smiled. She added dried basil and oregano and parsley. The sauce was starting

to smell good. She added dried spaghetti to the now-boiling water.

"I have to say, I'm a little amazed," he said. "I mean, I could have managed to feed us, but it wouldn't have been anything like this."

"Just some pasta with roasted vegetables," she said.

Ten minutes later, they were sitting down at the table with bowls of steaming pasta in front of them. He dug in. "It's delicious," he said.

"Yeah, it's pretty good," she said, sounding satisfied. "I like to cook. Sometimes, I forget how much until I do it."

"Favorite meal to cook?" he asked.

"Brunch."

"Walk me through brunch at your house."

"Well, let's see. You'd arrive," she said.

"With flowers," he interjected.

"Of course," she said, sounding amused. "Lilies, my favorite. And you have your choice of mimosas. You can be traditional—champagne and orange juice—or perhaps something more daring, like a raspberry lemonade mimosa."

"Love lemonade. Makes me think I'm at the county fair."

"No, no," she said. "This is a very elegant brunch. No corn dogs on the menu. There will be a cheese plate to nibble on while I put the finishing touches on the food."

"Am I helping?" he asked.

"You offer, but I shoo you out of the kitchen. Mingle, amuse the other guests, I say."

"I can juggle," he said.

"As long as it's not the crystal glasses on the table."

He sniffed the air. "Whatever you're cooking smells good."

"There's a spinach and cheese quiche. And some baked French toast with pecans and blueberries. Bacon and sausage—turkey, you know."

"Better for my heart."

"Your heart will not love the pastry tray, but every other part of you will."

"Did you bake the pastries?" he asked.

She frowned. "Oh, no. They were procured from a lovely little bakery down the block. They're sensational. Banana-nut muffins and cinnamon rolls and croissants laced with dark chocolate icing."

"I'm never going home."

She smiled. "Your turn."

He studied the ceiling. "It's dinner. Cocktails first. A nice pinot noir on the patio. Then I'm at the grill, showing off my man prowess."

"My knees are weak," she said. "Well, actually, my leg *is* broken."

"Shush. No reality. I'm at the grill, cooking some lovely bacon-wrapped filets. When they're a perfect medium rare, I bring out the baked potatoes—loaded, of course. And we sit down to eat."

"Oh, no," she said, her fingers to her lips in mock angst. "I forgot to bring you flowers."

"No worries. You brought chocolates instead."

"I did, didn't I? So smart."

"But I made dessert, too," he said. "A fruit trifle."

"You do not know how to make trifle," she accused.

"I do—buy an angel food cake and break it into bite-size pieces. Half of the cake goes in first, then add fruit. I like strawberries, blueberries and fresh peaches

if they're in season. Then mix up some vanilla pudding and pour half of that over the angel food cake pieces and fruit. Repeat everything you just did a second time. Then top it with some whipped cream. That is my award-winning trifle."

"It has won awards?" she asked.

"No," he admitted. "But it would if I entered it."

"You know the secret to a trifle?" she asked.

"I just described it," he said.

She shook her head. "The secret to a trifle is a pretty glass bowl so that you can see all the layers."

"I'll concede that," he said. "But wait, dinner is not over. There's an after-dinner cocktail."

"Port?" she asked.

He shook his head. "No one really drinks port, do they? We're having something with Irish cream and a dash of whiskey. And coffee, if you want it."

"Have you opened the chocolates I brought?" she asked.

"I can." He pretended to open a box of chocolates, and then he held out the imaginary box for her to take one.

"I do love a salted caramel," she said, picking a piece and popping it into her mouth.

"I'll take the dark chocolate," he said, playing along.

She sighed. "Lovely dinner at your house."

He looked at their empty pasta bowls. "Lovely dinner here. Thank you. I'll get the dishes."

"I won't argue," she said. "I'll get *Father of the Bride Part II* ready to go."

"Can't wait," he said dryly.

She winked at him. "I know you've been anxious for it."

He handed her the crutches and watched her make her way to the living room. Nope, he wasn't a bit anxious. Truth be told, he didn't want tonight to ever end. It had been perfect. She was perfect. He wanted to cook her dinner at his house. Every night. And wake up with her every morning.

Cart before horse. *Slow down, Weathers. She still has secrets.*

He told himself all that and more while he did the dishes. "Want something to drink?" he asked when he was finished cleaning up.

"Hot chocolate," she said.

He put water on the stove to heat. Then emptied two packets into two cups he pulled from the cabinet. He hadn't bought any marshmallows. They were going to have to rough it. When the water was ready, he poured it into the cups and stirred both. Then he carried them into the room and handed her one.

"Thank you," she said.

"Sure." He sat down on the couch. Held his hot chocolate with one hand and put his free arm around her shoulder. "This okay?" he asked, not wanting to make assumptions.

"Very," she said.

He'd told her that he'd been dating since he was sixteen. That was true. What he couldn't tell her right now was that he *felt* about sixteen again. Very, very unsure about next steps. He'd be breaking out with acne at any moment.

He wanted to kiss her again. Touch her.

But he did none of that. It was her turn to make the first move.

* * *

She loved sitting on the couch with Jamie, watching television, with his arm around her. She'd hoped he'd kiss her again, but they were halfway through the movie and…he seemed content to just hang out.

If she was smart, she'd be satisfied. The earlier kisses had been a little slice of happiness. She shouldn't want or expect the whole pie.

But, she argued with herself, if she didn't take a seat at the table and eat her fill, it would be a mistake. Because once he or she left, whichever came first, this *interlude* or whatever it was would be gone. And she was likely to be hungry for the really long time that it would take to get to know and trust someone else.

Circumstances had thrown them together. It was kind of crazy to turn her back on that.

Right?

Wrong. Pie could be very habit-forming. She'd be wanting a slice every night, maybe some for lunch, too. Better to not know what she would be missing.

Chicken. That's what she was. Jamie could fire up his grill and toss her on.

"What?" Jamie asked.

"I didn't say anything," she said. She really needed to keep those kind of thoughts to herself.

"You groaned. Are you feeling okay?" He put the back of his hand against her forehead.

She was hot, all right. "I'm fine," she said, dismissing his concern.

"Okay," he said, not sounding convinced.

"Do you think we could sit outside and listen to the waves?" she asked.

He frowned. "It's dark, and it's about forty degrees outside."

"We both have coats." At night she didn't have to worry about someone seeing them. And if she had to sit on this couch for another five minutes, she was going to do something that she might regret.

"I thought you liked the movie."

"I do. But I'll finish it later."

He sighed. "I'll put two chairs on the porch while you get your coat on. I'd suggest wearing your hat and some gloves if you've got them."

She was ready in just a few minutes. He was standing by the door with his own coat on. He opened it without a word, and she passed through. He held the door open while she found her chair. Then he shut it, plunging the small porch into darkness.

There was no moon. It was as if she'd sunk into a pool of darkness. But her other senses were in overdrive. She could smell the water and could hear the slap of it against the big rocks that lined the shore. She could feel cold air on her cheeks, her nose. She licked her lips, tasting the lingering sweet of the hot chocolate that Jamie had made her at the start of the movie.

She felt alive. And it was a pretty glorious feeling, since tomorrow it would be a week since she'd rolled her car and spent way too many minutes contemplating death. Jamie had saved her that day. And he'd saved her again when he'd come to the cottage.

She owed him a great deal, yet she continued to lie to him. It weighed on her. But the risk of telling him the truth could not be discounted. One of his best friends was a police chief. Could she have found a worse person to…what? Like? Lust after? Love?

That last one was crazy. Evidence that she couldn't be trusted not to make the mistake that he'd warned her about. What was it that he'd said to her? *I don't want your appreciation, your gratitude.*

She felt that, certainly. But there was more. She wasn't going to waste time trying to define it.

She turned to him. "I liked it when you kissed me." She believed in being frank.

"Okay."

It was easier to do this in the dark. "And I would like it if we could kiss again. And…"

He waited. "And?"

Her ability to be frank sometimes failed her. She must have paused too long, because he filled the silence.

"Well, then, yes to the kissing again," he said. "But you really did seem as if you were about to add something else."

"I was," she admitted. "I want to say that if you'd be so inclined, I'd be interested in more. I know it should happen organically in the best of worlds, but quite frankly, this isn't the best of worlds right now, and it might take a little more careful planning on both our parts."

"Give me a minute," he said. "I got behind at *organically.*"

"You did not."

"I've always had a fondness for careful planners." He sounded amused.

She'd proven herself the queen of careful planning these last few months, but that wasn't up for discussion. "It's a good trait."

"Indeed." He must have shifted in his chair, because the legs scraped against the wooden porch. "In your careful plan, what's the first step?"

"Obtain a medical opinion."

"Well, then, I guess it's lucky that I went to medical school," he said.

"In your expert opinion, Dr. Weathers, is there any reason that we can't…do this?"

"*This* is rather undefined as of yet, but in general, my professional opinion is that as long as both of us are exceedingly careful of your broken leg and equally mindful of your cracked ribs, there are no other significant medical risks."

She considered him. "I can think of one risk. Did you happen to pack any condoms?"

He laughed. "What you meant by *this* just got a whole lot clearer. I'm wrapping my head around that. And yes, I have some."

The path was clear. She really should be exuberant. Instead, she felt rooted to her chair, unable to move forward. "We can't do this."

"You haven't changed the working definition of *this*?" he asked, his voice cracking.

She'd have laughed if there was anything remotely funny about the situation. If she'd prided herself on being frank before, she better step up now. "We can't have sex until I tell you…something. Until I tell you the truth."

Chapter 13

He wanted the truth. Had been terribly disappointed when it hadn't previously been forthcoming. But now? Did it have to be *now*?

Once he'd fully understood her definition of *this*, his body had been ready. And now she was slamming on the brakes, and he was pretty much confident that he could stop but it wouldn't be without some serious wear and tear on the vehicle. "I'm listening," he said.

"Can we go back inside?" she asked. "I think this is the kind of conversation where we need to be able to see each other."

It was getting more interesting by the minute. He stood up and opened the door, providing them with some light. She went inside, and he quickly stacked the two kitchen chairs and carried them inside. He headed toward the couch.

She pointed to the chair across the room. "Could

you sit over there while we have this conversation? I...
I need some space."

He needed her to hurry up and get talking. "Of
course," he said. They got into their spots.

"My name is not Regan Jones. It's Layla Morant."

He hadn't expected to start here. And he was suddenly at a crossroads. Did he tell her that he already
knew this? Or pretend it was new information?

He evidently waited a second too long, because she
was moving forward.

"I'm not a waitress. I graduated from college with
a bachelor's degree in biology and a master's degree
in public health. I work at a lab in San Francisco as a
senior development specialist focusing on vaccine development."

"Okay," he said. There was no need to tell her he
knew most of this, he reasoned. It would gain him nothing and might make her trust him less.

"You don't seem that surprised."

"I told you just a couple days ago that as a doctor,
there was very little you could say that would surprise
me."

"I supposed that's true. I'm sorry I lied about who I
was. But I simply didn't see another alternative."

"Maybe if I had some background, this would make
more sense," he said. He desperately wanted the missing pieces.

"Regan Jones is a real person. I met her when she
wanted to participate in a paid clinical study that was
being conducted at the lab where I was working. She
didn't meet the criteria for the study, but she met my
needs."

"Your needs?"

"I had been thinking about disappearing for months. Had spent many hours researching the best ways to do it. You know, there are actually quite a few resources aimed at helping people go off the grid."

"And that's what you wanted to do?" he asked.

"Yes. But not for any political or social reason. I was afraid."

"Of?"

"Of a man named Douglas Glass. He was the chairman of the board of a company that I used to work for. I was part of a team that was making exciting progress in developing a vaccine for a novel virus. We were completing our final set of clinical trials when, suddenly, the data started to change. We saw information that we hadn't seen before. We couldn't explain the variances. Months and months of work was going to be shelved. This can happen in vaccine development, but I just didn't believe it. I pored over the data. I knew something wasn't right, but I couldn't find it.

"What I didn't realize was that the company was for sale. When the news became public that our vaccine hadn't panned out, the price dropped substantially. By more than fifty percent. We're talking billions, literally billions, of dollars in value, lost almost overnight."

Vaccine development had always been big money. Took big dollars to do it and, if successful, the rewards were enormous.

"The company was purchased, new management came in, new board of directors, many new employees. The project that I'd poured my soul into for three years was scrapped. But I couldn't let it go. On my own time, I reran data. I followed up with clinical subjects. Suffice it to say that I slowly pieced together that the

project had been purposefully ruined by a fellow scientist who'd left shortly after the new ownership took
over. Ultimately, it turned out that he'd not done it on
his own. He'd done it at the direction of Douglas Glass.
The scientist had received a payout of several hundred
thousand dollars, from Douglas Glass, who had gotten
a kickback of millions with the sale. It was pure sinful
greed that had destroyed the work of so many, and who
knows how many lives had been adversely affected."

"What did you do?"

"I didn't know who to trust at the new company.
Ultimately, I contacted federal law enforcement. A
grand jury was convened, and I was a witness. I was
scared to testify, because I thought I might be ruining
my career. There aren't that many big players in vaccine development, and I didn't want to be known as
the person who'd tattled to federal authorities. But they
assured me that grand jury testimony is confidential.
Ultimately, charges were brought against the company
that bought us, the scientist for scrambling the data, and
against Douglas Glass."

When Marcus had looked up Layla Morant online,
none of this had popped up. That made sense if she'd
testified to the grand jury versus in a courtroom where
information was more public. "That couldn't have been
fun."

She shook her head. "All I knew was that I didn't
want to let them get away with it. But I had no idea
how unhinged Douglas Glass really was. Ultimately,
he never once showed any remorse or even an understanding that it wasn't his supreme right to profit at the
expense of others. It was really frightening. But then
I realized that he could be absolutely terrifying. I was

following the trial in the newspapers, and I knew it was due to end soon. I was running in the park near my house when Douglas Glass approached me on the trail. Glass got close enough to tell me that when he got out of prison, he was going to kill me. He somehow knew that I'd been the person at the company who had put it all together. I imagine he paid someone involved in the grand jury process for the information."

"You believed him? You didn't think he was bluffing?" he asked.

"I saw his eyes. He was serious. He meant it. I think he would have done it that day, but the trial was still going on, and there was the slimmest of chances that he wouldn't go to prison. I'm sure he regretted that once the verdict was read and he was led away in handcuffs."

"Did you report it?"

"I did. He was asked about it and denied it. It was my word against his. I could tell that everyone was skeptical that he'd said it. I think they thought that I was so angry that I was making things up. Finally, the judge, the prosecuting attorney and pretty much everybody else placated me by saying that *even if* he'd said it, he was just blowing off steam, that he was a white-collar criminal, not a killer."

"You didn't believe them."

"He'd already killed. Our vaccine would have saved lives. He didn't care about that, or about the people who were going to die. He was a privileged baby who couldn't believe that a lowly scientist had brought him down. I was confident that he meant what he said. I was also confident that he had the means and the connections to make it happen."

It was inconceivable that she'd done the right thing

and then she'd been threatened. Worse, not believed. "I'm so sorry that happened to you." It was inadequate, but what else was there to say? *It was wrong. Others failed you.* None of that mattered. Now. "So you made a decision."

She shook her head. "I *stumbled* into a decision. After the trial, I was a wreck. Worried all the time. I took a new job, wanting to sever all ties with my past. I moved. And the days ticked by. He'd gotten a two-year sentence. A lousy two years, because he'd had the best defense that money could buy. I knew time was running out. But I was no closer to a solution. And then Regan Jones, the real Regan Jones, walked into the clinic where I was working. I rarely did intake of medical histories, but our administrative assistant was absent the day that Regan Jones came in. It was startling when I met her. There's the old saying that everybody has a twin somewhere. Well, it felt as if mine had just walked in the door."

It was his chance to tell her that he'd met Regan, that she didn't need to convince him. But he stayed silent. How could he explain that he'd actually spoken to Regan?

"During the intake process, you get quite a bit of personal information about a person. Everything from where they live and have lived, what kind of work they do and have done, where they have traveled, lifestyle habits, et cetera. So I got to know a lot about her quite quickly. She progressed to the clinical phase, but after a series of blood tests, it was ruled that she didn't meet the criteria. It happens frequently, and I've seen a myriad of reactions. But when I gave the news to Regan, I could tell it was rather devastating. This was a clini-

cal trial where there was going to be a rather lucrative financial incentive to participants. She admitted that she'd been counting on the money, that she desperately needed the money. She said that her hours had been cut at work and she was about to lose her apartment. She asked me a question. A tough question."

Her voice had trailed off. She seemed lost in thought, like she was right back at the lab, having that conversation with Regan. "What was it?" he asked.

"She asked me if I ever just wanted to give up. Because she did." She drew in a breath. "It hit me that Regan Jones and I were very much alike. I had a good job, enough money, but every day, I felt as if I wanted to give up. And it dawned on me how Regan Jones and I could help each other." She stopped again. "I didn't say anything to her right away. That's not me. I'm a planner, a thinker. But I kept her number. And for weeks, I worked it out in my head."

"I imagine that was quite an interesting conversation once you decided to approach her," he said.

"Yeah. Sort of went like this—'hey, I know you don't really know me, but I've got a business proposition. I want to become you, in every way that matters.'" She smiled. "It wasn't quite that fast, or quite that bold, but you get the drift."

"It's kind of complicated, isn't it?" he asked, trying to keep his voice nonjudgmental. "Assuming a real person's identity."

"Yeah. And the logical question is, why not just try to purchase another identity, a made-up identity? There are people who supply those, right?"

"I imagine," he said.

"I imagined, too. But I didn't know any of those

people. That wasn't my circle of friends. I had no idea who I could trust."

"But you thought you could trust Regan?"

"I knew it was a risk, but Regan was the best of bad alternatives. I knew that one of my stumbling blocks in starting over somewhere would be finding work. To do that, you need identification. Identification that can be verified. My agreement with Regan allowed me to immediately have access to a driver's license that wouldn't be questioned because of our physical resemblance and a real Social Security number. With those two things, I could work, I could rent an apartment, I could have a credit card, I could start to rebuild a life."

"But she's also using the documents. I guess I see the potential for you to get tripped up with that."

"I know. I thought about what happens when Regan's employer reports earnings on her Social Security number and my new employer did the same. Some computer would flag it for review. But Regan was used to working jobs that paid cash and agreed to do so in the future. She won't file taxes. I'll file them in her name. It's pretty complicated, but when I told her the truth about why I needed to use her identity, she agreed. She'd had an abusive ex-boyfriend, so she understood the risks better than some. I was able to make it worth it to her financially because I'd inherited money when my parents died."

Regan had told him that she didn't know why Layla had approached her. Maybe that was her way of living up to the agreement, continuing to offer Layla as much protection as she still could.

"You seemed to have really thought it through. I wonder, however, how you'll be able to continue in

your profession. I'm assuming that Regan Jones doesn't have the education or professional certifications that you must have."

"It took me a bit to come to terms with that limitation. I've loved my jobs, loved my small contribution to the world of science. But that's also where Douglas Glass would think to look for me. So, no, I won't be going back to that. But there are all kinds of other jobs. Jobs that don't require more than a high school education, which is what Regan has."

"And you'll be happy over the long run with that decision?" he asked.

"I…don't know," she admitted. "It's very hard to think long run when your mind is obsessing over your immediate survival. I am focused on the present and maybe, on a very good day, the very near future. The *long run* is out there somewhere, but it's beyond my capacity to think about it too much."

It wasn't that much different than soldiers who were on active military duty. Survival could be an all-encompassing thought. "I get it," he said.

"Unfortunately, as well thought out as I believed my plan was, when it came time to put it into action, it was very difficult. I had to do it before I was fully ready because Douglas Glass got released from prison earlier than I expected."

She pulled at her blond hair. "In my go-bag is brown hair dye. That will help me better match the driver's license photo. But the physical changes are nothing compared to having to say goodbye to everyone without really being able to say goodbye. In a way, I was lucky. As I mentioned, my parents are both deceased, and I don't have any siblings. So there was no immediate

family that needed to know. I had friends and work, of course, and I've offered up believable excuses to both about why Layla is suddenly gone." She paused. "You're the only person besides Regan and me who knows the truth."

He felt sick. That wasn't exactly true. Marcus knew. And in the law enforcement world, he'd connected Regan Jones to Layla Morant, so there was no telling how many people really knew at this point.

"You look troubled," she said. "Maybe this is simply more than you can accept," she added, her tone dull.

Tell her. Tell her now. "I think what you did was very brave," he said instead. "You were afraid, but you didn't give up. You found a way. I am...humbled that you trust me enough to tell me."

She offered up a small smile. And an awkward silence fell upon the room.

He felt strung tight. "More movies?" he asked, nodding his head toward the television. The sound was down, but it was still on.

She shook her head, reached for the remote and flipped it off.

"More hot chocolate?" he asked.

Another slow head shake.

"Running out of options," he admitted.

"Perhaps you could continue to offer alternatives in the bedroom," she said.

Wow. This is what it felt like when your head exploded. "Are you saying what I think you're saying?" he asked.

She nodded.

He stood up, handed her the crutches and quickly snatched his hand back. He was shaking. "I'm...a little

nervous," he said. Nervous wasn't really right. He was unsettled because she had no way of knowing that he wasn't being absolutely truthful with her.

"Don't know how the parts go together, Doctor?" she asked innocently.

"I've got a fair idea," he said.

"What, then?"

He had missed his opportunity to tell her the truth when she'd first started talking. He'd wanted her story. But now it just seemed like he couldn't take them backwards. He would tell her. Just not right now. Let them have a few days, a few nights. She'd just started to trust him. He could not unravel that yet. But when he did, they would set about figuring a way out of this. "Please understand that I want you to be very happy about this decision when it's over. No regrets."

Her eyes warmed. "So let me make sure I'm clear. Whatever happens between us has absolutely nothing to do with the fact that you've provided medical care, and when it's over, I must be happy with no regrets. Anything else?"

She was yanking his strings. Very effectively. He wanted her. Badly. That he could be honest about right now. The rest, definitely later.

"Yeah. Two more things," he said. "One, go a little faster on those crutches, and two, I'm in charge."

Chapter 14

I'm in charge. The words sent a trickle of anticipation up her spine. She had a rather delicious feeling that *just following doctor's orders* was going to take on a whole new meaning.

Her blood ran hot in her veins, and her breasts felt full and heavy. It made her seem uncoordinated, and it took her longer than usual to get to the bedroom. He had time to make a side trip into the bath to retrieve a condom.

He tossed it on the bed. "Lie down," he said, his voice almost guttural.

She sat, handed him her crutches and then carefully swung her legs up. She lowered her head to the pillow and looked up at him.

"You have too many clothes on," he said. He was standing next to the bed. His breaths were shallow and fast. It felt good that she wasn't the only one physically affected.

"Waiting for instruction," she baited.

He slowly shook his head, as if amazed at her cheekiness. "Well, then, take off your shirt."

She undid the top button of her light blue oxford shirt. Then another. His eyes followed her hands. When all the buttons were undone, she slowly let the two sides fall away from her middle. He stared at her stomach. Then his eyes moved upward, to her bare breasts. She'd ruled out wearing a bra with cracked ribs.

He seemed to have a profound appreciation for the view. She was grateful that most of the bruising on her ribs had faded.

"Beautiful," he whispered, confirming the look in his eyes. He sat on the edge of the bed, twisted his upper body so that he could lean over her, and very gently touched her with his tongue, running a trail from an inch above her belly button to the middle of her breasts. Then outward, to the nipple of her right breast. He caught it in his mouth and she swore she saw fire.

And he took his time. The man might be in charge, but he was in no hurry, giving both breasts equal attention. At some point, she lost her shirt completely. When he finally lifted his head, she was fumbling with the zipper on her jeans.

"Did I tell you to take off your pants?" he asked, his voice low, seductive.

If she didn't, and if he didn't touch her in the next sixty seconds, she was going to lose it. "May I?" She accepted that he'd reduced her to begging.

"No. Me," he said.

He unzipped, and she lifted her hips so that both jeans and undies could be removed. His hands were

hot against her skin, and he was ever so careful around her injured leg.

"Are you going to take the brace off?" she asked, looking down at her almost naked self.

He shook his head. "No. Safety first," he said. "It stays on."

Speaking of safety, he still had *all* his clothes on. "Am I the only one in the room who is going to get a chill?"

He smiled. "In due time. Remember, I'm in charge."

And then he showed her what that really meant. It meant that he was fully focused on her, on her pleasure, on learning every inch of her body with his fingers and his tongue. He did all the moving, while she had the pleasure of lying still and simply being devoured.

Her orgasm shattered her. He rode it through, his mouth on her breast, two fingers inside her. When it was over, she closed her eyes, drawing in breaths that made her sore ribs hurt. But the pain didn't matter. Nothing mattered. She was complete.

Seconds passed. She opened her eyes. He was lying in bed next to her, upper body propped up on his bent elbow.

"Okay?" he asked.

"I'm not sure many guys in charge willingly give up the lead," she said, fully aware that her pleasure might have come at his expense.

"I'm not many guys."

That was pretty darn obvious at this point. "Still, I'd like to return the favor." She spread her legs a bit wider.

"We have to be careful of your leg," he said.

"You will be," she said confidently. She reached for the buttons on his shirt. "I know you're in charge and all that, but it's time for you to get naked."

He did. And he was hard and ready, and she wanted him with an intensity that almost robbed her of speech. "Take me," she said, handing him the condom.

He put it on, and his hands were shaking. "Who's in charge now?" he whispered ruefully, his mouth close to her ear as he carefully lowered himself onto her and settled between her spread legs.

"Neither of us," she gasped as he pushed into her.

"Both of us," he said.

Then neither of them talked for a good long time.

They slept. He had no idea how long, but it was still dark when he awoke. They were both still naked, and Layla was half on top of him, using him like one big pillow. He rather liked it.

He used his hand to gently smooth back the hair from her face. She stirred. "What time is it?" she asked.

"Does it matter?"

"No," she said, snuggling even closer.

"How are the ribs?" he asked.

"Still there."

It was her standard answer. Probably sore, he thought. As careful as he'd tried to be of her, ribs seemed to feel everything. "Want some pain reliever?"

"Nope." She reached down and cupped him with her smooth hand.

The response was pretty much instantaneous, and he could feel her body shake as she laughed. "That was fast," she said.

"Yeah." If he'd wanted to pretend that the first time hadn't knocked his socks off, that option was gone now. "Medical marvel," he added.

"Marvelous," she corrected. She moved carefully

to her back. "I'm hoping you packed more than one condom."

He thought there were about a half dozen in his bag. "Underpromise and overdeliver," he said. "I'll be right back."

He almost ran to the bathroom and brought back the whole strip of condoms. He'd been reluctant to do that before, not wanting to make assumptions. But she was laying her cards on the table. He liked that.

"I've got a thought," he said, standing next to the bed.

"You can think in that condition?" she said with a straight face, looking at his erection.

"Think, walk, talk, chew gum," he said. "Willing to trust me with something?" he asked, holding out his hand.

"Of course." She took his hand and let him pull her up from the bed. When she was standing, she reached for her crutches.

"You're not going to need those," he said. "Spread your legs."

She did.

He wrapped his arms underneath her bottom and lifted her. She automatically wrapped her legs around his waist. "Good girl," he said. "Now just let your leg hang. This way there's no weight on it." Then he walked with her until her back was against the bedroom wall.

"Ready?" he asked.

"Oh, God yes," she said.

He shifted her and settled her on him. He went deep, and it wasn't fifteen strokes later that she was convulsing in his arms. "That's right, darling. That's right," he murmured, his mouth close to her ear. When she was spent, he held her in position, letting her rest. And

when she had her breath, he picked up the pace. When he came, it felt as if he was flying without a plane. Absolutely soaring.

It was a fact. He was never, ever going to be the same.

When Layla next woke up, it was hours later, and morning. They were in bed. She remembered Jamie safely depositing her on the mattress after he'd taken her against the wall. Just the memory of that, the carnal intensity of it, flooded her face with heat. It didn't help that the room smelled of sex, that she smelled the same.

"What's wrong?" he asked.

She hadn't realized he was awake. "Nothing," she said.

"You were wrinkling your nose. Sort of cute, like a bunny."

"Boy, you're really good with the after-sex chitchat, aren't you? 'You look like a bunny.'" She added air quotes around the last sentence.

"What are you, a politician? You're misquoting me. I said that you look sort of cute, like a bunny."

"Tomato, to-mah-to."

"Speaking of tomatoes, are you hungry?"

"Yeah, but I need to get cleaned up first. I really want a shower. I am desperate for a shower."

He considered her. "Okay, we'll make it work."

"Really?"

"Yeah. I'll get in with you. That way you can stand on your good leg and put a hand on me for balance."

A day ago that solution wouldn't have worked, because she'd have been uncomfortable with him seeing her naked, and he was too much of a gentleman to ever

suggest it. But now, things were different. "It sounds like heaven," she admitted.

"We'll take your brace off and wrap plastic grocery sacks around your bandages to keep them dry. I saw a bunch in a kitchen drawer. They won't work perfectly, but it won't matter because I can redress the wound after you're done."

"Redress the wound," she repeated. "More of your very sexy banter."

"You don't talk in the shower, do you?" he asked, almost under his breath.

"You wish."

In the end, they both got clean, but they ran out of hot water because he took his time soaping up and washing every part of her body, and then he gently washed her hair. "I'll bet this shower wall is every bit as sturdy as the bedroom wall," he whispered, his lips close to her ear.

It was tempting, but they didn't have a condom in the shower and she wasn't taking a chance of getting pregnant. It was bad enough that she was going to be alone. Alone and with a baby was even worse. "Another time," she said. "You have to feed me."

"To think," he mused as he reached behind her to shut off the lukewarm water, "a few days ago, you had to be coaxed to eat."

He'd changed that and so much more. "Perhaps you need to note it in those paper notes that you've been keeping. *'Patient has regained her appetite.'*"

"And her sarcastic wit," he added, handing her a towel to dry off.

She laughed. It was amazing that she felt so normal standing here naked. She'd never had this level of com-

fort, of intimacy, with anyone before. The idea that she might never have this again hit her hard, making her suck in a sharp breath, which her mending ribs protested.

"What's wrong?" he asked.

He was so attuned to her. That's what made him such a wonderful lover, so able to be careful with her physically, yet at the same time drive her to desperation before a final touch of his tongue or a perfectly angled thrust took her over the edge. "Just hungry," she said. "Did I hear you say that you're cooking?"

"If you're doing dishes."

"Done."

Four days later, when Jamie woke up, with Layla once again sprawled on top of him, he took a minute to reflect upon the week. It had flown by in a blur. When he and Layla were not making love, they were cooking or watching television or sitting outside looking at the stars.

He'd run out of condoms fairly quickly, which had necessitated a trip to the store. There was a small grocery about fifteen minutes north that met his needs. It also allowed him to buy a few more groceries so that they had more choices.

He'd not pushed her for more answers—hadn't wanted to do anything that would upset the balance that they'd so easily achieved.

"Good morning," she said, stroking her hand down his chest. "Sleep well?"

"Yeah. I had a dream that I took you flying."

"Oh, I'm pretty sure you did that," she said suggestively. "Before we went to sleep."

"Not that kind of flying," he said, giving her bottom a light pinch. "Although that's extraordinarily nice, too. But flying in my plane. Where do you want to go? You pick the place."

"I have no idea."

"Come on, there must be something."

She seemed to be thinking. "I've always wanted to visit all the Great Lakes. Maybe start with Lake Michigan. Have breakfast in Wisconsin and lunch in Michigan. That kind of thing."

"We could do that."

She smiled. "It seems very decadent."

"Now you're the one who is confused. Decadent was what we did before we went to sleep."

She kissed him. "You're right. I need coffee."

He sighed. "I'll go start a pot."

"Fine," she said, stretching. "I'll meet you in the kitchen."

Ten minutes later, he handed her a cup. "I want to take you on a date," he said. "It's Saturday night. Traditional night for a big date," he added, trying for blasé.

She looked up from her cup. "For days we've been living together and sleeping together. I think we officially skipped dating."

He shook his head. "We might have skipped *over it*, but that doesn't mean that we have to miss it altogether. We can circle back. I think dinner at Widow's Peak would be a good start." He had to be back at work on Monday. That meant that he would need to leave tomorrow. He needed to tell her the truth tonight, so that would give them some time to talk about next steps.

"I don't have a dress," she said.

He considered that. "One minute," he said. He

picked up his phone, and it took him just minutes to find what he was looking for. "There is a gift shop inside Widow's Peak. On the website it says, 'fashionable ladies' clothing.'"

"You think they'd have an LBD?"

"That sounds like it's an explosive device, so I'd say no."

She laughed. "Little black dress."

"Explosive in a whole other manner," he said knowingly. He very much liked her naked, but he suspected in a sexy little black dress, she might make his heart stop.

She sipped her coffee. He could tell she was considering the suggestion, so he kept his mouth shut. Finally, she set her cup down. "I'd like to modify the suggestion somewhat."

"Okay." He was flexible. As long as they talked tonight.

"I want you to cast my leg."

She needed that done. No argument there. Was he the best to do it? Probably not. But could he do it and do it well? He thought so. What she wasn't saying was that she was also aware that time was running out. "I need casting materials."

"If you went back to Knoware, could you pick them up and bring them back?"

"I could."

"Would you?"

Hell, he'd attempt to move mountains for her. Putting on a cast was nothing. "Of course. I'll leave now." He pushed his chair back. "Is there anything else you want?"

"May I borrow your phone?" she asked.

He pushed it toward her. She typed, then put the

phone up to her ear. "Hi. I'm calling to see if you carry black dresses for women?"

She listened.

"Excellent. Could you set aside the sleeveless black knit in a medium for Regan? Someone will be in to pick it up this afternoon. How much is the total?" She listened. "My...uh...my friend will be paying with cash. Thank you." She hung up. "Can you swing by Widow's Peak either on your way there or your way back?"

"Done." When he was home, he'd get his own clothes for dinner. He cleared the dishes from the table and put them in the sink. "You'll be okay here by yourself?" he asked.

She smiled, but it did not reach her eyes. "You have to go back to work on Monday. That means you're leaving tomorrow. I'm going to be alone then."

He did not want to have this discussion now. He wasn't quite ready, the atmosphere wasn't right and he wasn't prepared. He had to make a stop at Tiddle's Tidbits and Treasures first. Maybe he'd get lucky and Erin wouldn't be working. If not, well, there was no hoping that she wouldn't tell Marcus about his purchase. It was a risk he was willing to take. Debating Layla about the choices she made before he was fully prepared was too great a risk. "I guess that's true," he said. "I'll see you in a couple hours."

"Let me get you some cash for the dress," she said, heading to the bedroom.

"I've got it," he said.

She shook her head. "After all you've done for me, you do not need to buy me clothes. Just wait a minute."

He didn't argue. Just accepted the eighty dollars when she came back. Then he walked out the door and

around the cottage. Then it was up the long road to the parking lot behind Widow's Peak. When he'd driven to the store earlier in the week, he'd been relieved that there hadn't been any nasty notes on it from hotel management that he didn't have a hotel parking sticker in his window. The same was true today. He suspected that they weren't watching the parking lot very closely this time of year. But just in case they were busier than he thought, he took the time to duck into the hotel. He walked up to the hostess at the front of the restaurant. "Can I make a reservation for tonight?" he asked.

"Of course. What time, sir?"

"Seven. For two."

"Your name, sir?" she asked, adding the information to an electronic tablet.

"Weathers. Jamie Weathers."

She gave him a bright smile. "We'll see you tonight at seven. Are you celebrating anything special?"

He really hoped so. But he wasn't letting the cat out of the bag before he'd asked Layla. "Just a nice dinner with somebody I care about."

"We'll make sure you have a lovely evening."

He thanked her, knowing that only one thing would make it a truly excellent evening. He left the restaurant and found the gift shop. The clerk inside had already bagged the dress. He used the cash that Layla had insisted he take.

Then he was back in his vehicle and headed toward Knoware. His first stop was at Tiddle's Tidbits and Treasures. Since Erin had taken over running the store for her sister, who was home with a new baby, there'd been a few changes. One had been the addition of engagement rings. She'd been surprised when she got engaged

to Marcus that there was nowhere in Knoware to buy a diamond. Her selection was small, but she had good taste and every item was of excellent quality. He was confident that she'd have something he liked. Hopefully, Layla would feel the same.

If she didn't, she could pick out her own ring later.

That was, of course, assuming she said yes. He wasn't willing to let his mind seriously consider any other alternative.

He opened the door of the store. Erin was working. She looked up from the shelf she was straightening and gave him a big smile. "Hi. This is a nice surprise. Need chocolate? Have you been bad at work again and need to make amends?"

"I am never bad, and I do not make amends. I simply ensure ongoing compliance and gleeful effort with regular chocolate fixes." It reminded him of the first real dinner he'd shared with Layla at the cottage, when they'd described their perfect meals. He'd cooked her steaks and loaded baked potatoes. She'd pretended that she'd brought chocolates. "I do need a box, though," he said, pointing at a selection that he always enjoyed.

Erin started wrapping the box. "Did you hear that they caught the people behind the downtown break-ins? A trio of eighteen-year-olds. They were doing it just for the heck of it."

"Great news," he said. That had probably been keeping Marcus busy this week, which was why he hadn't heard from him.

"Anything else?" Erin asked, walking toward the cash register.

He looked around the store to make sure that there

wasn't anyone else inside. "Yeah. I'd like to look at your engagement rings."

Erin's mouth opened, then shut. Then she pressed her lips together. "I am going to kill Marcus. He hasn't even mentioned that you were serious about someone. Who's the lucky lady?"

"No one you've met. Actually, Marcus doesn't know." He leaned over the glass case and examined his choices. One caught his eye immediately. "Can I see that one?"

She pulled it out and held it in the palm of her hand. "This is my favorite," she said. "Just over a carat white solitaire, with a smaller diamond on each side, all set in fourteen-carat yellow gold. It's so delicate, yet so classy."

Just like Layla.

She discreetly flipped over the price tag so that he could see it.

It didn't matter. He was only ever going to buy one of these. "I'll take it," he said.

"We can size it for..." Her voice trailed off.

"Layla," he said. "Her name is Layla."

"We can size it for Layla at her convenience." She gave him a big smile. "I'm happy for you, Jamie. And I can't wait to meet Layla. I imagine she's got to be pretty special to snag a guy like you."

"She's very special," he said.

"Can I tell Marcus?" she asked.

"You're going to regardless of what I say," he said, giving her his credit card.

She rang up the sale. "You're right. But I'd much rather do it with your permission."

"Permission granted." His phone would be ring-

ing tonight for sure. Marcus was likely to have some thoughts about the engagement.

She cut off the price tag and then put the ring inside a box. "Want a bag or you going to carry it in your pocket?"

"Pocket is good," he said, slipping it into his jeans pocket. He'd be changing clothes before tonight, but there was no way he was forgetting this. "Thank you, Erin."

"Thank you. My sister told me I was crazy when I ordered that ring, that it would never sell. You've proven me right."

"Happy to be of assistance. I'll see you soon," he said. "I'm anxious for you to meet Layla."

"Likewise," he heard her say as he walked out the door.

He drove to the hospital. It was a Saturday afternoon, so there wasn't a lot going on in the emergency department. He waved at a few folks and said hello, but he didn't stop to talk. He got what he needed and slipped out the door before anybody could engage him in conversation.

He considered avoiding his office but in the end decided that he'd rather have a heads-up on the number of messages and the files that needed his attention. He unlocked his office door and was surprised to see Caitlin Rose. She was at her desk, dressed casually, with a stack of folders in front of her. "Hey, what are you doing here on a Saturday?" he asked.

She shrugged. "It was a crazy week, lots of interruptions. Dear Husband went hunting this morning and so I had the day to myself. Decided to tackle what I could. And I wasn't expecting you. You've been a very good

vacationer this time, Dr. Weathers. I have not seen the flurry of emails or telephone calls that normally accompany a stay away from the office. Have you been ill?" she asked, not sounding all that concerned.

"Some things never change," he muttered, loud enough that she could hear it.

She laughed. "I missed you. I did. But I was so glad that you were getting away. Truly away. What have you been doing?"

Like most people, the number of individuals that he had absolute trust in was limited. Didn't need all his fingers to count them. But Caitlin made the list. Without reservation.

And he wanted to tell someone.

Maybe not everything, but enough so that she could render some advice.

"I've been staying in a cottage, near Widow's Peak."

"One of those along the coast, below the cliff?"

"Yeah."

"Did you rent it online?"

"Yeah," he said automatically. How they came to be at the cottage wasn't a salient detail. "Not alone."

Her mouth made the shape of a circle, but she said nothing.

"Remember the trauma call that came in on Wednesday afternoon, before Thanksgiving? It was raining and I took Mobile One."

"Yes, of course. I was worried about you."

"I spent the week with her, the woman who was in the accident." He paused. But Caitlin said nothing, as if she knew that there had to be more. "And tonight I'm going to ask her to marry me," he said in a rush.

Her smile was immediate. "I knew it would happen like this."

"Like what?"

"That you'd find the right person and you'd immediately know. You wouldn't be like my son, who dated his girlfriend for seven years before he figured out he wanted to marry her. You would know. It's the very decisive nature of yours. You trust your instincts."

"I hope they aren't failing me now," he said.

"You have doubts?"

"None. But I might be rushing her. And there are… complications."

"Is she married?"

"Of course not," he said.

"Dying?"

"Pretty sure I prevented that."

"Then I suspect the complications can be worked out. You're not only decisive, you're a problem solver. The bigger the problem, the happier you are. You love a challenge."

"Usually true," he admitted. "Although in this case, I'd prefer that the complications weren't there."

"Are you going to let it stop you?"

"Hell, no."

"There is going to be widespread disappointment within the hospital and the community among all single women who've held out hope. You know you're the last of what many considered to be the three most eligible bachelors in town. What do Blade and Marcus think?"

"I haven't told them yet. Well, officially anyway. I got a ring at Tiddle's from Erin Price."

"So Marcus knows, and I'm sure he's already called Blade."

"I'll circle back with them in a few days," he said. "They'll understand."

"Of course they will."

"Want to see the ring?"

"You have to ask?"

He pulled it out of his pocket and opened the box. "I hope she likes it."

"It's perfect, Jamie. Absolutely stunning. What's your plan? Take your plane up and trail a big banner that says *Marry Me*?"

He shook his head. "Dinner, a nice bottle of wine, a reasonable and quick discussion."

"You want it to be tidy?"

"I guess. It just feels so right to me," he admitted, "that it's hard to imagine that it won't feel the same to her."

Caitlin got up from behind her desk and came around and hugged him. "I know you're the boss and we're in the office, but I love you like one of my own kids. She'd be a fool not to see how lucky she is. And Jamie, one thing I'm confident of is that you would never fall for a fool."

He let those words roll around in his head while he drove to his condo. He didn't bother pulling into the garage. Instead, he parked on the street. He couldn't resist one more peek at the gorgeous ring before he stuffed it back into his pocket. He hoped she loved it.

He hoped she said yes.

He got out, unlocked his door and went inside. It took him just a few minutes to gather clothes and dress shoes appropriate for that night. He put everything in a suit bag. Then he glanced through the mail that had gathered while he was gone and didn't see anything that needed

his immediate attention. The condo looked good, but it also seemed very empty, very quiet, and he realized that in just a few days, he'd gotten very used to living with Layla, very used to hearing her voice, her laugh, her sighs of pleasure.

He was back in his car within ten minutes, anxious to return to the cottage. He really didn't think that Layla would run again. And he was confident that she could safely get about on her own. But still, he'd feel better when he was back with her.

His phone rang, and he checked the number. Marcus.

He wasn't surprised. Had known that Erin would immediately call Marcus, who had likely immediately called Blade first. *What the hell is our friend up to? Did you know about this?*

Now he was reaching out to the source. And it was a rare occurrence that Jamie let Marcus's calls roll to voice mail. But he did today. He wasn't ready yet to have the discussion. Not before he'd convinced Layla. Not before they had a plan.

He got to the outskirts of Knoware and settled in for the drive, anticipation humming in his veins.

"He's taking a similar route as to what you described," the man said, keeping his eyes on the SUV that was a half mile ahead of him.

"Excellent," Douglas Glass said. He was in the library, and his mother was somewhere in the house. Still, he kept his voice quiet. She had no idea that he'd hired an old acquaintance to watch Jamie Weathers's condo. And for days he'd been waiting to hear that the man had shown up. Now, he had. And they weren't going to lose him this time. "Keep me posted."

"I will. Still the same plan?"

"Yes." He wanted information about where the doctor was headed and, if at all possible, once he reached a destination, confirmation that Layla Morant was also there. Then he'd take over.

With pleasure.

"Fine," his acquaintance said. "I'll be in touch."

Douglas put his phone down and reached for the decanter of whiskey that his mother always kept at the ready. But he pulled his hand back. No more drinking today. He needed to be sharp. Precise.

Ready to make his next—and final—move.

Chapter 15

Layla was excited about getting a cast on her leg. Yes, it would be heavy. Yes, it would be awkward. But it would provide necessary protection for her healing fracture. In six weeks or so, she'd have to find somewhere to have it removed. She'd have left here long before then. For all she knew, the owners of the cottage came back over the holidays. She intended to be gone by the third week of December at the latest.

She hadn't told Jamie this. She would have if he'd asked, but he seemed reluctant to want to talk about next steps. Only once had they talked about his going back to work on Monday. But that had been before they'd... had sex, made love?

Yes, there was a difference.

Not that that really mattered. He was going back to work on Monday. She knew what kind of schedule he worked, knew his commitment.

He wasn't going to have time to worry about her. Maybe he'd squeeze in a trip or two north before she moved on, but really, what was the point? Better to rip the bandage off, right? She had a big, ugly shadow looming over her, and there was no way that she was taking that into Jamie's world. She couldn't live under her real name. That would make it so easy for Douglas Glass to find her. But to live as Regan Jones was to ask Jamie to live a lie alongside her. That would not be fair to him, and after a while, he'd regret it.

The more she thought about it, the more she figured the right thing to do was to say goodbye to Jamie tomorrow—for good. It would be so hard on her—she'd already given up so much, and to have to again give up something that was important to her seemed almost too much to ask. But she would do it. For him.

He deserved better than her. He deserved the best because he was the best.

She closed her eyes, thinking a nap would be nice. Truth be told, she hadn't been getting all that much sleep the last few days, with Jamie reaching for her every few hours. But she hadn't said no. Had not wanted to. She could handle being tired. She was storing up memories that were going to have to keep her warm for a long time.

She did not wake up until she felt the side of the bed dip under a person's weight. She looked over at Jamie, who had crawled into bed with his clothes on. "What time is it?" she asked.

"Almost three," he said.

"Oh my gosh. I slept for hours."

"Good that you had a nap. I got everything I'll need for the cast."

"Before you put it on, is there time for one more shower?"

He seemed to consider the question. "The shower where I get to see you naked?"

"Yes."

"The shower where I get to hold your naked body?"

"Yes," she said, rolling her eyes.

"The shower where I get to pretend that I'm some kind of superhero because I'm the only thing between you standing or going down?"

"Superhero?" she asked.

"Everybody has a different definition," he said. "So, yeah, sure. We can shower." He leaned in and kissed her. "I can help you out of your clothes right here." He started to unbutton her shirt.

"That is helpful," she said.

"Underpromise and overdeliver," he said, falling back on an old line.

She lifted her head to whisper something in his ear.

His cheeks felt hot. "You've got a dirty mind, darling. But I'll do my best." And that was why, this time, he'd take a condom with him into the shower.

In the end, his best was three orgasms that shattered her. It was between the first and second that she'd finally gotten soaped up. They had come back to bed still wet, and the sheets had gotten very damp. A good contrast to the raging fire of lust in her body.

She opened one eye and was gratified that he appeared as spent as she. He was flat on his back, his forearm resting on his forehead, and his chest was perhaps not heaving, but the man was definitely trying to catch his breath.

She put a hand flat to his hard stomach. "That was nice."

"Nice is extra sour cream on my baked potato," he said, not opening his eyes. "Nice is not having to wait for an oil change. This was not that."

No. It had been fundamentally raw and unchoreographed. It had likely ruined her. Sex in the future would always suffer in comparison. That realization must have caused a physical response, because he opened his eyes.

"You just tensed up. Are you in pain?"

"No," she lied. Emotional pain, sure. But now was not the time to discuss it. They still had the evening ahead of them. One last night. She wasn't going to spoil it. "In a bit, we'll get up."

"Sounds good," he said, pulling her close.

"Then we'll do my cast."

"It's a plan."

They slept and when it was time to get up, he led her to the kitchen table and helped her get onto it. Both legs dangled from the side. She wore just her panties.

He studied her. "Why don't all my patients come dressed like you?"

"You might have to sleep with all of them, and quite frankly, you'd be a withered nub of a man."

"Never say 'withered nub' to me again," he teased, kneeling before her. "I'm going to put a fresh bandage on your incision, and then we'll give your skin some additional protection with a cotton sock, very appropriately called a stockinette, and then more padding before we apply the fiberglass cast."

"Sounds as if you know what you're doing."

"Skin protection is as important as getting the bone

set correctly," he said. "The cast will go from here," he said, pointing midarch of her foot, "to here." He moved his index finger up her leg, stopping just below the knee. "We'll take our time making sure that your foot is positioned correctly, at a nice ninety-degree angle, to prevent any additional damage to tendons or ligaments."

She looked at the incision as he unwrapped the bandage on her leg. Her leg was still black and blue, but the incision itself looked better, she supposed. "What do you think?" she asked.

"Healing," he said.

He was focused on his task, so she stopped asking questions and watched him work. He moved efficiently, almost impersonally. But still gently. He taped the bandage in place, and then he slid what appeared to be a very long cotton sock onto her leg. He left just her toes free, and it ended at her knee.

"What's that for?" she asked, looking at the plastic dishpan of water.

"To soak the fiberglass paper."

She watched as he cut open small foil packages and pulled out the roll of fiberglass. He placed it in the water, waited maybe thirty seconds and removed it, squeezing out the extra water. Then he started wrapping her leg.

Five minutes later, of more of the same, she had a cast.

He looked up. "How's it feel?"

"Heavy," she said.

"Of course. Other than that?"

"Fine. I thought you said that you didn't do this very often."

"I don't. But it sort of came back to me. Give it fif-

teen more minutes, and it should be hard enough for you to move around. Make sure you can wriggle your toes."

She did it, and he smiled. "Very good. When you sleep, we'll put a pillow under your foot. That will help with blood flow and reduce swelling."

"I know something else that helps blood flow," she said suggestively.

"That's not the area of your body that I casted," he said, rolling his eyes. "Thank the good Lord." He stood up. "I'm going to go get dressed for dinner while you let that dry a bit more. Your dress is right here," he said, handing her a package with Widow's Peak Gift Emporium printed on it.

She waited until he was out of the room before opening it. When she pulled out the dress, she was pleasantly surprised. It was a simple black knit, but the material was a bit thicker than some she'd seen, and it would be easy to pull on and off over her head. It would definitely fit. She checked for a price tag, and when there was none, she slipped it over her head and stuck her arms through.

It felt odd to have a dress on after wearing her pajama pants and a cami for days. Or being naked. How quickly she'd gotten accustomed to being naked.

She heard the bedroom door open, and Jamie came down the hall. *Oh my.* She'd seen him in scrubs, jeans, shorts and sweatpants and a T-shirt. She had not yet seen him dressed up in a freshly pressed light blue shirt and gray dress slacks. He was so handsome. "You look nice," she said.

"As do you. How does the dress fit?"

"Good. Can you help me down from the table?"

"Yeah." He tapped on her cast. "Good to go," he said, giving her a hand.

She stood, feeling oddly off-balance with the extra weight on her leg. But it felt good to know that the healing bone now had more protection.

He handed her the crutches. "How's it feel?"

"Great. Thank you," she said. "Will my bill be coming in the mail?"

His eyes got warm. "Oh no. I'll hand deliver it. Probably tonight. Demanding payment."

She laughed. "I can't wait." She was a little nervous, she had to admit, to be going out in public with Jamie. It was a risk. But a small one. They were an hour away from Knoware, it was the off-season and it was one dinner.

One more memory. Worth it.

She looked at the cast, which covered at least half her foot. "I guess there's no getting a shoe on tonight."

"The downside of a cast," Jamie acknowledged.

"Just as well. I don't really have dress-up shoes with me. But I've got some black flats. Let me go slip one on, and then I'll be ready to go."

Jamie checked his watch. "Perfect timing. Our reservation is at seven."

"What time will you be home?" his mother asked, standing at the bottom of the stairs.

Not tonight, thought Douglas. Maybe not even tomorrow. But he wasn't sure how much to tell her. She was so touchy about his absences. "I don't know, Mother. I haven't seen these particular friends for years."

"You're risking getting sent back to jail."

He really didn't think so. "Mother, it's Saturday. To-

morrow is Sunday. The day of rest. No state bureaucrat employed by the California prison system is going to be following up to catch parole violators."

"You don't know that."

She was sometimes so very difficult to live with. But as long as he stayed, she supported him in a lifestyle that he was very much accustomed to. A lifestyle that had been taken away from him by that bitch Layla Morant. Yes, prison was over but now as a convicted felon, his opportunities to make it on his own were much more limited. No one was calling to ask him to be a board member now. When his mother died, he'd be flush for life. No worries. Until then, he'd have to grit his teeth. Most of the time she was quite tolerable. It was just this that seemed to run her off the rails. "I know you worry, Mother. And I appreciate your concern. I will be fine. I promise."

He worked hard to keep his tone neutral, his voice modulated. But in reality, he was brimming with excitement. He was going to find Layla Morant. He was confident that Dr. Fly-his-own-plane Weathers would lead them right to her. Since the call twenty minutes earlier from his friend, he'd been flying high himself, no plane needed.

He needed to get on the road now. That way, when confirmation came from his friend that the bitch had been found, he'd be well on his way. If he was wrong, he'd simply return home.

But he wasn't wrong. Very soon, he was going to deliver on the promise he'd made.

Chapter 16

Widow's Peak dining room looked different at night. It was the very same space where she'd enjoyed her cinnamon roll and coffee, but the dim lights, candle-light, white tablecloths and four-piece string quartet in the corner made it seem very different. The holiday decorations that she'd seen earlier had been pretty during the day, but with all the lights lit, they were almost magical. "I'm really, really glad they had an LBD in the gift shop," she said under her breath as the maître d' led them to their table.

"You'd have been fine in your pj's," Jamie said.

"You think so?" she asked, amused.

"They're cute," he said. "With their little lavender flowers."

"Cute or not," she said, thinking she might keep them forever, "I'm grateful to be wearing something else.

This was a good idea." The dining room wasn't over-flowing with people. More than half the tables were oc-cupied, but the acoustics were such that it wasn't hard to hear each other. It was low risk.

A server approached, introduced himself and asked about cocktails. Jamie pointed at a bottle from the wine list, she nodded and the server smiled at their choice. Minutes later, they had filled wineglasses in front of them.

"A toast," Jamie said.

She picked up her glass. "To?"

He considered. "To you. To your continued recovery. To the future."

She'd toast it, throw a penny in a fountain or wish upon a star. Whatever might change the fact that a future seemed bleak without Jamie in it. But she was not going down that path tonight. There'd be time for that tomorrow and all the days after. "To the future," she said.

Their server returned, and they ordered. Jamie got a steak, and she ordered the salmon. "Red meat?" she teased as the server walked away.

"Occasionally. All things in moderation," he added. He leaned forward. "Except sex," he added softly. "There should be lots and lots of that."

"I have to admit," she said, "it's been rather restorative."

A short time later, the server had returned with her tomato bisque soup and his Caesar salad. Jamie waited until he'd left the table. "You just wait until all the other physicians catch on and start prescribing it for the common cold. The world is going to be a better place."

He was such fun. So talented. And smart. A genu-

inely nice guy. Her soup felt thick in her throat, and she swallowed hard. "You told me before that you're intending to go see your parents in Florida over the holidays. Are your parents big decorators?" she asked, pointing at the tall tree in the corner.

"My dad more than my mom. He really likes the outside lights. Inside, there will be a tree, but it won't be crazy. My two brothers, along with their wives, live nearby, so it's a houseful when we're all there. My mom was disappointed when I couldn't come at Thanksgiving. If I don't get there at Christmas, I don't want to face that next phone call."

"Best Christmas ever?" she asked, after their server had cleared away the dirty dishes from the first course.

He laughed. "I have no idea."

"Come on. There wasn't one year where you got what you absolutely wanted? That you could not have imagined getting a better Christmas gift?"

He shrugged. "I don't know. I remember being pretty psyched about a bike one year. I was probably eleven or twelve. How about you?"

"The year I was eight. I got a kitten."

"A real one?"

"Yes. She was gray with four white feet."

"And you named her Stockings?" he asked.

She shook her head. "I named her Georgia."

"That is not a cat name."

"I beg your pardon," she said.

He was saved from answering, because their server delivered their entrees. Everything looked delicious. More wine was poured, and they began eating. It was after dessert had been cleared that there was finally a lull in the casual conversation.

She yawned and quickly covered her mouth.

"Are you tired?"

She shrugged. "Not bad. And this was lovely. I am one of those people who really loves Christmas music," she said, with a nod toward the quartet. "And these four were really good."

"As was that chocolate cake," he said. "I'd come back just for that."

They wouldn't be back. Not together. Perhaps he'd bring another woman here someday.

"Hey, what's wrong?" he asked.

"Nothing," she lied. "It's probably time to go."

"Okay." He took care of the check, and they were on their way out of the restaurant five minutes later. "Do you mind if we take a closer look at that tree?" he asked, pointing to the one in the far corner. It was decorated with gold bows and beads.

There was a small sitting area off to the side, and no one was there. He motioned for her to take a seat. She did.

Then he knelt on the floor in front of her and pulled a small black box from his pocket. He opened the box to show her the most exquisite diamond ever.

Her chest felt tight, and it hurt to take the shallowest of breaths.

"Layla Morant, this last week has been the best week of my life. Because you were by my side. I want that forever. I want you, forever. Please say that you'll be my wife."

Say something. He willed it but still, she did not. She alternated between staring at the ring and staring at him. He glanced around, making sure that nobody

was watching them or, God forbid, catching it all on a cell phone.

"Layla," he said gently.

She shook her head. "No. I'm sorry. It's impossible."

He'd been prepared to meet some hesitation given the story she'd shared, but her tone was resolute, final. Unacceptable. "Layla, listen to me. We can undo what's been done thus far. You don't have to go on living as Regan Jones. You can be Layla Morant and you can be my wife."

"I won't be safe. You won't be safe."

"Don't worry about me. I will keep you safe. Douglas Glass won't get within fifty yards of you, ever."

"There's no way to ensure that." She swallowed hard. "Don't you think I examined the possibilities every which way before I made the decision to give up my life? Nobody but me believes he's capable of it, that he'll carry through with his threat. That much was obvious."

"I believe you." He did, although he also thought it was possible that she'd made Glass into a more desperate character than he really was. Perhaps time had cooled his anger? Perhaps the knowledge that he would be sent back to prison if he stepped over the line would make him set aside past hates.

"Do you know how one of the housekeeping staff at the hospital described you?" she asked.

"Uh…no," he admitted, bewildered by the change of subject.

"Local hero."

He waved a hand. "That's because of this photo in the—"

"No," she interrupted. "It's because everybody knows you and appreciates you. I am not the person that some-

body like you should marry. I'm an albatross. I'll simply weigh you down."

"You're being ridiculous," he said, getting mad. This wasn't going at all like he'd hoped.

"I'm not," she said, her voice rising. She looked around, as if suddenly aware, too, that they were in a public place. "Listen," she said, more softly. "This past week was…wonderful. Even though I was sick as a dog at the beginning." She wet her lips. "You saved my life. More than once. I owe you. I—"

"I told you from the very beginning," he said, his tone perhaps harsher than he intended. But this was going so wrong. "I wasn't collecting on a debt."

"I know," she said, holding up her hand. "And I never felt that way. If I had, I'd have never told you the truth about my situation. I took a big risk doing that. My secret is no longer a secret. Because you know."

He had to tell her. Right now. "About that," he said, keeping his voice very low. "I knew that your real name was Layla Morant before you told me."

She blinked fast. "What?"

"Marcus was able to find a photo of the real Regan Jones in some police records."

"She didn't have a criminal history. I checked."

"She'd been arrested but eventually the charges got dropped. They had a booking photo."

"That doesn't explain how you knew my real name," she said.

He wasn't surprised that she'd keyed onto the salient facts so quickly. She was very smart. "Marcus and I went to Oakland, and we met with Regan Jones. She told us."

Layla sucked in a breath, and her beautiful gray-blue

eyes were tumultuous with emotion. "Just like that, she told you?"

"I gave her my card and told her that it was a medical emergency. We convinced her that neither Marcus nor I was any threat to her or to you."

"Marcus is the chief of police. Of course he's a threat to me," she said, her tone resigned. "Reason one hundred that *we* would never work out. He's your best friend. He's never going to think that I deserve you. I would never measure up."

"Marcus will understand when he knows the truth." He felt certain of it. But right now, Marcus didn't have the benefit of that knowledge and had acted accordingly. "There's something else," he said.

"Wait, don't tell me. He's put my picture on wanted posters and I'm on the wall of every post office."

She was so close that it was startling. "Well, not quite. I don't think that's how it is done anymore. But you left us with the impression that you were headed toward Canada. As such, Marcus felt a responsibility to let law enforcement know that you were a person who should be detained for further questioning."

"What?" she practically sputtered.

"You purchased someone else's identity. I now understand that you had a need, but we didn't know that at the time the decision was made. I thought it was the right thing to do," he added. He wasn't putting this on Marcus. He'd been the one insistent upon trying what they could to find her. He'd done it for the best of reasons, but it didn't appear that she was buying into that right now.

"I can't believe this. You've...got law enforcement

hunting me." She stopped. "Are they looking for Regan Jones or Layla Morant?" she asked.

"Both," he said.

She ran her hands through her short hair. "I really can't believe this. Everything I've done, everything I've given up, you've undone. And you've been lying to me. I couldn't make love to you until I told you the truth. But you, oh, no, you had no compunction. You had already unraveled my life, but you said nothing."

He closed the ring box and put it back in his pocket. "Listen, Layla. We can talk about this. Make this right."

She stood up and reached for her crutches. "I'm going back to the cottage."

It would probably be better to have the conversation there. He pulled his keys from his pocket.

"Oh, no. By myself."

"Layla," he pleaded. "You can't walk back to the cottage on crutches at night. It's too dark, too dangerous."

She let out a huff of air. "Now you're worried about danger to me."

That hurt. But he wasn't going to let her be ridiculous. "I'm going to get my SUV, and then I'm going to drive you back to the cottage. I won't come in."

"You need your things."

"I'll get them tomorrow." By then, she'd have had a chance to calm down. They could have a rational conversation. That wasn't happening tonight.

"Fine," she said.

The temperature had dropped considerably since they'd arrived, he realized as they made their way to the parking lot. It was likely not much warmer than the high teens. His vehicle had barely even started to warm up when they reached the cottage.

She hadn't complained about the cold. Hadn't said a word to him. He put his SUV in Park and turned to her. "Layla, I'm sorry." About how the conversation had gone. About how angry she was. About not being honest before this. So many things.

"I want your cottage keys" was her response.

This was killing him. He pulled them from his pocket and tossed them in her lap. He wasn't going to fight about keys. "Layla, I need you to know just one thing."

She turned to look at him, and he got the awful sense that this might be the last thing she ever intended to listen to him say. He better make it good.

"I love you," he said. "I think I started to fall in love with you from the minute we met. And every day we spent together, that love grew. What we shared this week isn't common. It's special. I'm not walking away from it. I can't. And I won't let you, either. This isn't over."

Chapter 17

This isn't over.

He was wrong. It was. And she desperately needed to think about next steps. But she couldn't think, couldn't reason, couldn't plan. Couldn't do all the things that came naturally to her scientist mind. But now, safe inside the small cottage that had been her refuge this past week, she could cry.

She did it with gusto, without restraint. She cried until the tears dried up and all she had was rough, panting sobs that tore at her tender throat. Her head ached and fatigue weighed her down, making it difficult to move from where she had initially landed on the living room couch. At some point, she slept. Fitful dreams of a fanciful wedding where blood dripped from her veil and her groom was faceless.

She woke up at twenty past one in the morning. The cast on her leg felt heavy, and she realized that she'd

failed to keep her leg elevated when she was sleeping, as Jamie had instructed. That thought threatened to set off a new set of tears, but she blinked them away. She'd had a good cry. It was probably therapeutic. But more was just a waste of her time, her energy, her future. She needed to think.

She had a target on her back, both as Regan Jones and Layla Morant. She would need to be even more cautious. Using the Regan Jones credit card was fraught with danger now. She had to assume that it was flagged in the system and that law enforcement would follow up on any transactions. But the good news was that she had thousands of dollars in cash with her. She could still go to Seattle, find an apartment and get a job. She'd have to be careful about where she chose to work because she wouldn't want a background check to trigger attention from anyone. But there were still small employers who likely didn't have sophisticated pre-employment processes.

She could still live under the radar. She'd just have to be more careful. Thankfully, she'd been smart enough not to tell Jamie her true destination. He still thought she was Canada-bound. It was going to be tricky getting her cast off when the time came. Medical facilities required identification. She'd been successful delaying it at Bigelow Memorial because she'd come in as an emergency transport. But if she showed up to have a cast removed, a routine procedure, they'd insist.

At least any reputable place would.

But maybe she could find someone to help her. There had to be training programs for cast technicians in Seattle. Perhaps she could find someone who was

studying but had not yet graduated to do it for the right amount of cash.

She shook her head. Lies upon lies. Buying services and people. This was not the life that she'd envisioned before she had crossed paths with Douglas Glass.

It was time to leave the cottage. Not only did it feel terribly empty without Jamie, it suddenly felt very risky. She would walk up to Widow's Peak tomorrow and assess her options. She might be able to get a ride with someone, as she'd done leaving Knoware. If that didn't look like a possibility, she could always pretend that she was a guest and ask the doorman to order her a taxi. One way or another, she intended to get to Seattle tomorrow and start the process of building her new life.

It was the middle of the night, and she knew that she should be sleeping, but there was simply no way. She would clean the cottage, erasing all signs that she and Jamie had ever been there as best as possible. She intended to leave an unsigned note and money for the homeowner to cover the repair to the window she'd broken when entering as well as the canned goods they'd consumed.

She looked around, debating where to start. Every room was a minefield with memories of her time with Jamie. The bedroom where they'd made love. The living room where they'd watched the movies. The kitchen where they'd cooked together and teased each other with descriptions of their favorite meal. The bathroom where she'd had the most sensual experience of her life in the shower.

No good choices. But delaying wasn't going to help anything. She stood up, got her crutches under her arms

and walked into the kitchen. There, next to the coffee-pot, was something that hadn't been there before.

Candy. Wrapped in lovely paper with a sticker that said Tiddle's Tidbits and Treasures. Oh, what the hell. She tore into the box and opened it. Put the first piece, a salted dark chocolate caramel, in her mouth. It made her remember that ridiculous conversation she'd had with him about the perfect dinner at his house. He'd cooked steaks. She'd brought the chocolate.

She spit the piece out into the garbage.

She might never eat chocolate again.

She opened the cupboard under the kitchen sink. She grabbed the cleaning products that she needed and set to work cleaning the counters and the stove. When she got to the refrigerator, she was very grateful that they'd used most of the food that Jamie had originally brought with him. She pragmatically sorted what she could take with her in her go-bag. She had room for the oranges and grapes, and it would give her some fruit to eat along with her peanut butter and jelly sandwiches. The rest would have to go in a garbage bag, and she'd dump it at Widow's Peak tomorrow.

She finished the kitchen and headed into the bedroom. Now that she'd gotten started, she felt better. To do something, anything, was better than to constantly be reliving the conversation with Jamie. To be reliving the exhilarating and terrifying experience of seeing that beautiful ring. Reliving the crushing pain when he'd admitted that he'd been lying the whole time, that he'd known she was Layla Morant well before she'd ever told him.

Douglas was very tired. So tired that he was driving with the window open so that the fresh, cold night

air hit him hard. It was noisy, and he didn't like that. Since he'd been a small child, he'd preferred the quiet.

It was nearing three in the morning, and there was little traffic on the highway. He'd just passed a sign that said Knoware was four miles. His destination was an hour north still.

He had to keep going. As he'd expected, his contact had provided confirmation that Dr. Weathers and Layla Morant were together. They had gone to dinner at some place called Widow's Peak. How lovely. It was good to have a nice last meal.

They'd returned to the small house where they were staying, but Weathers hadn't even gotten out of the vehicle. Just Layla had gone inside. Weathers had driven off. His contact did not know where, had decided it was more important to continue to watch the house, because that's where Layla was.

His contact was right. He didn't care about the doctor. Yes, he wanted him out of the way, but beyond that, he was unimportant.

He wondered if the two of them were sleeping together. Hard to deny that Layla Morant was very attractive. Smart, too. Too smart for her own good.

She was going to have to pay for that. Pay for the lost months when he'd been confined to a cage. Pay for all the indignities that he'd suffered in prison. For the brutality that he'd endured, the memories he carried. He could give firsthand testimony that minimum security did not equate to a safe place. But he would not do that. No one would ever know.

He had too much pride, for one thing. And as important, no one must know that he continued to harbor as much hate in his heart today as he had when he'd first realized that it was this woman, with her calm de-

meanor, her impressive credentials and her damning evidence, who had swayed a grand jury to indict him.

No, as tired as he was, there was no sleeping for him. He would keep going.

And he would kill her.

Jamie lay in his bed, eyes staring upward, unable to distinguish where the wall ended and the ceiling began in the dark, unfamiliar room. How had the night ended so badly, with Layla walking away from him, shutting him out of the cottage, of her life, of their future?

The ring was on the bedside table. And while he couldn't see it in the dark, he imagined that the diamond was blinking, a silent code mocking him. *You idiot. You lied and you put the woman you love in danger.*

He was going to fix this. That had been the only thing going through his head when he'd let her get out of his vehicle. He'd waited until she was safely inside and then driven away, intending to find a place nearby to park his vehicle for a few hours, while both of them got some sleep and some much-needed space from one another.

So that they could go at this again.

So that they could see solutions rather than incriminations.

But he realized pretty quickly that it was going to be a very cold night in his vehicle, so he'd driven back to Widow's Peak and rented a room. The gentleman behind the desk had asked whether he needed assistance with his luggage. Given that he had nothing but the clothes on his back, a billfold and a diamond ring in his pocket, he'd declined. Once he'd found his way

to the room, he'd showered and now lay naked between the soft sheets, his mind whirling.

He would go back in the morning. And they would talk. Reasonably.

Maybe it had been a mistake to broadcast the names of Layla Morant and Regan Jones to law enforcement. But when he and Marcus had made that decision, he'd been consumed with concern about finding her, about making sure she was okay. He'd had no idea about Douglas Glass or any of that.

But you should have assumed she had a good reason.

That was the bodiless, toneless voice in the corner of his brain.

But I didn't know her then.

He was arguing with nothing. He was losing his mind.

You should have trusted her.

That was the crux of it. He hadn't trusted that her motivations and actions were pure. He'd looked at the facts presented, which, in his defense, was part of his training, and he'd made an assumption. And perhaps if he'd told her the truth at the time she'd opened her heart and told him about Douglas Glass, then he could have saved the situation.

He'd been afraid.

That did not sit well with him. It wasn't a character trait that he often associated with himself. And now the absurdity of the situation didn't escape him. He'd been afraid before. Now he was truly terrified that he'd lost her forever.

He loved her.

He closed his eyes. In the morning, he'd figure out a way to convince her.

* * *

Layla lay in the dark and considered her options. The cottage was clean, and her go-bag was repacked and ready to go. She was fully dressed in jeans and a T-shirt. The shoe that she would wear on her right foot was carefully placed next to her bed so that she could slip it on in the morning.

She could go now. She had a phone in her bag that she could use to call a car service. But that just felt so unsafe. She'd be getting into a stranger's dark car in the middle of the night in the middle of nowhere. It was the equivalent of going into the creepy basement when you heard a strange noise down there. Probably stupid.

And a car service would want her credit card in advance. Now she knew that using the Regan Jones credit card was dangerous. Better to wait until morning, when she could go back to Widow's Peak and get the doorman to help her. If the hotel called for a car, she could pay cash when they arrived.

It was killing her to wait, to simply do nothing when her instinct was to run. But a few more hours would not hurt. She should sleep. She was going to have a big day of traveling tomorrow.

She closed her eyes.

Layla woke up to a pounding on her door. It was still dark, and she felt disoriented. She'd only been asleep a short time, she thought.

Jamie. She'd taken his keys, and now he was forced to knock.

But she just didn't see him as the type to demand entrance.

"Layla Morant, this is the county sheriff. Open the

door. We need to speak to you immediately. There's been an accident."

What? Oh, God, no. Not Jamie.

She got out of bed, grabbed her crutches and went to the door. Her heart was practically beating out of her chest. "Who? Who was in the accident?"

"Open the door, ma'am. We can tell you everything. Please don't delay. The victim is asking for you."

Jamie. "I need to see some identification," Layla said, trying to keep her panic under control.

"Of course. Open the door and I'll slip it inside. There will be a phone number you can call on the business card to verify that we were sent here to inform you."

Her hands fumbled with the bolt lock. Then she turned the knob and opened the door just inches. She put her hand up so that the officer could see it.

And then the door flew back, and she lost her grip on her crutches and fell to the floor. And she realized she'd made a terrible mistake. Because there before her stood her worst nightmare.

Douglas Glass.

Chapter 18

The bitch had picked the ends of the earth to escape to, Douglas thought as he stared at her. And what the hell had she done to her leg?

He pointed his gun at her. Oh, how he loved seeing the fear on her face. "Sorry, I lied," he said.

"How did you find me?"

"It wasn't that hard." It hadn't been. The drive had been as long and tedious as he'd remembered as a child, and he'd been so very tired. But the directions had been good. His contact had told him that as soon as he saw Widow's Peak on the cliff above him, that he should start looking for the row of seaside cottages.

She was in the fourth one. Lavender.

His contact had no way of knowing that he'd arrive in the middle of the night, when it would be impossible to tell the colors. But he'd also told him about the plywood on the window. That had been a helpful tidbit.

As had been the verification that the doctor had left. After seeing the highway sign for Knoware, he'd spent a few minutes thinking about Weathers being on the same road, just going a different direction. *Hope I see a crash.* He'd put the mantra to music in his head and hummed along. Anyone who had helped Layla Morant was no friend of his. Indeed, it put you square in the enemy camp.

He'd been less than fifteen minutes from his final destination when it had come to him. He would knock on the door, as a cop would do, and tell her that he had news of an accident. Few people could turn away from that.

It was rather brilliant, he thought.

And it had worked. He'd worried that she might recognize his voice. They'd had little previous conversation, but he had been interviewed multiple times on television as he'd pleaded his innocence, hoping to sway public opinion in his direction. He'd disguised it by punching out the bottom of his paper coffee cup and then speaking through it, in a modified bullhorn fashion.

Again, no wonder he had little patience with most people. They simply weren't as bright.

"What happened?" he asked, pointing to her leg. She was still sprawled on the floor. He sat on the couch.

She didn't answer.

"Whatever," he said. "It's not like I care." He looked around the small cottage. "Quaint," he said. "Nice place to die."

He appreciated that her face lost color. But to her credit, she didn't plead or beg. The only thing, however, was that it really wasn't a great place to kill her. First

of all, he didn't know who all knew that she was here. Weathers did, for sure. And while he'd left for the night, perhaps he was expected back early tomorrow morning. "When is your friend expected back?" he asked.

"My friend?"

"Your doctor friend. Handy to have around, I suppose, when you're injured. Handy for me, certainly, because that's how I found you. He led me right to you."

"He'll be back. Very soon," she added.

He didn't think so. Certainly not until morning and he didn't intend to be hanging around until then. But he needed to be careful.

If her body was found too soon, before he could return to San Francisco, it would make it harder for him to deny culpability. If he was home when the police arrived, his mother would provide an alibi. He was confident of that. But if they got there before he did, there was a chance that she'd be so angry with him that she might do or say something that she would regret later. But by then, he could be back in prison.

He needed to kill her somewhere else. Someplace her body wouldn't be found for a long time.

He could hear the waves crashing on the shore. He could knock her out and toss her into the ocean. Make it look like a midnight swim went badly. But who swam with a cast on their leg? And she might wash up onto the shore far too soon. He knew very little about ocean currents.

Push her off a cliff? That was another option. But same risk. He assumed this area was heavily hiked. Just his luck, someone would see her body right away.

He was so tired. It made it hard to think. All he knew was that he needed to get her away from this place. He

didn't feel up to driving one more mile. She could drive, he supposed. But then the risk was too great that in the coziness of the passenger seat, he'd be lulled to sleep.

He looked at his watch. Just past four. He made his decision. "Get up," he said.

She considered him. "I'll need a hand," she said finally.

"For God's sake," he muttered. He stood up and pointed his gun at her with his right hand. Then he extended his left.

She took it and awkwardly pulled herself to her feet.

"Is there rope here?" he asked.

"I have no idea," she said.

"Well, then, I guess we'll have to look," he said sarcastically. He motioned for her to go to the kitchen where he opened every drawer. Then he saw the door next to the refrigerator. When he opened it, he saw the tools in the far corner. There was a roll of twine. "This will work."

He pointed for her to return to the kitchen and to sit on the kitchen chair. "Put your arms behind you," he said. Then he tied each arm to the chair. He did the same with her good leg, wrapping the twine around her ankle and securing it to the chair leg. He left the casted leg alone. She wasn't going anywhere. And to make sure, he took her crutches with him when he went into the living room. He lay down on the couch.

The whole time she said nothing. That unnerved him somewhat, because he was used to his mother, who had an opinion and a comment about everything. "I want to know what happened to your leg."

"I broke it," she said.

"How?"

"In a car accident."

Perhaps that was how she and Dr. Jamie Weathers had gotten connected. He thought about verifying that and realized that it didn't matter. "Pity. Probably slowed you down."

She said nothing.

"I'm going to sleep now," he said. "After that, we'll take a little ride."

Layla was terrified. And so angry with herself. Why had she unlocked the door? But when he'd said that the victim was asking for her, it had hit her so hard. It was just over a week ago that she'd been in an accident, praying that somebody would come. Jamie had saved her. She wasn't going to turn her back on him now.

But it had been a stupid mistake, and now she was tied to a chair, watching Douglas Glass sleep on the couch.

It had been a gut punch when he'd said that Jamie had led him right to her. But she'd realized, even in the midst of her despair, that Jamie certainly hadn't intended to do that and had been unaware that he'd been followed. From the very beginning, he'd done everything he could to save her. He wouldn't have knowingly led danger to her door.

She'd told Douglas Glass that Jamie intended to return, hoping that it might scare the man away. But it hadn't.

When he'd told her to get up, she'd seen her first opportunity. She'd asked for a hand, repulsed by the idea of touching him, but still, she had done it, because she'd hoped that she could drag him onto the ground. Then she had intended to fight with every fiber of her being.

But he'd held the gun on her and she'd been afraid that he would either shoot her or even that it might go off by accident.

He'd said they were going for a ride. Where the hell did he intend to take her? While it wasn't great, every minute she stayed alive was another minute when she could figure out a solution, figure out a way to attract someone else's attention or get herself out of the situation.

She cursed her broken leg. It put her at such a disadvantage. She could not run. At the same time, she was grateful for the cast. If she got banged up some, her leg might still be okay because of the protection the cast offered.

How had he known to follow Jamie? Now that the immediate terror of being literally knocked on her butt by Douglas Glass was past, she could think of logical questions. Had he somehow stumbled upon the real Regan Jones and she'd overshared? Had he somehow learned of Jamie's and his friend Marcus's interest in Layla Morant and put the puzzle pieces together?

She realized that it really didn't matter. She'd always taken his threat seriously, even though others had not. She'd heard the intent in his voice, seen the hate in his eyes. It had forced her to alter the course of her life. And stupidly, she'd thought it would be enough. Had spent countless hours thinking through the moment that Douglas Glass discovered that Layla Morant was no more. Not at work. Not at her condo. No credit card activity. No phone. No trace.

She'd somehow convinced herself that he'd give up at that point. That he'd figure out that he had won after all. He would not have had the pleasure of inflicting the

final blow, but for all practical purposes, she was dead. Layla Morant was gone.

She'd underestimated his need for revenge. He wouldn't be satisfied with anything less than being the one to end it.

She was going to have to end him. That was the only way this was ever going to be resolved.

Jamie slept fitfully. The beds at Widow's Peak were comfortable enough, but he'd been unable to quiet his mind. He picked up his phone to check the time. Twenty-two minutes after five.

It was too early to go see Layla. She'd be sleeping.

He reached for the remote and turned on the television. Channel surfed for fifteen minutes before turning off the power and tossing the remote to the side. There were no coffeepots in the room, but he recalled that the night clerk had said that coffee was available twenty-four hours a day in the lobby. He'd shower, get dressed, get a cup of coffee, and by then, it should be close to six. He wasn't waiting any longer.

The night had been pure agony, and if he had his way, it was going to be the very last night that he ever spent apart from Layla. On the nights he covered the emergency room, she could bunk in the doctors' lounge so that he could sneak in to see her.

That was the first funny thought he'd had in hours, he mused as the hot shower soothed his muscles. Okay, perhaps there'd be other nights they'd be apart. But she would never be angry and upset with him again. He'd give her no reason to be. He was going to spend the rest of his life making sure she was happy.

He only had the clothes he'd worn to dinner, so he

put them on again, feeling way too dressed up. He took the elevator to the first level and found the coffeepot. He poured himself a cup, added some cream and sipped. The lobby was almost empty. There was one other early riser, a woman. She was elderly, perhaps mideighties. She stood before the big windows, staring outside, drinking her own coffee.

Maybe she'd escaped a snoring husband. That was one point in his favor, he thought—he was pretty sure he didn't snore. He'd been on plenty of overnight jaunts with Blade and Marcus over the years, and he was confident that one of them would have gladly pointed out the shortcoming.

Maybe he should start a list of positive attributes.

But before he went there, he was going to profusely apologize for not having been a hundred percent honest with her. She'd deserved it, and he'd fallen short. It would never happen again.

He walked back to the coffee station to top off his cup and came face-to-face with the woman. He motioned for her to go first.

"Lovely morning, isn't it?" she said.

He hoped it was indeed lovely. "Yes," he said.

"I saw you in the restaurant last night," the woman said. "Your wife is very beautiful. How did she break her leg?"

Not my wife, he started to object. *Not yet*, he amended. If he had his way, she would be. "Car accident," he said.

"Oh, I'm sorry to hear that. Well, I hope she has a quick recovery. This is a good place to while away the hours."

"I'll let her know," Jamie said, smiling at the woman. As he walked by the registration desk, the middle-aged

woman standing there smiled at him. "Good morning," she said.

"Morning," he said. So far *these* two women had been very nice. He could only hope that his encounter with the next woman went half as well. He walked out the back door of the hotel, filled with resolve.

His vehicle was cold, but he didn't wait for it to warm up before taking off. He drove down the paved road to the highway and, within a minute, was pulling into the driveway of the lavender cottage.

The bedroom window blinds were down as usual, but he could see that there was a light on in the room. Good, she was up. He couldn't wait to see her.

He got out and knocked on the door. It reminded him of how he had knocked on the door that very first time.

But this time he did not hear the telltale thump of her crutches on the wood floor.

He knocked again. "Layla, it's Jamie," he said. "Please open the door."

No response. "Come on. We have to talk about this," he said, feeling foolish on the porch. It was still not yet light and must have been low tide, because even the waves were not hitting the rocks with much force or noise. It made his voice seem even louder.

He pounded on the door.

"Layla, I'll kick the damn door down if I have to," he yelled.

Still no response. This was childish. He picked up his foot and kicked at the door. Once. Twice. On the third kick, it flew open.

Chapter 19

She was not in the living room or the kitchen. He ran down the hallway. Not in the bedroom or the bathroom. He ran back to check the small utility room off the kitchen. Empty. What the hell?

She was gone. She had no vehicle. She could have walked, he supposed, but not very far or fast in the dark on crutches. She had no phone. Or did she? Perhaps in her duffel bag.

He ran back to the bedroom and saw the strap of her duffel bag peeking out from underneath the bed. Without hesitation, he pulled it out. It was locked. He ran to the utility room, got a box cutter from one of the drawers and ran back to the bedroom. He slashed the bag open. It was full. A loaf of bread. Peanut butter and jelly. Fruit. He tossed that aside. A phone. A few clothes. Some other things that looked a bit like camping gear.

He opened zippers. Money. Her identification as Regan Jones. He felt the lining and, after a minute, found the hidden zipper. More money.

She'd been packed to go. This food had been in the kitchen cupboard and the refrigerator yesterday. Her extra clothes had been in the closet. But sometime last night, she'd packed her duffel bag in anticipation of leaving.

And then she'd left but hadn't taken her bag. The bag that she'd been fiercely protective of since the first moment he'd met her.

It made no sense.

And he was filled with an awful sense of dread. It threatened to take him under, but he called upon his training. No, he was not a detective, but he was a physician, trained to look for signs and symptoms and to draw logical conclusions. He needed to do that now.

Her coat was not in the closet. He was going to assume she had it on. But if she'd taken the time to put her coat on, why had she left her duffel bag? Because it was too heavy? No. She'd gotten it here when she was in much worse physical shape than now.

She'd left it because she wanted someone to find it. Wanted him to find it.

She'd known that he'd come back this morning and she'd reasoned it out that he would assume that something was very wrong if she hadn't taken her duffel bag.

There were no signs of struggle in the bedroom. Or the bathroom, he said to himself as he did a slow walk through the cottage. Living room was fine. Kitchen was… He stopped. The chairs were spaced differently. Instead of one chair on every side of the rectangular table, there were two chairs on the one side, leaving an end open.

He checked the refrigerator. Empty and cleaned. Then the cupboards. Same. He'd expected that since he'd seen the bread and other food items in her duffel bag.

As he passed by the garbage, he lifted the lid. Emptied.

Almost. What was that? He looked closer. Three pieces of twine. All about the same length.

They hadn't used any twine when he'd been here. He did not touch it. Instead, he pulled out his cell phone and took a picture. He opened the door to the utility room. There was a tied-up garbage bag. He undid the tie. He recognized the contents. It was the garbage from the last week. The candy he'd bought at Tiddle's was on the top.

He pieced together her evening. After he'd left her off at the door, she'd come inside. At some point, she'd cleaned the cottage, going so far as to empty the refrigerator and set aside the garbage. She'd packed her duffel bag.

Then something had happened. Something that had required three pieces of twine.

Then she'd left. Without the garbage that she'd prepared for disposal. Without her duffel bag. Without a great deal of money or a phone.

Someone had taken her. He was confident of it.

And he was pretty damn sure he knew who.

She thought they'd been driving for at least forty-five minutes. However, she didn't have her watch on, nor did the car have a clock. They were headed south, she was confident, because the sun had come up to their left. Exactly where they were was unclear. Douglas Glass had started off on the same highway that the linen truck driver had used when she'd first come to

Widow's Peak. But fifteen minutes into their trip, he'd turned off. The road was still paved but appeared to be a lesser used highway.

Ten minutes ago, she'd seen a billboard advertising Gertie's Café in Knoware, and she'd gotten excited. She remembered that Jamie had mentioned the café as someplace that he went with friends. She could get help there. But the sign had said turn at the next crossroad, and Douglas Glass had blown past the intersection.

She sat in the passenger seat of the old Mustang convertible, her hands in her lap, her wrists not only tied together with the twine that he'd brought with them, but he'd used an additional piece to secure them to the hard plastic part of the seat belt. It put her arms and her right shoulder at an odd angle to her body, and it was very uncomfortable. The vinyl top was up, but wind still whistled through the aged seams, chilling the car.

It was not the kind of car that she'd ever associated with Douglas Glass. "Is this yours?" she asked. It was the first thing she'd said to him since they'd started the trip.

"My mother's," he answered, not taking his eyes off the road.

"No GPS?" she asked. It was evident by the paper map that was open, half on his lap, half edging over onto her seat. The car was too old, but most people she knew used their phones to navigate anyway.

But not people who didn't want their movements tracked.

Douglas Glass was tense. Had been ever since he'd awakened from his nap on the couch and announced that it was time to leave. She'd been awake the whole time he'd slept. Thinking. Planning.

She'd asked where they were going, but he'd told her

to shut up. After he'd untied her from the chair and tossed the remains of the twine into the garbage, she'd pushed the kitchen chair back to the table. But in a different spot than before. He hadn't noticed.

"I'll need my coat," she'd said.

"Fine," he'd responded, as if surprised. She realized then that he'd come to the door last night without even a jacket, evidently warmed by a misguided need for revenge.

He'd followed her to the bedroom, where she'd gotten her coat out of the closet. When she put it on, she'd waited for him to check the pockets, but he hadn't. Instead, he'd walked over to the window, pulled back the blinds a bit, as if checking to see whether it was light yet.

It hadn't been. But the light in the bedroom was on, and the strap of her go-bag was peeking out from under the dust ruffle of the bed. She had prayed that he would not notice it and had not breathed easily until they were out of the bedroom.

Jamie had said that he'd be back, that they weren't done. He would find the bag. He would be able to piece together that she'd left it behind. He would know that she was in trouble.

As painful as last night's conversation had been, she was so thankful that they'd shared everything. He'd spring into action, that was for sure. Her job was to stay alive long enough to give him time to find her, since her leg significantly hampered any escape attempt. That being said, if she got the chance to ram her crutches down Glass's throat and save herself, all the better.

"Where are we going?" she asked.

"Shut up," he said. "Don't talk to me."

She was pretty sure the guy didn't have a plan. It

was encouraging in one sense but worrisome in another. Would he do something erratic, something that she had no time to prepare for?

It was odd, because for the last twenty months, she'd been terrified that Douglas Glass was going to find her and make good on his threat to kill her. So terrified that she'd been willing to leave her life behind and start over. But now that it had happened, while it was still awful, she was buoyed by the fact that she wasn't trembling or crying in the corner.

"My head is killing me," he said. "I need to eat. There was no food in that damn place you were at. Not even any damn coffee."

That was because she'd put most of it in a garbage bag that was still sitting in the utility room or she'd packed it in her go-bag, which he'd missed. If he'd been thinking, he should have wondered what she'd been eating and where her other clothes were. Or thought it was odd there were no toiletry items in the bathroom. Should have definitely searched her for a phone or asked about it.

It seemed as if Douglas Glass was a big-picture kind of guy, not one to care too much about the details. She was going to use that. She had a phone and money. If she could get away from him, she could call 911.

"There was a billboard back there a little ways. Advertising a café. In Knoware," she said, keeping her voice calm. She didn't want to oversell it.

"Not backtracking. We're south of that. Got to keep going south."

Jamie called Marcus from his car. When his friend answered, Jamie didn't waste any time. "I need your help. I think a man named Douglas Glass, who was

sent to prison due in part to Layla Morant's testimony, has kidnapped her from a cottage near Widow's Peak. Glass is from San Francisco. I need to know everything about him. I need to find her."

"Okay, okay," Marcus said. He did not ask him to repeat anything. Marcus would have gotten it on the first pass. "Do you have any idea of where he might be? Even a direction he might be heading?"

"No. But there is somebody who might. I'll call you in ten minutes." He hung up. He was already pulling into the parking lot of Widow's Peak. He ran into the hotel and up to the registration desk. It was the same person who had been there a half hour earlier. "There was a woman here this morning. She was standing at the window. It was still dark outside. I need to speak to her."

"That would be Mrs. Willowby. She's a long-term guest. First coffee drinker of the morning," the clerk added.

"Please, can you call her? Tell her I need to speak with her. Tell her I'm the man who was having coffee this morning. Please. It's important. Someone's life may depend upon it."

She looked startled, but she did not hesitate. She quickly tapped on her computer screen, and then she was picking up her phone. "Mrs. Willowby, there's a gentleman, another guest, in the lobby. I think you may have met him this morning. Anyway, he says it's very important that he have a word with you. Would you be able to come back down to the lobby?"

It was less than two minutes later that the elevator dinged and Mrs. Willowby stepped out. Jamie walked up to her. "Thank you," he said. "My name is Dr. Jamie Weathers. This morning, you were standing at the win-

dow. From that view, you can see the road below, and the cottages that sit across from the road. I'm looking for a woman who might have left the fourth cottage, the lavender one. Did you see anything?"

"I didn't see a woman," she said.

"But you did see something?"

"I saw a car. Pulling out of one of the driveways toward the middle of those eight cottages. Couldn't see who was inside, but I think there may have been two of them. You know, I look out those windows every morning, and I can't remember ever seeing activity at the cottages. Not at this time of year. I guess that's why I noticed."

"What direction did it go?"

"South."

"Can you describe the vehicle?" he asked, not having much hope.

"A 1965 Ford Mustang. Red with a white vinyl top."

He wanted to hug her. "You're sure?"

"I had one. People get the '65 and '66 mixed up if they don't remember that the '65 had a vertical bar on the front grille. I could see it quite plainly when it made the turn out of the driveway."

"What time was this?" he asked.

"What time did the two of us bump into each other at the coffee station?" she asked.

"Around ten minutes to six."

"I'd say about fifteen minutes before that."

He felt a surge of energy. He wasn't that far behind them. "You've been extraordinarily helpful," he said. "Thank you."

"You're welcome. If you're around tomorrow, let's have coffee."

He wouldn't be here tomorrow. He hoped he'd be somewhere with Layla safe in his arms. But he needed to find her first. He was dialing Marcus by the time he got outside.

When his friend answered, Jamie spoke quickly. "I think she's in a red convertible Mustang, a 1965, with a white vinyl top. Headed south from here."

"That makes sense," Marcus said. "I found a location for Douglas Glass in San Francisco. He lives with his mother. She owns a 1965 Mustang. I tried to call the phone number associated with the license plate, but it just rings. So I called a friend, and he's going to do a home visit for me. I should know more in twenty minutes."

"Thank you."

"What are you going to do?"

"I guess I'll head south," he said. It was the only thing he knew to do. It wasn't a great plan, because they could jump off the highway at any moment, but for now, it was the best idea he had.

"Knowing his vehicle is huge. I'm requesting backup from the county and state police. Barricades will be set up. We'll get him, Jamie. We will."

"Thanks, Marcus." Jamie hung up before he voiced his concern that the barricades would be of little use if Glass had already harmed Layla.

Please, please, still be alive, he prayed as he pulled out of the parking lot and onto the highway.

Because he'd said he was hungry, she wasn't too surprised when he abruptly swerved off the road and pulled into the parking lot of a twenty-four-hour truck stop and diner combination. He parked in the far corner of the lot, not near any other cars, but where he could

see the telephone number painted on the front wall. He called in his order. An egg and bacon sandwich on whole wheat toast with a large coffee. When he ended the call, he turned to her. "Sorry, no last meal for you, Layla. I'm not stupid. They might do an autopsy afterward, and I don't want the contents of your stomach telling them anything."

He said it so calmly, so matter-of-factly, that it helped her get past the image of her body lying naked on a sterile surface while a pathologist cut into her. Douglas Glass was not right in the head. He was worried about the contents of her stomach, but at the same time, he clearly had not thought through the plan of killing her.

"I understand," she said. She rubbed her one shoe on the floor mat of the car. "I imagine my clothing is picking up all kinds of fibers that will lead them back to this vehicle. And who knows what kind of trail this thing leaves," she said, carelessly motioning to her cast.

He paled. "Shut up," he said. He glanced at his watch. After a few minutes, he undid his seat belt. The vehicle was too old for electronic locks. It had the old-fashioned lock on the door. He reached across her and engaged it. Then he got out, locking his own door behind him.

She was alone. But it was doing her absolutely no good. If he'd simply tied her wrists together, she'd have use of her fingers and might have been able to lift the lock. But that option had been taken away from her. Nor could she get to her phone that was in her coat pocket. It was so close. She wanted to scream in frustration.

She did. As loudly as she could, hoping to attract some attention. Surely, someone would hear her.

But there was no one parked nearby. Minutes went by before suddenly a vehicle pulled into the lot. It was

a new-looking black SUV. It headed straight toward the convertible and parked next to her.

They would help her. She would be saved. She turned to the window. "Help me. I've been kidnapped. Please, help me."

A lone woman, perhaps in her late sixties or early seventies, was in the vehicle. She stared at Layla, no emotion on her carefully made-up face.

"Help. I. Need. Help. Call the police." Layla leaned toward the window as far as she could. She spoke clearly. If the woman couldn't hear her, she should at least be able to read her lips.

Still no response.

Oh, God. What was the chance of this? It was a nightmare.

From the corner of her eye, she saw Douglas Glass emerge from the restaurant carrying a brown sack and a white insulated coffee cup. Dismay crossed his face as he saw the vehicle parked next to her. His steps faltered, and he stopped.

Yes, this would end it. Yes, yes. Hope roared through her.

But then Douglas Glass squared his shoulders and started walking again. But not to the Mustang. He veered toward the black SUV, and Layla saw the woman roll down her window.

That was when she knew that she was definitely going to die.

Chapter 20

Douglas Glass said nothing when he got back inside the Mustang. His conversation with the woman had been brief, less than two minutes.

It had affected him, however. When he brought the cup of coffee up to his lips, his hands were shaking. Badly. And he no longer seemed interested in his breakfast, which he'd tossed aside.

"Who was that?" She was pretty sure she knew, but she needed him to say it.

He didn't answer. He started the car, waited until the black SUV pulled out and then followed it.

They got back on the highway, still heading south. They'd gone less than two miles when the vehicle ahead of them made an abrupt left turn. They followed suit. They were in the middle of nowhere. No longer on paved roads. All gravel. They drove for another mile

or so before the SUV made another quick turn, this time to the right. A half mile up the road, she saw a big once-white, now-gray barn surrounded by several smaller sheds. There was no house on the property, and it appeared the buildings hadn't been used in years.

The woman ahead of them drove toward the barn. It was probably easy going for the SUV, but the Mustang, lower to the ground, lurched and bumped along, making Layla think that it would be a miracle if the vehicle didn't get caught up in the overgrown grass.

The black SUV stopped, and the woman got out. Douglas Glass opened his door, but the woman put up a hand, as if telling him to stay put. She walked over to the big hanging door and slid it to the right. She opened her purse and pulled out her cell phone, then appeared to use the flashlight option to examine the interior of the barn. She stepped back, turned to look at them in the Mustang and motioned them to pull in. It was dimly lit inside, with natural light coming from the many windows on the sides of the building.

Inside, it was a cavernous structure, with a high ceiling and what might have been a hayloft at one time. Now the high shelf was empty. There were cement stanchions for livestock lining both sides. Empty now, but evidence that this had at one time been a thriving operation.

Layla glanced at Douglas Glass, to gauge his reaction. He didn't appear to be surprised or even wondering why his mother—or so Layla assumed—had led him to this place. He wasn't looking around; rather, he was just staring at his hands, which were still on the steering wheel.

"Where are we?" she asked.

"A place that I thought had been torn down twenty years ago," he said.

Now she was really confused.

With a sigh, Douglas Glass opened his door. He got out, walked around the car and opened Layla's door. He used a small pocketknife to cut the twine that held her to the seat belt. "Get out," he said.

"I need my crutches."

He reached behind her to get them from the back seat. By the time she was out of the car, the older woman was standing less than ten feet away. Waiting.

"Ms. Morant," the woman said.

So very formal. "Mrs. Glass," Layla responded, taking a guess. She'd never seen Douglas Glass's mother, but the resemblance between the two of them was obvious. Same closely spaced eyes. Square jawline.

"I regret that it's come to this," Mrs. Glass said.

"It doesn't have to be this way," Layla said, thinking that maybe she could reason with this woman.

"Unfortunately, it does." The woman unsnapped the purse that was hanging off her left arm and pulled out a gun. She looked at her son. "Dougie, you look surprised. You didn't realize that I had another? This one isn't registered and can't be traced, unlike the one you so rashly took from my bedroom yesterday."

"I should have said something," Douglas Glass said. His tone was conciliatory, as if he was trying to win back his mother's approval.

"You shouldn't have taken it or made this journey. But you don't listen, Dougie. You don't learn. And I'm tired of it. I'm not going to spend my retirement years waiting for your next truffle up. It was a disgrace when you were imprisoned. And visiting you required me

to…" Her voice trailed off, but she visibly shuddered. "Anyway," she said, recovering. "I simply won't do it again."

"Mother," Douglas Glass said. "You won't have to. I'm not going to get caught."

"You will," she said, sounding tired and beaten. "You will."

Layla's head was reeling. It was a family drama unlike anything she'd ever seen.

Now the woman turned to look at Layla. "How did you like the car?"

"What?" It was such an unexpected question that she wasn't sure she heard right.

"I asked how you liked the car. I've had it since I was a teenager. All original." She chuckled. "Well, with the exception of the tracking device that I added three days ago."

Layla glanced at Douglas Glass. He had not known about the tracking device, that was clear. And he was angry.

"Go home, Mother. Let me deal with this," he said.

"You don't deal with anything," she responded, her voice angry. "You mess things up, and then I'm left to deal with them. I'm tired, Dougie. I'm really just so tired. You've disappointed me for the last time. A mother should love her son, and I do. But I will not allow you to ruin all the good years that I have left."

And then she lifted the gun and shot him.

It was a shot straight to the heart, and Douglas Glass did not linger.

The woman had killed her own son. And she did not look terribly sorry.

"I did what I had to do," Mrs. Glass said, no emotion

in her voice. She pointed the gun at Layla. "He gave me no choice."

Now what? It was hard for Layla to think when her nose and throat were filled with the stench of blood and other bodily fluids oozing from Douglas Glass. The man had been going to kill her. She would have killed him first if she'd had the chance.

But, still. It was a tough thing to see. For her, anyway. Mrs. Glass was checking her watch. Then she looked at Layla.

"You don't need to do this," Layla said, not certain what Mrs. Glass intended, but she doubted that it was going to be good. "I can just forget about this."

Mrs. Glass laughed. "My dear, you will run to the authorities at your first chance. Sit," she said. She had the gun pointed at Layla's heart, and Layla knew she wouldn't miss.

"Please," Layla said.

"Sit. I do not have time for this."

Layla got to the ground. If she'd been going to kill her, why had she bothered having her come inside the barn?

She opened her handbag a second time and took out a pair of handcuffs. Layla's hands were still tied together, in front of her body. But Mrs. Glass didn't look at them. Instead, she put one cuff around the ankle of her good leg and locked the other cuff around a stanchion pole.

"I'll be back," she said.

"Where are you going?" Layla asked, not believing her. Was she leaving Layla here to slowly starve to death? To sit in the dark when the coyotes came at night and devoured her son, only to move on to Layla?

"As much as it pains me, I'll have to get rid of the Mustang. Your DNA is inside it."

It was the same argument that she'd made to Douglas Glass not that long ago.

"I was smarter," Mrs. Glass said. "I thought to bring plastic. However, I did not anticipate the need for an accelerant."

An accelerant? Gasoline. She was going to torch her car. The barn. Her son's body. Layla. "Our bodies will be found. People will connect my death to your son. Even though he's dead, the stigma will carry over to you." It was the only argument she could think of based on the limited conversation she'd heard.

"You forget about the plastic, dear. I'm not leaving your dead body here. I'll wrap you up, take you a good ways up the road and roll you into a ravine. By the time you're found next spring, the police may suspect that your death had something to do with Dougie's, but there will be no proof, nothing that definitively says the two of you were together. By then, everyone will believe my sad story of how Dougie was so distraught over his prison experience that he drove up to his great-uncle's old farm, a place he had wonderful memories of, where he committed suicide."

His great-uncle's old farm. That's how Mrs. Glass had known about it. That's why Douglas Glass hadn't even looked interested in the interior of the barn. He'd been there before. "They can detect that an accelerant was used to start the fire," she said.

"Well, perhaps Dougie did that before he shot himself to ensure death, or perhaps sometime later a vagrant did it. It doesn't matter. As long as I can't be definitively

tied to the event, I won't be charged. I'll simply be the grieving mother."

Douglas Glass hadn't been a details kind of guy. It appeared that Mrs. Glass didn't share the same limitations.

The woman walked out of the barn and out of Layla's sight. Layla heard a vehicle start and then the crunch of tires on gravel. The sound faded, and she was all alone.

Waiting to die.

Chapter 21

Jamie's phone rang. It was Marcus. "What do we know?" he answered.

"We know that there's nobody home at the Glass residence."

"Coincidence?" Jamie asked.

"I don't know. My contact knows a bit about the Glass family. Mother is really well-known in San Francisco. She's a mover and a shaker of sorts. Likes to be recognized for her philanthropy. She was profiled for an article in the newspaper several years ago, and one of her business acquaintances described her as one of the most cunning and calculating businesswomen he'd ever had the pleasure of meeting."

Cunning and calculating. Had Douglas Glass inherited those traits from his mother? Or was he simply a rich spoiled brat who couldn't rest until he'd gotten his

revenge? Jamie wasn't sure what to hope for. Each was dangerous in its own way. "Do you have a description of Mrs. Glass or her vehicle?" he asked.

"Of the vehicle. It's an SUV. A Black Mercedes GLS." He rattled off the license plate, and Jamie scribbled it on a piece of paper. "She's also got a firearm permit for a nine millimeter," Marcus added.

"Okay, thanks," he said.

"Where are you?" Marcus asked.

"In the air."

"How the hell did you manage that?" Marcus asked.

Some fast talking and a bit of luck that the flight instructor at Widow's Peak airfield showed up early for work every day. He'd remembered Jamie from meeting him at the charity event and had been willing to lend him his own plane. "Long story, but I'm about twenty miles south of Widow's Peak. No sign of a red Mustang."

"Okay. Another ten miles or so, you should start to see the first roadblocks. I'd given police the information that you should be allowed through, but I guess that's not necessary now."

"I'll be in touch."

"There's one other thing," Marcus said. "I did a property search on both Douglas and Francine Glass, his mother. Douglas doesn't have anything. Francine has her house as well as several exclusive rental properties in San Francisco. And, oddly enough, she owns three hundred acres in Washington State. About thirty minutes from Knoware."

"Send me the GPS coordinates," Jamie said. It might be worth a look since he was so close.

"Will do."

Jamie hung up and heard his phone ding with a text. He plugged the coordinates in and realized that he was less than ten minutes of flying time from the spot. He changed course, heading that direction.

And there it was. Saw an old barn, but he didn't see any activity. He continued circling. And then he saw a black vehicle off in the distance. He wasn't an expert on car models, but he was fairly confident this was one of the new Mercedes SUVs.

He told himself to breathe. Crashing the damn plane wasn't going to do him any good. He also forced himself to maintain his altitude. Didn't want to scare her.

He called Marcus. "I have Mrs. Glass," he said when his friend answered. "She's traveling at a pretty good clip, heading east on a gravel road. And I'm pretty sure she's headed toward an old barn that is about two miles out that matches the GPS coordinates you gave me."

"I'm fifteen minutes away. Is Layla with her?"

"I think she's alone."

"No sign of a red Mustang?"

"No," Marcus said. He had a bad feeling about this.

"Okay. On my way." Marcus hung up.

Jamie had just seconds to decide what to do. He could stay in the air, watching from above and be powerless to stop anything. Or he could make a calculated guess that Mrs. Glass was headed for the barn and land the plane now. There was a thick stand of trees that separated the barn and adjoining property from a now-picked corn-field on the other side.

It would be a rough and difficult landing. The plane might be damaged. He could get hurt.

He'd made rough and difficult landings before. He'd

replace the plane if it came to that. And any amount of physical risk was worth it to potentially save Layla.

He cut his speed and his altitude just enough. Made a wide circle. Got lower. And landed.

He'd been right. It was rough enough to jar some fillings loose. But when the plane came to a stop, both the aircraft and he were still in one piece.

Go, go, go. The voice inside his head was screaming at him.

He unbuckled, got out and headed for the trees.

He was just emerging from the other side when the SUV turned into the lane, some two hundred yards away. He stepped back, staying hidden. The car stopped near the barn door.

A woman got out, opened the rear door of the SUV and pulled out a roll of something. Plastic, he thought, as he watched her unroll the material and spread it on the ground near her vehicle. Then she reached inside the back of the SUV again, this time pulling out two red gas cans—the type they sold at gas stations to motorists who'd run out and needed to ferry gas to their vehicles.

Was Douglas Glass inside with Layla? Had he run out of gas and called his mother for assistance? And she'd driven all that way to help.

Absurd.

Douglas Glass had left the cottage about an hour ago. If he'd come from San Francisco, he'd driven all night. His mother, too. She'd had to have been on the road shortly after he was in order to be here now. Were they working together?

The woman took several steps toward the barn, a container in each hand. She was wearing black gloves. Jamie expected her to enter, but she stopped short of

going in. Instead, she set one container on the ground and began pouring from the other. He had to assume it was gasoline. She was liberally dousing the lower boards of the barn. What the hell?

She kept going until she'd apparently emptied the container. Then she tossed it aside. Picked up the other and went inside the barn.

And Jamie's really bad feeling got a little worse.

Mrs. Glass had left the door open, which let in enough light that Layla could easily see the woman had accomplished her mission. There she was, gas can in hand.

She'd been gone less than fifteen minutes, but that had given Layla plenty of time for regrets. And there was a list. Most of them had to do with Jamie. Regret that they hadn't had more time together. Regret that it had ended badly. Regret that she hadn't been in a position to say yes to his marriage proposal. Regret that she hadn't told him that she loved him.

He'd deserved to know that.

Regret that they weren't going to have a life together, raise their babies together, grow old together. She had heard a plane flying overhead and remembered their last morning in bed. Regret that he wouldn't get to take her flying across the Great Lakes. There'd be no breakfast in Wisconsin and lunch in Michigan. When the noise of the plane had abruptly faded, she'd felt that her last link to Jamie had vanished.

"Hello, dear," Mrs. Glass said cheerily, as if she'd gone to the store for a carton of milk. And she hadn't even glanced at the dead body of her son. It appeared that in her mind, she'd dealt with it, and now it was over.

She wouldn't lose a moment of sleep over Layla's death. Wouldn't care about Layla's regrets.

"I've already used one of these on the exterior. Should be a real nice blaze," she said conversationally. She set the container on the dirt floor. She reached into her pocket and then tossed something toward Layla. It was a key for the handcuffs. "Unlock yourself."

She did. And then used the bars of the livestock stanchion to get herself to her feet. She balanced with her weight on one leg. "I need my crutches."

Mrs. Glass tossed them to her. "Let's go."

"Where?"

"Just outside. I've got everything ready for you."

"I'm not going anywhere with you," Layla said.

"Well, then, dear, I'll shoot you where you stand."

"No, you won't," Layla said. "Because I'll bleed, and then my blood is going to be in this dirt. Even if the fire burns the structure, the dirt will remain. A lab analysis will prove that I was here. That my death is connected to your son's death."

Mrs. Glass narrowed her eyes. Then sighed. "Truffle you, dear." Then she walked up to Layla and grabbed her upper arm, as if she intended to drag her out of the barn.

It was the opening Layla had hoped for. She swung the crutch under her other arm upward, catching Mrs. Glass across the forehead. The woman's grip faltered, and Layla lunged at her, taking her to the ground. She might have a broken leg but she was thirty years younger, had more muscle and was more agile. And she was fighting for her life.

She punched the woman and was bringing her arm

back for another strike when someone grabbed her from behind.

"Whoa, whoa, whoa. You've got a wicked hook."

Jamie.

She turned to look. But he wasn't looking at her. He was solely focused on Mrs. Glass, and he had one foot on her arm and used his other to kick her gun away. "Are you injured, Layla?" he asked, eyes still on Mrs. Glass.

"No. Oh, Jamie. Where did you come from?"

"I sort of dropped in. In time to see you challenge her to the middleweight championship."

She laughed. It felt glorious. She stopped when she heard a vehicle approaching.

"That's our reinforcements," Jamie said. He waited until he heard car doors. "Marcus?" he yelled.

"Yeah," came the reply.

"You're late. I think that means you're buying breakfast at Gertie's."

Then the barn was full of people. Jamie stepped away from Mrs. Glass, letting Marcus take charge. He wrapped his arms around Layla and led her to the other side of the barn. "You're not hurt? You're sure?" he asked, holding her at arm's length and running his eyes from her head to her toes.

"My hand is a little sore," she admitted.

"That's why they wear gloves in the ring," he said, bringing the fingers of her right hand up to his lips and kissing them.

"They'll probably swell up," she said. "I guess… I guess it's a really good thing that an engagement ring goes on your left hand."

He drew in a breath, looking hopeful. But then he

shook his head. "How can you want to marry me? I wasn't truthful with you. I knew you were Layla Morant. My secrecy and the actions that Marcus and I took put you in danger."

She nodded. "There's something else."

"What?"

"Douglas Glass found me because he somehow followed you to the cottage."

"Oh my God," Jamie said, his voice sounding choked.

"The only reason I'm telling you that is because I don't want it to come up later. We're done with secrets, and regrets. I don't care about any of that. Lies were told. By both of us. Mistakes were made. But here's what I know to be true. You saved me. More than once. And this past week, even though I was sick and injured, was still wonderful. Because of you. I've spent some time regretting that we weren't going to have a future. I was wrong to send you away last night. You told me that you loved me. Well, I love you, Jamie. So very much. And while I want my life back, I don't want it if you're not a part of it."

He stared at her for a long minute. "You're amazing," he said finally.

She shook her head. "Just trying to measure up to the guy who under-promises and over-delivers."

"I guess it's a good thing that I happen to have a ring in my pocket."

She felt a rush of joy spread through her body. "Just happen to? What is this, some sort of corny romantic comedy?"

He pulled the ring out, opened the box and slipped it onto her finger. "You bet it is. Starring Jamie Weathers and Layla Morant."

Epilogue

"Six, five, four, three, two, one." Horns blew, whistles shrilled, balloons floated, tinsel rained and couples kissed. "Happy New Year, Mrs. Weathers," Jamie said, holding her tight.

"Happy New Year," she said, blinking back tears of happiness. It wouldn't be the first time she'd cried. Not even the first time in the last hour. Just looking at Jamie in his black tux, looking so happy, tended to make her a bit misty-eyed.

Earlier that evening, the minister, standing in the big bay window of Widow's Peak lodge, had pronounced them husband and wife, and they'd sealed it with a kiss. Guests had toasted the happy couple. Blade and Daisy had been there; upstairs in one of the rooms slept their twin boys, under the watchful eyes of their teenage sisters. Marcus and Erin, too. Erin was toasting with

water, because she'd just found out they would be welcoming their first child next summer.

Jamie's parents and his brothers and their wives had made the trip to Washington, too. They could not have been more welcoming or excited about her joining the family.

Gertie Biscuit had driven up from Knoware. She'd given Layla a lovely pearl barrette for her hair, saying that she'd worn it when she'd married her own husband almost fifty years earlier. Caitlin Rose had come, with her husband. She'd cleared Jamie's schedule for a few days to allow for a short honeymoon. They'd officially rented the lavender cottage from the rightful owners. Everything strictly legal now, she'd told Jamie.

Even her friend Becky and a few of her former coworkers at Weber Labs had flown in for the occasion. They'd been sorry to lose her to the Knoware Health Department. She'd no longer be working in vaccine development but rather using her talents to assess and respond to public health issues and emergencies. She was so excited about the next chapter of her life.

A life that was going to be so different than the one she'd imagined just months before. It was sometimes still hard to believe that the nightmare was over. Douglas Glass was dead and his mother was in prison for a long time. She would likely die there.

"It's time to cut the cake," Jamie said, his voice close to her ear.

She pressed a hand to her stomach. "No one wants cake," she said. The chefs of Widow's Peak had outdone themselves on dinner.

Jamie shook his head. "It's our last official duty of the night before we can sneak out."

"Well, when you put it that way," she said, thinking of the pleasures that lay ahead. "Find me a knife."

* * * * *

Don't miss the first two books in Beverly Long's
Heroes of the Pacific Northwest series,
A Firefighter's Ultimate Duty *and*
Trouble in Blue, *available now wherever*
Harlequin Romantic Suspense books are sold!